P. G. Wodehouse

'The ultimate in comfort reading because nothing bad ever happens in P.G. Wodehouse land. Or even if it does, it's always sorted out by the end of the book. For as long as I'm immersed in a P.G. Wodehouse book, it's possible to keep the real world at bay and live in a far, far nicer, funnier one where happy endings are the order of the day' _Marian Keyes_

'You should read Wodehouse when you're well and when you're poorly; when you're travelling, and when you're not; when you're feeling clever, and when you're feeling utterly dim. Wodehouse always lifts your spirits, no matter how high they happen to be already' _Lynne Truss_

'P. G. Wodehouse remains the greatest chronicler of a certain kind of Englishness, that no one else has ever captured quite so sharply, or with quite as much wit and affection' _Julian Fellowes_

'Not only the funniest English novelist who ever wrote but one of our finest stylists. His world is perfect, his stories are perfect, his writing perfect. What more is there to be said?' _Susan Hill_

'One of my (few) proud boasts is that I once spent a day interviewing P.G. Wodehouse at his home in America. He was exactly as I'd expected: a lovely, modest man. He could have walked out of one of his own novels. It's dangerous to use the word genius to describe a writer, but I'll risk it with him' _John Humphrys_

'The in... ...readers of all ages, sh...

'A genius . . . Elusive, delicate but lasting. He created such a credible world that, sadly, I suppose, never really existed but what a delight it always is to enter it and the temptation to linger there is sometimes almost overwhelming' *Alan Ayckbourn*

'Wodehouse was quite simply the Bee's Knees. And then some' *Joseph Connolly*

'Compulsory reading for anyone who has a pig, an aunt – or a sense of humour!' *Lindsey Davis*

'I constantly find myself drooling with admiration at the sublime way Wodehouse plays with the English language' *Simon Brett*

'I've recorded all the Jeeves books, and I can tell you this: it's like singing Mozart. The perfection of the phrasing is a physical pleasure. I doubt if any writer in the English language has more perfect music' *Simon Callow*

'Quite simply, the master of comic writing at work' *Jane Moore*

'To pick up a Wodehouse novel is to find oneself in the presence of genius – no writer has ever given me so much pure enjoyment' *John Julius Norwich*

'P.G. Wodehouse is the gold standard of English wit' *Christopher Hitchens*

'Wodehouse is so utterly, properly, simply funny' *Adele Parks*

'To dive into a Wodehouse novel is to swim in some of the most elegantly turned phrases in the English language' *Ben Schott*

'P.G. Wodehouse should be prescribed to treat depression. Cheaper, more effective than valium and far, far more addictive' *Olivia Williams*

'My only problem with Wodehouse is deciding which of his enchanting books to take to my desert island' *Ruth Dudley Edwards*

The author of almost a hundred books and the creator of Jeeves, Blandings Castle, Psmith, Ukridge, Uncle Fred and Mr Mulliner, P.G. Wodehouse was born in 1881 and educated at Dulwich College. After two years with the Hong Kong and Shanghai Bank he became a full-time writer, contributing to a variety of periodicals including *Punch* and the *Globe*. He married in 1914. As well as his novels and short stories, he wrote lyrics for musical comedies with Guy Bolton and Jerome Kern, and at one time had five musicals running simultaneously on Broadway. His time in Hollywood also provided much source material for fiction.

At the age of 93, in the New Year's Honours List of 1975, he received a long-overdue knighthood, only to die on St Valentine's Day some 45 days later.

*Some of the P.G. Wodehouse titles to be published
by Arrow in 2008*

P. G. WODEHOUSE
Hot Water

arrow books

Published by Arrow Books 2008

1 3 5 7 9 10 8 6 4 2

First published in the United Kingdom in 1932 by Herbert Jenkins Ltd

Arrow Books
The Random House Group Limited
20 Vauxhall Bridge Road, London, SW1V 2SA

www.rbooks.co.uk

www.wodehouse.co.uk

Addresses for companies within The Random House Group Limited can be
found at: www.randomhouse.co.uk/offices.htm

The Random House Group Limited Reg. No. 954009

A CIP catalogue record for this book
is available from the British Library

ISBN 9780099514152

The Random House Group Limited supports The Forest Stewardship
Council (FSC), the leading international forest certification organisation.
All our titles that are printed on Greenpeace approved FSC certified paper
carry the FSC logo. O   nd at

Hot Water

I

THE town of St Rocque stood near the coast of France. The Château Blissac stood near the town of St Rocque. J. Wellington Gedge stood near the Château Blissac. He was reading his letters on the terrace outside the drawing-room.

A passer-by, given the choice between looking at Mr Gedge and at the view beneath him, would have done well to select the latter, for this tubby little man constituted the only blot on an impressive landscape. The Château was on a hill, and from its terrace the ground descended sharply through many-coloured gardens and shrubberies till it reached the lake. Beyond the lake lay sand-dunes, and beyond these glittered the harbour, dotted with boats at anchor.

The town itself was to the left, a straggling huddle of red roofs and white walls in the centre of which, raising a golden dome proudly skywards, stood the building which had made the place the popular resort it was – the Casino Municipale. For St Rocque, once a tiny fishing village, has become in recent years a Mecca for those who enjoy watching their money gathered in with rakes by sad-eyed croupiers.

Mr Gedge, reading his correspondence, did not see the

spreading prospect. Nor did he wish to. He was not fond of St Rocque, and this morning it would have seemed less attractive to him than ever, for three of his letters bore Californian postmarks and their contents had aggravated the fever of his homesickness. Ever since his marriage two years ago and the subsequent exodus to Europe he had been pining wistfully for California. The poet speaks of a man whose heart was in the Highlands, a-chasing of the deer. Mr Gedge's was in Glendale, Cal., wandering round among the hot dogs and filling-stations.

To him, grieving, there entered a trim and personable young woman whom, after a moment of blinking, he identified as Medway, his wife's maid.

'Moddom would like to see you, sir.'

'Eh?' said Mr Gedge. He had already paid his morning visit to the Big Chief. 'Why?'

'I fancy moddom has decided to take the afternoon boat to England to-day.'

Mr Gedge started.

'What!'

'Yes, sir.'

'How long is she going to be gone?'

'I could not say, sir.'

It was a point on which Mr Gedge was anxious to obtain early and authoritative information, for much depended on it. St Rocque, normally, he found a boring spot, but there is one day in the year when it pulls itself together and gives of its best. This is on the occasion of its founder's birthday, which is piously celebrated by a Costume Carnival of impressive proportions. The Festival of the Saint was due next week, and until this moment Mr Gedge had had not even a faint hope of contributing his mite to the revels. Now, for the first time, it seemed as if something might be done about it. He stuffed his letters in his pocket and hurried into the Château.

A lover of the old and quaint would have admired the Château, dating as it did from the late fourteenth or early fifteenth century. The only feeling it gave Mr Gedge was that its architect must have been cock-eyed. Mouldering stone with spiky turrets stuck on all over it was not his idea of a house. And while its interior had been modernized, or what these French called modernized – electric light and two bathrooms – it was not at all what he had been accustomed to in Glendale, California.

He found Mrs Gedge in the Venetian Suite, a large apartment with a heavily carved ceiling which always looked as if it were going to come down and bean you. She was sitting up in bed, dictating letters to Miss Putnam, her social secretary, a thin, colourless feather-weight with horn-rimmed spectacles and an air of quiet respectability.

Mrs Gedge herself would have fought in the light-heavy division. She was a solidly built, handsome woman a few years younger than her husband, and you could see from a glance at her why he always did what she told him to. Even in repose, her manner was forceful. Of her past life before their marriage, except that she was the widow of a multi-millionaire oil man named Brewster who had left her all his multi-millions, Mr Gedge knew nothing. He sometimes thought she might have been a lion-tamer.

With a slight gesture of her hand she caused Miss Putnam to melt into thin air, and raised herself on the pillows.

'What,' asked Mr Gedge, taking the chair vacated by the secretary, 'is all this about your going to England? Medway tells me you're sailing on the afternoon boat.'

'I have had a letter from my lawyer in London. There has been some trouble about English Income Tax, and he says he must see me.'

'How about your ticket?'

'Miss Putnam is attending to that. I want you to run down to the drug store and buy me some seasick remedy. You had better get Philipson's Mal-de-Mer-o.'

'All right.'

There was a pause. Mr Gedge coughed nonchalantly.

'Going to be gone long?'

'About a week.'

'Ah!' said Mr Gedge.

A purposeful gleam lit up his prominent eyes. There and then he had resolved that he would attend the Festival of the Saint, and not only attend it but attend it right. For if anybody thought that he couldn't lay his hands on a pair of pyjama trousers and one of his wife's blouses and wrap a scarf round his head and present a life-like picture of an Oriental potentate, whoever was of that opinion, felt Mr Gedge, was mistaken in the last degree.

'Well, sir,' he said, 'I guess it's going to be lonesome without you. Yessir, it'll be lonesome all right. But I'll make out some-how,' he added bravely, for the Glendale Gedges have the right stuff in them.

'You won't be lonesome. Didn't I tell you?'

'Tell me what?'

'I have invited some people to stay at the Château. They will be arriving the day after to-morrow.'

Something of Mr Gedge's quiet happiness left him. He was not one of those men who enjoy playing the host. A lot of nosy visitors about the place, moreover, might hamper his movements.

'Quite a small party. Senator Opal and his daughter....'

'Old Opal!'

'. . . and the Vicomte de Blissac.'

'What!'

'I have never met him, but I believe he is a very charming young man.'

Mr Gedge corrected this view.

'A very charming young wild Indian. Never sober, they tell me.'

'I know all about that, and I have given orders that no alcohol is to be served in the Château during his visit. His mother's main reason for sending him to us is that she wants him to have a few weeks of complete abstinence.'

'Say, what is this joint? A Keeley Cure Institute?'

'I am very glad the Vicomte is able to come. There are several things about this house that I wish to discuss with a representative of the family. The Vicomtesse gave me to understand that the plumbing was in good repair. It isn't. It's terrible. And there's that leaky cistern upstairs.'

'So when he arrives,' said Mr Gedge morosely, 'I suppose I meet him on the doorstep and say, "Come right on in, Vicomte. We can't offer you a drink, but step up and take a look at our leaky cistern." That'll make a big hit with him.'

He rumbled wordlessly for a while. Then a sudden and unpleasant idea seemed to strike him.

'What is all this?' he asked suspiciously. 'What's the big idea back of it all? Filling up the place with Vicomtes and Senators – there's something behind it that I don't get. Why the Vicomte? How come the Senator?'

Mrs Gedge was silent for a moment. Into her manner there had crept a sort of strained alertness, like that of a leopard crouching for the spring.

'It is all quite simple,' she said. 'The Vicomte's mother has great influence with the French Government.'

'What of it?'

'Any friend of hers would be welcomed by them.'

Mr Gedge, who had no intention of spending a week-end with the French Government, said so.

'And Senator Opal is so powerful in Washington that he can practically dictate appointments.'

'What appointments?'

'Well, for instance, the appointment of American Ambassador to France.'

'Who's going to be Ambassador to France?' said Mr Gedge, mystified.

He could not have asked a more convenient question. It enabled Mrs Gedge to place the salient facts before him crisply and without further preamble.

'You are,' she said.

2

The spectacle of a human being in agony is never an agreeable one. It were well, therefore, to linger as briefly as possible over the description of J. Wellington Gedge, as this terse remark crashed into his consciousness, first gaping, then gurgling, then gasping, and then shooting from his chair as if Miss Putnam had left a pin in it. It would be best, also, for the historian to touch but lightly on his utterances, from the first strangled 'Gosh darn it!' to the final, anguished 'Be human!'

Of his frenzied circling of the room and the culmination of that circling in noisy collision with a small table laden with glass and china we will say, following out this policy of reserve, absolutely nothing.

It will be enough to hint that he was deeply moved. There are some who crave for the honours their country can bestow. Mr Gedge had never belonged to their ranks. He was not an ambitious man. The thought of being Ambassador to France filled him with a sick horror.

If this awful thing went through, it meant that years must pass before he saw California again. And those years would be spent in a city which he had disliked at sight and in the society of just the sort of people who gave him the heeby-jeebies. And a sudden grisly thought came to Mr Gedge. Didn't Ambassadors have to wear uniforms and satin knickerbockers?

'But I don't want to be an Ambassador!'

Mrs Gedge seemed to regard this as a mere animal cry, the wail of some creature of the wilds licking its wounds.

'There's nothing to being an Ambassador,' she said soothingly. 'It's just a matter of money. If you have money and there are important people like the Vicomtesse de Blissac and Senator Opal behind you . . .'

A very faint ray of hope illuminated Mr Gedge's darkness.

'I suppose you know,' he said, 'that old Opal hates my insides? We had a fuss over a golf game once and he's never forgotten it.'

'I heard about that. But I think you'll find that he will use all his influence in your support.'

'Why?'

'I had a letter from him this morning which gave me that impression.'

'What did he say?'

'It was not so much what he said. It was the general tone of the letter.'

Mr Gedge looked at his wife sharply. Her face was wearing that disquieting half-smile which always indicated that she had something up her sleeve.

'What do you mean?'

'Oh, nothing,' said Mrs Gedge. She was, as her husband had frequently had occasion to notice, a secretive woman. 'I am going to see him when I get to London to-morrow, and I think you will find that everything will be all right.'

'But why in the name of everything infernal do you want me to be an Ambassador?'

'I will tell you. When I married you, my late husband's sister Mabel made herself extremely unpleasant. She seemed to consider that a woman who had been Mrs Wilmot Brewster ought to be satisfied for life. I'm not sure that when Wilmot died she would not have liked me to commit *suttee*.'

'Do what?'

'I was only joking. Commit suicide. When an Indian dies, his widow burns herself on the grave. They call it *suttee*.'

A rather wistful look came into Mr Gedge's face. It was just his luck, he seemed to be thinking, that an unkind fate had made the late Wilmot Brewster a Californian and not an Indian.

'So I made up my mind that you should be the next American Ambassador to France. I should like to see Mabel's face when she reads the announcement in the papers. A nobody, she called you. Well, the Ambassador to France isn't a nobody.'

Despite the fact that his chin receded and his eyes bulged, J. Wellington Gedge had a certain rude sagacity. There might be things of which he was ignorant, but this he did know, that if a man is a pawn in a row between women it is futile for him to struggle. For a few tense moments he sat picking at the coverlet and staring silently into a grey future. Then he heaved himself out of his chair.

'I'll go get that Mal-de-Mer-o,' he said.

3

At about the time when Mr Gedge was starting to toddle down to the drug store, a tough-looking man in one of those tight suits which somehow seem to suggest dubious morals had entered the cocktail bar of the Hotel des Etrangers.

The Hotel des Etrangers is not far from the Casino Municipale. In fact, it is so close that a good sprinter can lose his money at the tables, rush over and get some more at the desk, and dash back and lose that all in a few minutes. St Rocque is proud of the Hotel des Etrangers, and justly. It has all the latest improvements, including a garden for the convenience of guests wishing to commit suicide, a first-class orchestra and cuisine, telephones in the bedrooms, and on the ground floor an up-to-date cocktail bar presided over by Gustave, late of Chez Jimmy, Paris.

The bar at the moment of the tough man's arrival was empty except for a dark, slender, beautifully dressed person of refined and distinguished appearance who was reading the Continental edition of the *New York Herald*. It was as he lowered the paper for an instant to knock the ash off his cigarette that the tough man uttered the pleased whoop of one who has sighted a familiar face.

'Oily!' he cried.

'Soup!' exclaimed the other.

They shook hands warmly. In their native America they had perhaps been more acquaintances than friends, but there is always enthusiasm when exiles meet in a foreign land.

'Well, you darned old horse-thief!' said the tough man.

In describing his companion thus, he had spoken figuratively. Gordon Carlisle did not steal horses. A specialist in the Confidence Trick, he would have considered such behaviour low.

'You old dog-stealer!' he replied.

This, too, was mere playful imagery. Soup Slattery had never stolen dogs. He was an expert safe-blower.

'Well, well!' said Mr Slattery. 'Fancy running into you!'

He sat down at the table. His face, which in repose resembled a slab of granite with suspicious eyes, was softened now by a genial smile. He had not actually parked his gun in the cloak-room, but he had the air of a man who has done so.

'What you doing here, Oily?'

'Oh, just looking around.'

'Me, too.'

They turned for a space to converse with the waiter on the subject of beverages. This question settled, the reunion was on again. It was some time since they had met, and they had much to discuss.

Old days passed under review. Old names came up for mention. Reminiscences of Plug This and Shorty That were exchanged. Soup Slattery showed Mr Carlisle the scar on his fore-arm where a quick-drawing householder of Des Moines, Iowa, had pipped him a couple of years back when he was visiting at his residence. Mr Carlisle showed Soup Slattery the nasty place on his left leg where a disappointed investor in Australian gold-mines had bitten him. It was only after some half-hour of these confidences that the talk took on a softer and more sentimental note.

'Got the little woman over here with you?' asked Mr Slattery.

'Little woman?'

'I met some guy, forget who it was, told me you were married to Gum-Shoe Gertie.'

Gordon Carlisle had a somewhat melancholy face. At these words, its melancholy deepened.

'No,' he said.

'This guy said you were.'

'Well, I'm not.'

He spoke a little sharply. Then, as if feeling remorse for having snubbed a well-meaning friend, he explained.

'Gertie and I had a fight.'

He brooded for a space. Then the urge to pour forth his troubles overcame reserve.

'Just about nothing,' he said bitterly. 'A trifling misunderstanding you would have thought could have been put right in a couple of words. She'd had to go to hospital for a few weeks with a broken leg, and while she was there it happened that I saw something from time to time of a girl friend of hers. Purely on business. And when she heard about it, she went haywire. I kept telling her the whole thing had been strictly on the up-and-up, but she wouldn't listen. One word led to another, and in the end she hit me over the head with a vase and went out of my life. That was a year ago, and from that day I've not set eyes on her. Women are tough.'

'You bet they're tough,' agreed Mr Slattery. 'You never know where you are with them. You take me, for instance. Boy, could I write a book! The slickest partner I ever worked with goes and leaves me flat without so much as giving me her telephone number.'

'I'm sunk without Gertie.'

'I'm sunk without this dame. Julia her name was.'

'Professionally, I mean.'

'Professionally's what I mean. There wasn't any of the hearts and flowers stuff between Julia and me. You never met Julia, did you?'

'No.'

'Well, she was just the best inside worker a safe-blower ever had. Used to get herself invited to these swell homes, and could get away with it, too, because she had style and class and read books and all. To hear her talk you'd of thought she was in the Social Register.'

'Gertie . . .'

'Julia,' said Mr Slattery, manfully holding the floor, 'worked with me for years. And then one day – four years ago almost to this very minute – she told me out of a blue sky, as you might say, that she was through. Just like that. No explanations. Just gave me the Bronx Cheer and beat it. And me who had split Even Stephen with her on every deal, never chiselling, never holding out on her, no, not so much as a dime. Seems to me sometimes, the squarer a guy is with these beazels, the worse they treat him. Well, sir, off she went, and I've never been the same since. I've gone down and down, as you might say.' Mr Slattery hesitated. 'Shall I tell you something, Oily? I even do stick-up work now.'

'You do?' said Mr Carlisle, and though he tried to keep the note of disapproval out of his voice it crept in. He hoped he was no snob, but there are social grades and degrees in the world of crime, and everybody knows that stick-up men are not quite.

Mr Slattery flushed.

'A guy's got to live,' he argued.

'Oh, sure,' said Mr Carlisle.

There was a rather constrained silence. When Mr Slattery spoke again, it was evident that he was anxious to re-establish himself in his companion's eyes.

'It isn't as if I wouldn't open a safe if I could. There's a big job right here in this town I'd take on to-morrow, if only I'd got a partner to do the inside work.'

Mr Carlisle was interested. He forgot his disapproval.

'Right here in this town?'

'About a mile out. Joint called the Chatty-o Blissac.'

Mr Carlisle shook his head.

'Don't know it. I'm a stranger in these parts.'

'It's up that hill past the Casino. Some American dame has rented it. I'll bet she's got ice.'

'You don't know.'

'Must have – a dame that can rent a great place like that.'

'Probably keeps it at her bank,' said Mr Carlisle, whom misfortune had made a pessimist.

'Yeah, I guess so. Not that it's any use getting worked up about it. I couldn't do a thing, anyway, me not having an inside worker.'

'Well, I could do the inside stand,' said Mr Carlisle on a brighter note. 'If it comes to that, why couldn't I do the inside stand?'

'How are you going to get inside? You see,' said Mr Slattery, 'that's how it goes. A man's helpless.' He drained his glass and rose. 'Well, I'll be taking a little stroll. You staying on here?'

'Might as well be here as anywhere,' said Mr Carlisle gloomily. The industrial depression had affected his spirits considerably.

Mr Slattery passed out into the sunlit street, walking aimlessly towards the harbour. And it was as his wandering feet brought him to a narrow and unfrequented alley that he observed immediately ahead of him a small tubby man reading a letter.

For a moment Mr Slattery hesitated. Then, with a half-sigh, he produced his automatic. The task before him was distasteful, but these were times when every little helped. He sidled towards the tubby man.

'Stick 'em up!' he said.

4

Mr Gedge stuck them up. He would have been glad to oblige anyone so big and ugly even without the added inducement of an automatic pistol. He was conscious of a sinking sensation akin to that which his wife's eye sometimes induced in him and, mingled with alarm, a tender pang of commiseration for anyone so deluded as to regard holding him up as a step on the road to wealth.

Mr Slattery, who had been doing some brisk exploring with his left hand, now appeared to have learned the sickening truth. A look of chagrin came into his gnarled features, and the tip of his broken nose twitched in obvious disillusionment. His whole aspect was that of one suddenly brought face to face with the facts of life.

'Haven't you *any* dough?' he asked querulously.

'Not a cent,' sighed Mr Gedge.

Mr Slattery grunted unhappily. Mr Gedge was an opulent-looking little man, and he had hoped for better things. Replacing the pistol in his pocket, he pushed his hat back with a sort of Byronic despair. The movement caused Mr Gedge to utter an exclamation.

'Say! I've seen you before.'

'Yeah?'

Mr Slattery spoke indifferently. He rather gave the impression that he felt that nothing mattered now. All this trouble and fuss, and not even lunch-money at the end of it.

'Aren't you the fellow who stuck me up one night in Chicago?'

Mr Slattery eyed him dully. He seemed to be saying that one meets so many people.

'What were you wearing?'

'A grey business suit with an invisible blue twill.'

'I don't place you. Sorry.'

'Sure you do. A cop came along and you made me put my arm through yours and stroll along as if we were old friends. We sang, don't you remember?'

'Sang what?'

'"Pale hands I loved beside the Shalimar." You took the bass.'

Mr Slattery's face brightened suddenly.

'Why, that's right. I remember now. Well, well!'

'It's a long way to Chi.'

'It sure is.'

'They told me your name, too. It'll come back to me in a minute.'

'Who told you my name?'

'The cops, when I described you. I've got it. Soup Slattery. One of the cops said it sounded like Soup Slattery, and another cop said yes, he wouldn't be surprised if it wasn't old Soup, and then they went on playing checkers. The only thing that seemed to puzzle them was that you should be holding people up on the street. They said you were an expert safe-blower.'

'I sometimes do a bit of stick-up work on the side,' said Mr Slattery with a touch of stiffness. 'Any objection?'

'None,' said Mr Gedge hastily. 'None whatever. It's all right by me.'

He may have been going on to cite the classical precedent of Michelangelo, who refused to be satisfied with one branch of

Art; but at this moment his companion returned to the main point at issue.

'*Why* haven't you any dough?'

'I never have.'

'You look rich enough.'

'My wife is rich. Immensely rich. Her late husband left her millions.'

'And you slipped in and copped off the widow? Did pretty well for yourself.'

Mr Slattery spoke disapprovingly. He was a man of sentiment, and when he saw one of these cold, commercial unions in a motion-picture he always hissed.

Mr Gedge sensed the unspoken slur.

'I did not marry my dear wife for her money,' he said warmly. 'I was a rich man myself at the time of our wedding. But unfortunately I played the Market. . . .'

There was nothing of the austere in Mr Slattery's manner now. He was eyeing Mr Gedge with warm-hearted interest.

'Were you caught in the big crash?'

'Was I! Lost every dollar I had.'

'Me, too,' said Mr Slattery, wincing at the memory. 'Hot zig! Those were the days! Like going down in an express elevator, wasn't it? Did you have any Electric Bond and Share?'

'Did I!'

'What did you buy it at?'

'A hundred and sixty-seven.'

'A hundred and sixty-nine – me. How about Montgomery-Ward?'

'Mine cost me a hundred and twelve.'

'So did mine.'

'General Motors?' asked Mr Gedge eagerly.

'Say, let's talk of something else,' said Mr Slattery.

For a few moments the two financiers let their thoughts stray silently back into the past. Mr Slattery sighed.

'Well, I'm mighty glad to have met you again, Mr – what was the name?'

'Gedge. J. Wellington Gedge. And I've certainly appreciated meeting you, Mr Slattery. How about coming and having a little drink?'

A touch of the old moroseness returned to Mr Slattery's manner.

'What do you mean, coming and having a little drink? You haven't any money.'

'Lend me some,' said Mr Gedge.

It had been no part of Mr Slattery's plans when he set out that morning with his gun to finance his victims, but there was something so appealing in the other's voice that a sort of *noblesse oblige* spirit awoke in him. He handed over a hundred francs.

'You couldn't make it two hundred, could you?'

'Sure,' said Mr Slattery, though not very heartily.

'I'll tell you what,' said Mr Gedge, inspired. 'Give me a level thousand, and then that'll be a nice, round sum.'

Mr Slattery peeled a *mille* off his slender roll, but his manner as he did so was not vivacious. He seemed to be wondering what had ever given him the impression that sticking people up in the street was a sound commercial venture.

5

Seated with his new friend at a table in one of the little cafés near the harbour, Mr Gedge became communicative. For many months he had been yearning for a sympathetic ear into which to decant his troubles, and now he had found one. This charming safe-blower, he decided, should hear all.

'Yessir,' he said. 'That's how it is. My wife has all the money, and I'm simply the Hey-You around the place.'

'Is that so?'

'Yessir. The Patsy, that's what I am. Just the squidge. You wouldn't be far out if you said I was only a bird in a gilded cage. Whatever Mrs Gedge says, goes. I want to live in California. She insists on coming to France. Do you think if I had any money I'd be living in a dump like the Château Blissac? No, sir. I'd be back in Glendale, where men are men.'

Mr Slattery gave a little start.

'Do you live at the Chatty-o Blissac?'

'Yessir. Right there at the Château Blissac.'

Mr Slattery chewed his lower lip thoughtfully. The discovery that this little man was residing, even if only in the modest capacity of a bird in a gilded cage, at the house which had been so much in his day-dreams, had stirred him a good deal. He could not have said just what he hoped would develop from their acquaintanceship, but he certainly felt that it was worth taking trouble to conciliate him. He cocked an eye politely.

'Do you now?' he said. 'Well, well!'

'Yessir. Mrs Gedge insisted on renting it, and I wouldn't give you a nickel for the place. It makes me sick. And that's not the half of it.'

'No?'

'No, sir. Do you know what?'

'What?'

'When she told me this morning, you could have knocked me down with a feather. What do you think?'

'What?'

'You'll never guess.'

'What?'

'Do you know what she told me this morning?'

'How the hell should I know what she told you this morning?' said Mr Slattery, momentary irritation causing him to deviate from his policy of courtliness. 'Do you think I was hiding under the bed?'

'She told me I've got to be American Ambassador to France.'

Mr Slattery considered this.

'You won't like that.'

'I know darned well I won't like it. Ambassadors have to wear uniforms and knickerbockers . . . the sissies.'

'And cocked hats.'

'Cocked hats?'

'Sure. I've seen them in the news-reels. And they get kissed all the time by Frenchmen.'

It had been Mr Gedge's belief until he heard these words that he had explored to their ultimate depths the drawbacks to representing his country in an ambassadorial capacity. He now perceived that the last and most hideous of them had escaped his notice. He sat for a moment paralysed. Then words poured from him in a frenzied tumult.

'I won't do it! I just won't do it. No, sir! I'll get me a little capital, enough to start again on, and then I'll defy her. Yessir, that's what I'll do – defy her. I'm very fond of my dear wife, but I'll walk right up to her and defy her. Here's what I'll say: "Look-ut!" I'll say, "I've got enough to start again on now, and I'm independent, see? And I don't intend to be Ambassador to France," I'll say. "The quicker you forget that Ambassador stuff, the better, because it's all wet. And what's more, talking of France," I'll say, "I'm getting out of it on the next boat and going back to California, that's what I'm doing. If you want to stick on in France, stick on," I'll say. "But I'm going right back to Glendale. Yessir!"'

Mr Slattery, though not an unkindly man, was practical. It is his type that discourages dreamers.

'Where,' he asked, 'are you going to get your capital?'

In the exhilaration of building air-castles Mr Gedge had overlooked this point. The fire faded from his eye.

'You couldn't lend me a little, could you?'

Mr Slattery said he could not.

'I shouldn't want more than ten thousand. If I could lay my hands on ten thousand, I could get back everything I lost.'

Mr Slattery said that if he ever saw ten thousand dollars he would take each individual bill singly and kiss it.

A mad rebellion at Fate's unkindness seemed to sting Mr Gedge.

'It's so unjust!'

'What's unjust?'

'Why, well, look. Do you know what?'

Mr Slattery begged his companion not to keep asking him if he knew what.

'Well, *do* you know what? When I married Mrs Gedge I was a rich man....'

'You told me that.'

'Yes, but I didn't tell you this. I covered that woman with jewels. Well, when I say covered her...Anyway, I gave her a darned lot. Sixty thousand dollars' worth, at least.'

Mr Slattery was impressed. Sixty grand, he agreed, was pretty good gravy.

'Think what those sixty thousand fish would mean to me now! Think what I could do with them!'

'Ah.'

'I tell you,' said Mr Gedge, trembling with self-pity, 'when I see Mrs Gedge swanking around in those jewels I can understand how men become cynics.'

For an instant the significance of the remark did not seem to penetrate to Mr Slattery's consciousness. He said 'Ah' again in rather an absent voice, and refreshed himself from his glass. Then, suddenly, he jumped as if something hot had touched him.

'Swanking around? Do you mean she's got them with her?'

'Yessir.'

'Right there at the Chatty-o?'

'Yessir.'

There was a pause.

'Keeps them in a safe, I suppose?' asked Mr Slattery casually.

'When she isn't wearing them.'

Mr Slattery fell into a rueful silence. He was thinking of what might have been. If only his lost Julia were with him now, he mused, how swiftly she would think up some plan for getting into this Château and working the inside stand. Lacking her gentle aid, it seemed to him that he was helpless.

Of course, there was Oily. Oily had expressed himself willing to do the inside work. But how was he to make Mr Gedge's acquaintance and so qualify for an invitation to the Chatty-o? It was the difficulty of establishing that first link that saddened Mr Slattery. He could scarcely introduce Gordon Carlisle to Mr Gedge. He was not a very intelligent man, but even he could see that a prospective visitor to the Château Blissac would require better credentials than an introduction from a stick-up man and expert safe-blower.

He drew in a deep breath. The thing seemed cold, after all.

He was aroused from his meditations by a stirring in the seat opposite. Mr Gedge was making preparations for departure.

'You going?'

'Yessir. Got to get back.'

'What's your hurry?'

'Well, I'll tell you. Mrs Gedge is off to England to-day on the afternoon boat, and there'll be a lot of things she'll be wanting to talk to me about. Goodbye, Mr Slattery. Pleased to have met you.'

Mr Slattery did not reply. Although his granite face did not show it, inwardly he was tingling with rapture. It was as if there had been a belt of fog hiding the Promised Land from him and Mr Gedge had ripped it apart and brought the sun smiling through.

Historians relate of the mathematician Archimedes that on a certain occasion, having solved some intricate problem, he leaped from the bath in which he was sitting and ran through the streets crying 'Eureka! Eureka!' Mr Slattery was not in his bath, but if he had been he would certainly have left it now, and it is highly probable that, if he had known what it meant, he would have shouted 'Eureka!' For he had found the way.

A moment later he was out in the street, hurrying towards the Hotel des Etrangers.

6

Mr Carlisle was still in the cocktail bar. Mr Slattery made for his table.

'Oily,' he said, 'we're sitting pretty. The thing's in the bag!'

Mr Carlisle sat up alertly. His friend, he knew, was no idle talker. Seldom, too, was he as emotional as this. Strong and silent were the adjectives which sprang to the lips when describing Soup Slattery. If Mr Slattery was excited, it meant something.

'What thing? What we were talking about?'

'Sure. That Chatty-o. I've just run into the guy that lives there.'

Mr Carlisle's animation increased.

'How did you do that?'

'We happened to meet,' said Mr Slattery with a touch of embarrassment. 'And we got chummy and had a drink. And he says Mrs Gedge don't keep her ice at no bank. She's got it right there with her. In a safe she keeps it. Well, say! Show me the pete I can't open with my eye-teeth and a pin, and I'll eat it. And when I say that,' added Mr Slattery with justifiable pride, 'I'm not handing myself a thing.'

'But . . .'

'I know. The inside stand. How are we going to work it? I'll tell you. This Gedge dame is sailing for England this afternoon.'

He paused to allow the momentous information to sink in. A glance at his companion's face told him that he had not overestimated the agility of the other's mind. Mr Carlisle took his meaning instantly.

'I go on the boat and get acquainted?'

'That's right.'

'Easy.'

'You'd best tell her you're one of these French titled guys with lots of pull with the fellows that run the French Government. On account she wants her old man to be Ambassador to France, and she'll think you can help.'

'I'll string the beads till she thinks I own the French Government.'

'We're on a big thing, Oily, if you can work it. This Gedge tells me that ice of hers runs as high as sixty grand.'

Mr Carlisle licked his lips. A dreamy look had come into his face. Like Mr Slattery a short while before, he seemed to be gazing upon the Promised Land.

'If I'm not inside that Château in five days,' he said, 'I'm not the worker I used to be.'

CHAPTER 2

I

THE glorious weather which was making St Rocque's summer season such a success was equally glorious across the English Channel. Sunshine had flooded the grounds of the Château Blissac, and sunshine shortly after four o'clock on the following afternoon was flooding the streets of London. It turned the pavements to gold. It lit up omnibuses and the fruit-barrows of costermongers. It illuminated with its merry beams the faces of pedestrians, dray-horses and policemen.

Only Waterloo Station, that austere cavern, would have none of it. Wrapped in its customary decent gloom, it continued to resemble a cathedral whose acolytes fill in their time with a bit of steam-fitting on the side. And to-day the sombre note was intensified by the presence of large crowds of moist adults, accompanied for the most part by children with spades and buckets. For it was the beginning of what the papers call the Holiday Rush. London and its young, like Xenophon's Ten Thousand, were making for the sea.

Outside the gates behind which the management keeps the 4.21 express to Yeovil and points west, there stood a young man whose appearance did something to raise the lowered tone of the place. If not strictly handsome, he looked extraordinarily fit and healthy, and there was in his demeanour a cheerful contentment which marked him off from the droves of worried fathers who were so obviously wishing that they had remained bachelors. All this was new and entertaining to him. He had been in England only a few months, and he enjoyed every manifestation of English life. As he now detached two children, Ralph and Flossie, from his legs and handed them back to their parents, there was nothing of impatience in his manner, only a kindly solicitude. And if he would have preferred that another child, named Rupert, had selected somebody else's trousers as a strop for his all-day sucker, he gave no outward evidence of the fact.

As to his identity, if you read your Society Gossip, you will recall that the engagement was recently announced between Lady Beatrice Bracken (who is, of course, the daughter of the Earl of Stableford) and Patrick B. Franklyn (who is, of course, the well-known young American millionaire and sportsman). This was Packy. Beatrice was leaving London to-day for her father's seat, Worbles, in Dorsetshire, and he had come to Waterloo to see her off.

She came in view now, walking disdainfully through the crowd like a princess among the *Jacquerie*, a girl so spectacularly beautiful that you would have thought that even some of these perspiring parents with five children to look after might have spared her a glance. Beatrice's was a comeliness which had lent lustre to Biddlecombe Hunt Balls, where comeliness is comeliness, and never failed to attract attention even in the Royal Enclosure at Ascot or among the throng which parades Lord's Cricket Ground during the luncheon interval of the Eton and Harrow match.

Mary Mayfair, who conducts the page entitled 'A Little Bird in Society' in *Fireside Chatter*, had said of Lady Beatrice Bracken in a recent issue that at the last reception at the Spanish Embassy she had been *facile princeps* and *non plus ultra*, showing to superb advantage in a dress of the new opaline *crêpe royale* with the bias cut to stress the natural line of the figure. And Mary was right.

At the moment, nervous irritation was preventing her from looking quite her best. If there was one thing she disliked, it was having to travel by train during the tripper season; and if it was really necessary that she should revisit the ancestral home to help her father entertain his house-party, she thought he might have sent the car for her. But with petrol at its current price, the level-headed old man had been too smart for that.

A girl who seldom smiled, she greeted Packy with the merest twitch of the upper lip which had come out so well in the Lazlo portrait.

'What a mob!' she said disgustedly.

'I like it,' said Packy. 'All this is helping me to understand the spirit which has made England what it is. I can see now what they mean when they talk of the bulldog breed. There was one fellow came navigating by here just now with an infant in each hand and attached to each infant, mark you, a Sealyham on a string. The last I saw of them, the port-side child had got tangled up with the starboard Sealyham and the port-side Sealyham with the starboard child, and, take it for all in all, it was beginning to look like a big day for Dad. In my opinion, good clean fun, gratifyingly free from all this modern suggestiveness. By the way, how about your baggage?'

'Parker is looking after it.'

'And reading matter? Would you like me to race to the newsstand and get you something? There's just time.'

'No, thanks. I have a book.'

'She has a book. What is it?'

'Blair Eggleston's *Worm i' the Root*.'

'Blair Eggleston? Why does that name seem familiar? Have I met him somewhere?'

'I introduced you to him at the Young Artists Exhibition in Dover Street a week ago.'

'Of course, yes. I remember. A gosh-awful pill with side whiskers.'

The remark was one of those unfortunate remarks. It had the effect of increasing Beatrice's irritation.

'Don't talk like that,' she said in the voice which, much as he worshipped the girl, sometimes made Packy think that she must have governess blood in her. 'Everybody whose opinion matters regards Mr Eggleston as one of the leaders of the younger school of novelists.'

'Well, it's no good him going about boasting that I read him, because I don't.'

'You never read anything.'

'I've read all Edgar Wallace.'

'Well, you'd better read all Blair Eggleston. I do wish you wouldn't be like this. What on earth is the use of my taking all this trouble over you – trying to make you appreciate good books and pictures and so on, if you are going to talk like a Yahoo?'

'I'm sorry,' said Packy. 'You're quite right.'

He was full of remorse. A nice way, he felt contritely, to behave to a girl who had gone to such pains to get behind his spiritual self and push.

At Yale, where he had been educated, Packy Franklyn had been an All-American half-back, but he had tended, he fully realized, rather to under-nourish his spiritual self. He had given it the short end, and it was missing, he knew, on several cylinders. He was self-critic enough to be aware that, if there was a department in which he could safely be sold short, it was the department of the soul. How ill it became him, then, not to cooperate to the fullest extent with a girl who was trying to jack it up.

Apart from her beauty, what had fascinated him from the first about Lady Beatrice Bracken was the loftiness of her ideals. When it came to ideals, she had unquestionably got something. And of this loftiness of ideals she was giving him the benefit. Already she had toned down his natural exuberance quite a good deal, and he was not half sure that if she spat on her hands and stuck to it she might not some day succeed in almost curing the slight nausea with which picture galleries and concerts now affected him.

Yes, stiffish going though she might be at times, closely though her manner towards him might occasionally resemble that which, he felt, she probably employed when rebuking James, the footman, for bringing cold toast to the tea-table, she undeniably bore the banner with the strange device, Excelsior, and he writhed to think that he should have wounded her with his flippancy.

'I'm quite wrong about Blair Eggleston,' he said, 'I must have been thinking of a couple of other fellows. Now that I recall our meeting, I remember that I was greatly struck with his quiet charm. I will start reading him to-morrow.'

'I happened to meet him in Bond Street this morning,' said Beatrice. 'I told him that you would be at a loose end in London....'

'But I shan't.'

'What do you mean?'

'Well, now that you're going to be away, there doesn't seem much point in sticking on in a city which appears to imagine that Nature intended it for a Turkish Bath. I thought of chartering a boat and pushing off somewhere. I saw an advertisement the other day,' said Packy, becoming lyrical, for in his native land he had been an enthusiastic yachtsman, 'of an auxiliary yawl, forty-five feet over all, thirty-nine on water line, thirteen foot beam, Marconi rig . . .'

'I particularly want you to stay in London,' said Beatrice.

Her tone was final, and Packy eyed her with dismay. He had been looking forward to that yachting trip.

'But why?'

'Well, for one thing . . .'

She broke off, and stooped to rub an ankle which had just been kicked by a child named Ernie. And at the same instant there smote Packy vigorously between the shoulder-blades one of those hearty buffets which tell us we have found a friend. Turning, he perceived a lissom young man with green eyes and hair cut *en brosse* who beamed upon him fondly.

For a moment he was at a loss. The other's face, like his manner, was familiar; but, unlike his manner, only vaguely so. Then memory awoke.

'Veek!'

'My old Packy!'

It was eighteen months since Packy had last seen that effervescent young French aristocrat, the Vicomte de Blissac. Mingled with his delight at seeing him now was the feeling that he wished the reunion could have taken place a few minutes after the departure of Beatrice's train instead of a few minutes before. His friendship with the heir of the De Blissacs dated back to the brave old days in New York, and something told him that the other was going to start talking about them. And experience had taught Packy that where Beatrice was concerned it was better to keep the whole subject of the brave old days a sealed book.

However, she had stopped rubbing her ankle, so there was nothing to do but present this ghost of his dead past.

'Lady Beatrice Bracken. The Vicomte de Blissac.'

Beatrice bowed. In her beautiful eyes, as she did so, there was a stony look. Packy read its message. She did not approve of the old Veek.

It was not often that Lady Beatrice Bracken did approve of Packy's friends. It sometimes seemed to her that each was more repulsive and impossible than the last. She herself, except for a taste for the society of intellectuals, was exclusively County in her intimacies. Packy, on the other hand, as far as she had been able to gather, seemed to like everybody. You could never be sure when you met him that you would not find him hobnobbing with a prize-fighter or worse. The discovery that he was on cordial terms with this Vicomte de Blissac, of whom she had heard much from time to time, did nothing to diminish her already rather pronounced resemblance to a smartly-dressed iceberg.

'De Blissac and I saw a good deal of one another when he was in New York a couple of years ago,' said Packy, with that slight touch of the apologetic which your well-trained *fiancé* employs on these occasions.

'We hotted it up,' said the Vicomte, quite unnecessarily adding explanatory footnotes. 'We made whoopee. We painted that old town pink.'

His eyes, which had widened a little at the sight of so much beauty at so short a range, now left Beatrice. It was plainly Packy, the old friend, in whom he was really interested.

'So you got home all right, my Packy?'

He chuckled amusedly and turned to Beatrice, all smiles, as one imparting delightful news.

'When last I see this old *farceur* it is in New York, and he is jumping out of the window of a speakeasy with two policemen after him. Great fun. Great good fun. Do you remember, my Packy, that night when . . .'

'Are you off somewhere, Veek?' asked Packy hastily.

'Oh, yes. But do you remember . . . ?'

'Where?'

'I go to St Rocque. I catch the train at a quarter past four to Southampton.'

Packy sighed a sigh of relief.

'Well, do you? It's a debatable point. I don't know if you have happened to notice that it is now four-fourteen.'

'*Zut!*' exclaimed the Vicomte, and vanished like an eel into mud.

Beatrice was the first to break a silence during which the warm summer day seemed to cool off several degrees.

'You do know the most awful people.'

'Oh, the Veek's all right.'

'From what I have heard of him I don't agree with you.'

A porter opened the gates, and they passed through. They arrived at an empty first-class compartment, and Packy took up his stand at the door to repel intruders.

He had fallen into a meditative silence. He had just discovered, and was shocked to discover, that this meeting with the Vicomte de Blissac had affected him with a well-defined spasm of what the ancient Greeks called *pothos*, a sudden, deplorable nostalgia for that regrettable past of which the other had formed a part.

He fought it down. It was revolting, he told himself, that the *fiancé* of a wonderful girl like Beatrice should not be utterly contented with his lot. True, he and the Veek had had some pretty good times together in the old days, but how far, far happier he was now, a reformed character under the personal supervision of the most beautiful girl in England.

By way of helping to stifle the quite improper wistfulness which the sight of his old friend had aroused in him, he reached for her hand and pressed it.

'It would be so good for you,' said Beatrice, and Packy became aware that his reverie had caused him to miss her latest remarks.

'I'm sorry,' he said. 'I was thinking of something. What was that?'

'I was just saying that I wished you would try to make friends with somebody worth while, like Mr Eggleston. He is the sort of man I would like you to know.'

'I must give him a buzz some time.'

He turned aside to stare sourly at a grocer named Witherspoon who was showing a disposition to invade the compartment. And so forbidding was his eye that the latter quailed and passed on, taking with him Mrs Witherspoon and their four children, Percy, Bertram, Alice and Daisy.

'. . . at a quarter to five,' said Beatrice.

Once more Packy found that he had missed something.

'What's that?'

'Mr Eggleston wants you to meet him at a quarter to five in the lobby of the Northumberland Hotel. He is giving you tea.'

'What!'

'And I want you to cultivate him. He is a most interesting man, and he will do you a lot of good.'

A cloud had come over Packy's cheerful face.

'Have I really got to go and swill tea with this side-whiskered bird?'

'Don't call him a side-whiskered bird. Yes, you have. And the more you can be with him, the better. A friend like that will keep you from getting into mischief.'

Packy started.

'Mischief? Me!'

'You know perfectly well that, left to yourself, you would get into hot water of some kind the moment my back was turned.'

'I wouldn't dream ...'

'Have you forgotten what happened when I went off to Norfolk two months ago?'

'But I explained that – explained it fully. I got mixed up in a birthday party....'

'Yes, and I don't want you to get mixed up in any more. They were very upset about that at home. You know how particular Father and Mother are.'

Packy nodded penitently. Modern laxness, he was aware, had not touched the Earl of Stableford and his countess.

'Aunt Gwendolyn said you were a flippertygibbet.'

'A what?'

'A flippertygibbet.'

Packy drew himself up a little haughtily. Comment and criticism from his affianced he was prepared to accept. But when it came to her moth-eaten relations shooting off their heads ...

'That's all right what that old cat-fancier and cheater-at-solitaire says,' he replied with a dignity which became him well. 'Here's a little message which you can pass on to her from me. You can tell her... No, on second thoughts, perhaps better not. Just give her my love and say I hope it chokes her.'

He suspended his remarks in order to foil the attempt of an assistant cashier named Bodkin to muscle into the compartment together with his wife Miriam, his sister Louise, his caged parrot Polly, and what had the appearance of being the full strength of some juvenile school or college. There was, he assured them quite falsely, plenty of room further down the train, and the success of his arguments seemed to exercise upon Beatrice a softening effect. When she resumed the conversation, it was on a gentler note.

'I do hope you won't get slack while I'm away. I want you to keep on going to concerts and picture galleries.'

Packy quivered devoutly.

'Let 'em try to keep me out! That's all I say. Just let 'em try it.'

'They are doing you so much good.'

'You bet they are. I can feel the old soul swelling like a poisoned pup.'

'Yascha Pryzsky is giving a recital at Queen's Hall to-morrow.'

'Atta Yascha!'

'And there's that new play at the Gate Theatre they say is so wonderful. What I feel is that if you were going about with a man like Blair Eggleston . . .'

Packy patted her hand fondly.

'I won't let him out of my sight. If you want me to sop up tea with him this afternoon, I will sop it up till my eyeballs squeak. And day by day in every way I will haunt him more and more. He shall dress of a morning and find me lurking in his left shoe . . . . Hullo, you're off.'

The train had given itself a shake and was now beginning to slide along the platform. Packy trotted beside it. Beatrice continued to lean out of the window.

'Well, mind you do see plenty of Mr Eggleston.'

'I bet it'll seem plenty.'

'Don't miss Pryzsky.'

'I won't.'

'And see that play at the Gate.'

'I will.'

The train gathered speed. Packy removed his hat and waved it lovingly.

'And go and get your hair cut,' screamed Beatrice. 'You look like a chrysanthemum.'

The train bore her out of sight.

2

Packy stood on the platform, running an appraising hand over the back of his head. Yes, he saw what she meant. Slightly on the matted side, perhaps. Undoubtedly a suggestion of Absalom, the son of Saul. They had got the 4.21 off on the dot, so there would be ample time for him to look in at the barber-shop of the Hotel Northumberland before meeting the pill, Eggleston. He hailed a cab, feeling something of the valiant glow which comes to a knight who has been given a behest by his ladye and sees his way clear to the fulfilment of it.

The barber-shop of the Hotel Northumberland, which is situated in the basement of that well-known caravanserai, is as a rule a busy, bustling place, gay with the click of scissors and all the latest news about the weather. To Packy's surprise, it contained, when he entered it some minutes later, not only no customers but, oddly enough, no barbers either. A strange quiet enfolded the room, and the scent of bay-rum hung eerily over its emptiness.

But he was not in the frame of mind to devote much attention to the matter. He relished rather than marvelled at this solitude. Sitting down to wait, he gave himself up to long, loving thoughts of Beatrice.

A quarter of an hour later, he awoke to discover that the place was still entirely free from barbers.

For these apparently inexplicable mysteries there is always a solution. We cannot here go into the rights and wrongs of the case, though it was one fraught with great interest: we must content ourselves with stating that for some little while past disaffection had been rearing its ugly head among the hair-dressing staff of the Hotel Northumberland, with the result that at precisely four o'clock that afternoon a lightning strike had been called and the rebels had downed scissors.

Unaware of this, Packy continued to sit perplexed. And he had just decided to give the thing up and take his custom else-where, when the telephone rang at his elbow.

To ignore a ringing telephone is one of the few feats of which humanity has so far proved incapable. Packy took up the receiver, and instantaneously a loud and irascible voice with an American intonation nearly broke his ear-drum.

'Hello! Hello! HELL-O! Say, how many more times have I got to call up before I get a little service? Come on! Come on! If this is the way you run your hotels on this side, God help England! Do you think I've nothing better to do than sit here trying to get a blasted barber-shop on the wire? Come on! Come on! Come on!'

'Are you there?' enquired Packy mildly.

The Voice seemed to resent the question.

'Are *you* there, darn it! That's the point. I've been ringing for the last half-hour. What's the matter with you all? Deaf or something? This is Senator Opal speaking, from Suite 400.

I want a man up here at once. Senator Ambrose Opal. Suite 400. Send a man here immediately. I want my hair cut.'

It was on the tip of Packy's tongue to inform the other that by one of those coincidences which so often occur in life he himself was in precisely the same situation. But even as he opened his mouth to reveal this bond which linked them he became aware of a disturbing emotion.

He diagnosed it immediately. It was the Old Adam stirring within him once more.

In his unregenerate days, in that graceless past before Beatrice's beneficent influence had come to give his soul its Daily Dozen, such an opportunity for making a fool of himself would have enchanted him. With a good deal of dismay, he found that it was enchanting him now. Indeed, it was making his mouth water. Only the thought of Beatrice . . .

'Come on! Come on!'

And yet, would Beatrice wish him to reject an experience which could scarcely fail to enrich his outlook on life?

'Come on! Come on! Come on!'

Suddenly Packy's conscience was at rest. He wondered what he had been hesitating for. Beatrice, he saw now, would be the first to applaud the bringing of aid and comfort to a distressed Senator. To go and hack at this old buster's thatch would be to perform a kindly and altruistic act, very much the same sort of thing for which Sir Philip Sidney and the Boy Scouts are so highly thought of. He rather doubted if even Beatrice's aunt Gwendolyn could find anything in it to view with concern.

And there was another thing. This obviously must be the famous Senator Opal, the great Dry legislator, the man who had only just failed to put over the Opal Law, which was to have been about six times as severe as the Volstead Act. If he shrank from the proposed tryst, he would probably never get another chance of meeting this celebrity. And Beatrice was always saying how much she wanted him to meet the best people.

For Beatrice's sake, then, he must certainly see the thing through.

'I will be right up, sir,' he said respectfully.

3

Packy Franklyn was not an unreasonable young man. He knew that you cannot have everything just so in this world. Nevertheless, as he entered Suite 400, he could have wished that its occupant had been a shade less formidable. His first sight of Senator Ambrose Opal made him feel as if he had taken on the lion-barbering concession at a Zoo.

The sponsor of the Opal Law was a man of medium height and rather more than medium girth. He had the massive forehead which seems to go with seats in the American Senate. Above this forehead was a fine jungle of snow-white hair, below it a pair of jet-black eyebrows, and beneath these two piercing and penetrating eyes which even now were none too friendly.

'Come on, come on,' he said. It seemed to be his favourite expression.

He seated himself in a convenient chair, and Packy, having swathed him in a sheet, brought to bear what he could remember of the technique of the profession.

'Rather thin on top, sir.'

'No, it's not.'

'Scalp a little dry, sir.'

'No, it isn't.'

'Ever try a hot-oil shampoo, sir?'

'No. And I'm not going to.'

'Beautiful day, sir.'

'What?'

'The day, sir. Beautiful.'

'What of it?'

Rightly or wrongly, Packy received the impression that small talk was not desired. He addressed himself silently to his task, and for a few minutes only the snipping of scissors disturbed the calm of the apartment. At the end of that period the whole atmosphere of the place was suddenly brightened and improved out of all knowledge by the entrance of a girl. She came right in without knocking and sat down on the table.

Although betrothed to Lady Beatrice Bracken, Packy Franklyn had not wholly given up the good old custom of looking squarely at pretty girls. He looked squarely at this one, and found her charming. She had a nice round face that suggested possibilities in the way of dimples and nice black hair and a nice little figure and nice dark eyes. And when she spoke her voice was nice, too, giving her a full hand.

'Hullo, Father.'

'Hullo.'

'Having your hair cut?'

'Yes.'

Packy could put two and two together. The first portion of this dialogue had told him that here were a father and daughter, the second that there existed between them a healthy spirit of confidence and frankness. No concealments. No evasions. He liked it.

Not, he felt, that it mattered much whether he liked it or not. Except for a fleeting and uninterested glance, the girl had taken no notice of him whatever, and it was plain that she regarded him as mere background. That is one of the drawbacks to being a barber. Nobody ever takes any notice of you. In whatever exchange of thoughts might be about to take place, his own share, Packy foresaw, would be negligible. Just a be-scissored robot, that was what he was. It pained him a little.

The girl's behaviour proved this surmise correct. She ignored his presence completely. Swinging her nice little legs, she began to speak freely of her own affairs, and at the end of a few minutes he knew as much about them as she did.

Jane, to begin with, was her name. That, at least, was what the Senator called her, and he seemed a man you could rely on. Her name was Jane, and she had been shopping earlier in the afternoon and had found some lovely handkerchiefs, not at all expensive, at a place in Regent Street. She thought the weather great and admired the London policemen. She would have liked to remain longer in London, but that, Packy gathered, was impossible because she and her father were leaving on the morrow for France.

The Senator said he hoped the crossing would not be rough, and Jane said, 'Oh, no.'

'Why won't it?'

'Oh, it won't.'

'Never rough at this time of year, sir,' said Packy.

'Shut up,' said the Senator.

'Yes, sir,' said Packy.

His remark had had the effect of drawing the girl's attention to him, and she was looking at him with a puzzled expression on her face. Then the Senator went on speaking. It seemed that the prospective hardships of the journey were still weighing on his mind.

'What do these Gedges want to live in a place like that for? I hate sea trips on small boats.'

'What I want to know,' said Jane, 'is why we are going to stay with the Gedges at all.'

'Never mind.'

'Mr Gedge isn't such a great friend of yours, is he?'

'Gedge!' Senator Opal uttered a sharp, barking sound. 'I've no use for Gedge. A fellow who says he had a five on the ninth, and I saw him with my own eyes take four niblick shots in the gulley.'

He paused, brooding coldly over some past unpleasantness which seemed still to rankle. Packy found himself warming to this Gedge, whoever he might be. A man who could attempt to chisel Senator Opal in a golf game must have striking qualities of enterprise and determination.

'Well, do you like Mrs Gedge?'

'No, I don't. She's a pest. Do you know what she's always after me to do? Use my pull to get that pop-eyed husband of hers made American Ambassador to France! A fellow who's a cross between a half-witted fish and a pneumonia germ. Well, I don't think I shall have much more trouble about that. I wrote her a letter the day before yesterday, telling her in so many words that I didn't think a man who couldn't count his shots at golf was a fit and proper representative for my country in the capital of a great and friendly power. You let a fellow like Gedge loose in Paris as an ambassador, and first thing you know he'd be giving America a black eye by being deported for cheating the French President at backgammon.'

'Well, after that, isn't it going to be rather awkward, staying with the Gedges?'

'We are going to stay with them, so don't talk any more about it.'

This flat pronouncement seemed to depress the girl Jane. She bit her lower lip in manifest heaviness of spirit. Packy would have liked – in a perfectly nice way of course – to take her little hand in his and press it and tell her to cheer up.

'It's about time,' said the Senator stoutly, 'that someone taught that Gedge woman that money can't do everything.'

Jane burst into a sudden flood of eloquence. It was as if the word had touched a spring.

'Money! I wish there wasn't such a thing. A man I know says money destroys the soul, and I quite agree with him. He says that in the final issue only the artist counts, and I think he's right. If I were going to be married, I would want it to be some man who was intellectual and spiritual. A man who wrote wonderful books, for instance, I mean. A man all sorts of intellectual people looked up to for his intellect, I mean. A man with a great, unspoiled soul, I mean. I wouldn't mind if he didn't have any money. In fact, I'd much rather he didn't. It's a great mistake to marry anybody but a poor man. Constance Bigelow told me so. She married an artist with hardly any money, and she says it's wonderful being married to a man with hardly any money, because you appreciate little treats so much. She says she's sure it's the greatest mistake to marry anybody but a poor man. She says she knows a girl who married a rich man, and she's having an awful time. I think love is the only thing that matters – that is, if you marry an artist with a great, unspoiled soul, I mean, because ...'

'How about that valet?' said the Senator.

The abrupt change of subject seemed to disconcert the girl. She had evidently only begun to touch the fringe of her chosen theme, and the interruption silenced her as effectively as if her father had hit her on the mouth with a wet towel.

'Valet?'

'I told you to go to the Employment Agency and get me a valet.'

'Oh, yes. Yes. They're sending a round man.'

'How do you mean, a round man? Why a round man?'

Packy too, was a little mystified. He had never heard of obesity as a quality to be desiderated in valets.

'I mean a man round. They're sending a man round for you to look at.'

'Good. I suppose he'll be just another sub-human half-wit like the rest of them, but . . .'

Senator Opal's voice trailed away in a sort of rasping howl. A scratched phonograph record would have produced a similar sound. For the first time, he had scrutinized himself closely in the mirror opposite the chair, and it was plain that what he saw there was having a disastrous effect on his morale. Little bubbling noises proceeded from him, and his face deepened slowly to a ripe magenta. Then, after an instant in which time seemed to stand still, he bounded up and turned on Packy, red-eyed.

Packy understood his emotion and sympathized with it. What with being a novice with the scissors and having allowed his concentration to be impaired by the necessity of drinking in what these two had been saying about their private affairs, he had undeniably made something approaching a devastated area of that noble white mop. He had shortened it, yes, but he had shortened in a series of irregular ridges which, though picturesque and interesting, might, he realized, quite easily not appeal to an owner of orthodox views.

But though compassionate, he was not foolhardy. After the briefest and swiftest of looks at the fermenting legislator, he started to move towards the nearest exit.

'Here, you!'

Packy halted. He had not wished to halt, but that bellow would have stopped the Scotch Express.

'Look what you've done, you clumsy, dithering moron!'

'Now, Father!'

'Don't say "Now, Father!" Look what you've done,' thundered the Senator, waggling his head from side to side so that Packy should get the light and shade effects. 'I'll have you fired for this. Do you call yourself a barber?'

It was an occasion when only candour could serve. Packy had hoped to be able to remove himself before the necessity for tedious explanations arose, but as this was not to be he was frank and open.

'I'm glad you brought that up,' he said. 'No.'

'What!'

'You see, I happened to be waiting in the shop for a hair-cut myself when you telephoned. There were no barbers there, and there didn't seem any prospect of there ever being any, so I stepped into the breach. I thought it was the square thing to do.'

A strange, wordless sound proceeded from Senator Opal: and, having uttered it, he began to advance with so much meaning in his burning eye and twitching hands that Packy, though for three years he had faced without a tremor the massed attacks of footballers from Harvard, Princeton, the Army, Notre Dame, and other points, suddenly found himself undisguisedly in flight. Harvard, Princeton, Notre Dame, and the Army had not included a Berserk Senator in their teams.

The handle of the door came conveniently to his fingers. He turned it and passed through. It was not until he was in the elevator that he paused to mop a moist brow. He had something of the emotions of a rabbit that has just eluded a more than usually quick-tempered boa-constrictor.

He found that he was still in the possession of property belonging to the hotel – to wit, scissors, one pair. The sheet, he recalled, was lying on the floor of Suite 400. He could have gone back and got it, had he wished, but he did not wish. He went to the barber-shop, placed the scissors on the edge of a basin, mopped his brow again, and mounted the stairs to the lobby.

Blair Eggleston was there, looking at his watch.

4

Blair Eggleston was small and slim, and if you did not mind side whiskers and one of those little moustaches which resemble smears of soot, good-looking. He seemed nervous. There was not much of his moustache, but he was tugging at what there was. He regarded Packy with a glassy eye.

'Hello,' said Packy, forcing himself to a joyous enthusiasm which he was far from feeling. 'Here I am.'

'I beg your pardon?'

'I'm afraid I'm a little late.'

'I beg your pardon?'

'Beatrice said you were expecting me at a quarter to five, but I had to see a man about some hair.'

'Beatrice?'

'Lady Beatrice Bracken.'

'She said what?'

'That you were . . .'

Packy broke off. He perceived that he no longer had the good fortune to engage his companion's attention. He wondered if the other were always like this. If so, the task of laying the foundation of that beautiful friendship which Beatrice seemed to desire so greatly was going to be a man's size job.

'Can we by any chance have got the wires crossed?' he said. 'It *was* the idea, wasn't it, that we should pile on to a pot of tea together?'

Blair Eggleston's eyes suddenly lost their glassiness. He stiffened like a pointing dog. He reached out and clutched Packy's coat sleeve feverishly.

'Ah! There she is!'

Packy, following his gaze, saw that the elevator had just discharged passengers into the lobby. And among them with an unpleasant shock he recognized his late client's daughter. She was heading straight for them, and there came to him a strong conviction that the sooner he left this spot the better.

'Well, it's been great seeing you again,' he said hastily, 'but I've just remembered an important...'

His attempts to withdraw were foiled by the fact that Blair Eggleston, apparently unconsciously, was still attached to his coat sleeve with a limpet grip.

The girl was quite near now, and Packy was able to see that the nice little forehead which he had so much admired was puckered. He made another unsuccessful attempt to release himself.

'I really must be ...'

'Jane!' cried Blair Eggleston. 'What a time you've been!'

The girl made no reply. Her attention was riveted on Packy.

'You!' she said.

Up in the Senatorial suite, Packy had not been able quite to satisfy himself as to the exact colour of this girl's eyes. They were either black or a very dark blue. He was now in a position to settle the point. They were within a foot or two of his own, and he saw that they were blue – a vivid blue and constructed, as far as he could ascertain, of molten fire.

'You!' she said.

There are practically no good answers to the word 'You!' Packy did not attempt one.

'I don't know who you are, but it may interest you to know that you've probably ruined my whole life.'

Packy begged her not to say that. A foolish request, seeing that she had just said it. He also asked her what she meant.

'I'll tell you what I mean. Blair and I are engaged, and Father doesn't know anything about it yet. I went up there to try to coax him into a good temper before Blair broke the news, and now you've played this fool trick and got him madder than a hornet.'

Blair Eggleston seemed bewildered.

'I don't understand.'

'You will,' said Jane Opal grimly.

Blair Eggleston's was a face which even at normal times had always a certain intellectual pallor. As he listened now, this pallor became more pronounced. It was as if the young novelist had been cast to play the Demon King in a pantomime and had assumed for the purpose a light green make-up. His lower jaw drooped feebly, like a dying lily.

'You don't mean that after that I've got to go and ask your father's consent to our marriage?'

'Yes.'

'But you say he is extremely upset.'

'He was tearing up a sheet when I left,' said Jane.

She turned upon Packy with such whole-hearted ferocity that he jumped back a full foot. A moment before, he had been intending to palliate his rash act by explaining that it had been the outcome of a sudden whim or caprice. Eyeing Jane, he decided not to.

'Tearing up a sheet?' said Blair Eggleston in a dry voice.

'Into little bits.'

'I'm awfully sorry,' said Packy.

Jane asked him what was the good of being sorry, and for the life of him he could not tell her. He remained silent, pensively rubbing the scorched patch on his cheek where her eyes had rested.

A good deal of talk now followed in which he took no share. His companions were discussing the various points in his character which prevented him achieving ideal perfection, and on such occasions the well-bred man does not chip in. It was principally in order to avoid hearing any more of the girl Jane's penetrating word-portrait that he buried himself presently in thought. And, thinking, he saw that it might be possible to some extent to make amends for the evil he had wrought.

'Listen,' he said, taking advantage of the fact that girls, no matter how gifted as critics, cannot go on for ever without stopping to take breath. 'I may be a dangerous imbecile – I'm not saying I'm not – but if you'll only listen for a minute I think I can help you.'

It is possible that mere words might not have availed, but at this moment the girl Jane, who had been allowing her eyes to play silently over his face while she thought of what to say next, came before the meeting with a question.

'Aren't you Packy Franklyn?'

'Yes.'

'I've been trying to remember ever since I saw you upstairs. You reminded me of someone, and I couldn't think who it was.

I saw you score that touchdown against Notre Dame. Boy, that was a run!'

Her voice had lost its rancour. It was plain that she considered the revelation of his identity to have placed an entirely new complexion on the matter. What is lunatic behaviour in the ordinary man becomes mere playful eccentricity in a football hero.

'Do you remember when you sort of wiggled sideways and the fellow just missed you by inches?'

'I got the breaks,' said Packy modestly.

'Gosh, I was hoarse for weeks.'

Her voice and manner were now all amiability. In Blair Eggleston's, on the other hand, the old animosity still lingered.

'I cannot see,' he said stiffly, 'how Mr Franklyn's ability to run and – ah – wiggle sideways affects the matter under discussion.'

'No,' agreed Jane, reminded of her wrongs. 'Get back to the point. What were you saying about being able to help us?'

'I can give Eggleston a few tips which will improve his technique. I can see just how he is planning to go about this business of tackling your father. Left to himself he would creep in and grovel on the floor. All wrong. This asking-father's-consent stuff is pie, if you handle it right. What you need is front. Bright self-confidence.'

'It's quite true, Blair.'

'Look at me. Faced by an Earl. What did I do?'

'What Earl?'

'Never mind what Earl. It was the Earl of Stableford, if you must know, and a tough baby he is, as anyone in Dorsetshire will tell you. Well, what happened? I just charged in, slapped him on the shoulder, and said: "Hello there, Earl! I'm going to marry your daughter, so let us have no back-talk." Just like that.'

Blair Eggleston shuddered strongly.

'And it worked?' said Jane.

'Like a charm. Fellow's eaten out of my hand ever since.'

'I can't do it,' said Blair Eggleston.

'Of course you can.'

'Of course you can,' said Packy. 'Take a drink first. Take two drinks. Three.'

'Yes, and have Father sniff it! Haven't you ever heard he's a rabid Dry? If he thought Blair had been drinking, he would have him bumped off and dropped in the Thames by moonlight.'

Packy mused awhile.

'I've got it. Go and tell him you're a friend of Miss Opal's and say she pointed me out to you and told you I had mussed up his hair, and you were so mad you sailed right in and knocked me for a loop.'

'That would make him grateful,' explained Jane.

'He would be all over you,' said Packy. 'Then, when he's fawning on you and saying "My hero!" you slip him the big news.'

'H'm!' said Blair Eggleston.

'Or another method. Pretend to be an influential member of the Temperance Society of England and touch him for a ten dollar subscription. Then give him the works. By this means, whatever happens, you will be ten bucks up, at any rate.'

'Well, anyway,' said Jane, 'you'd better get action. It's no good standing here doing nothing. Maybe Father will have gone off the boil by now.'

'Sure to,' said Packy.

'Go on up, Blair, and get it over.'

'And if you fail,' said Packy, 'what of it? It will just be one more grave among the hills.'

The departure of Blair Eggleston seemed to remove a certain fevered something from the atmosphere. The conversation up to this point had been conducted in a tensely perpendicular attitude on the part of all concerned. Jane Opal now allowed herself to be led to an alcove where a couple of arm-chairs held out a promise of repose and comfort. She sank into one of these and looked at Packy interestedly.

'How funny us meeting like this,' she said.

'A scream,' agreed Packy.

'I mean, you were the idol of my girlish dreams when I was a kid.'

'I was in my prime then. A flick of the finger, a broken heart.'

'I used to go to football games and worship you. You certainly could teach those stevedores to take a joke.'

Rightly interpreting her to mean by this term the gentlemanly students of Harvard, Princeton, Notre Dame, and other intellectual centres, Packy simpered coyly.

'Your taste in idols seems to have changed,' he said. 'You appear to like them smaller and brainier nowadays. Incidentally, I wonder how Eggleston is getting on. About now, I should imagine, he is leaning on the bell and your father is shouting "Come on! Come on! Come on!" in that curious way of his that always reminds me of a gorilla thumping its chest.'

Jane knitted her brow anxiously.

'Father's a pretty hard egg, isn't he?'

'It is not for me to criticize your father,' said Packy primly, 'but I can tell you this – if he ever asks me to come down a lonely alley with him to see his stamp collection I shall refuse with considerable firmness.'

'I never realized till now that he was quite such a man-eater.

I've hardly seen him these last two years. I've been in Paris, finishing. I wonder if it was really wise to send Blair up?'

'Is he insured?'

'The trouble is, you see, Father has very decided views about the sort of man he wants me to marry. That's what has made us keep the thing a secret. He expects me to make a big match.'

'Some belted Earl?'

'It looks more like a belted Vicomte at the moment. He is taking me to visit some people named Gedge who live in a Château over in Brittany. It belongs to a French Vicomtesse, and I feel sure Father's real reason for going there is that her son will be there and he wants to bring us together. He practically said as much this morning. I can't see what else would take him to a place like St Rocque.'

'St Rocque? This fellow your father wants you to marry isn't the Vicomte de Blissac, by any chance?'

'Yes. Why, do you know him?'

'I was talking to him only this afternoon. Well, this is certainly where I can oblige with a word in season. You mustn't do it. You positively mustn't. I'm not saying a word against the dear old Veek, mind you. As a companion for a merry evening in the pleasure zone of a great city he stands almost without a peer. But if I were a girl I wouldn't marry him on a bet. He isn't the type. I love him like a brother, but he's the fellow who first suggested the title "What Fun Frenchmen Have". I should imagine New York is talking about him still. Even in circles which prided themselves on being a trifle rapid, his work was considered swift. My good kid, don't dream of marrying him.'

'I'm not going to. And don't call me your good kid. I'm going to marry Blair.'

Packy did not want to depress her, but he could not help looking doubtful.

'You think you are,' he said. 'But my experience is that you never know who you're going to marry in this world. I once thought I was going to marry a cabaret girl called Myrtle Blandish.'

'Were you engaged to her?'

'All signed on the dotted line. And then one day I got a letter from her saying that she had run off with a man named Scott or Pott or even – her handwriting was practically illegible – Bott. It just shows you, doesn't it? However, I can see now that it was the best thing that could have happened – except possibly for poor old Bott. A nice girl, but essentially a female Veek. It wouldn't have done. Her habit of never going to bed before five would alone have been enough to spoil the cosiness of the home.'

'And now you're engaged to Lord Stableford's daughter? Rather a step up.'

'Quite. Both socially and spiritually. They don't come more spiritual than Beatrice.'

'Is that her name? Beatrice what?'

'Bracken.'

'Not Lady Beatrice Bracken? I've seen photographs of her in the papers. She must be lovely.'

'Lovely! Say, have you ever seen Greta Garbo?'

'Yes.'

'And Constance Bennett?'

'Yes.'

'And Norma Shearer?'

'Of course I have.'

'Mix 'em together and what have you got? Beatrice.'

'And did you really say what you were telling us to Lord Stableford?'

'Well, not those actual words, perhaps. But I was firm with him, very firm.'

'And he crawled?'

'I had him pawing at my trouser-legs. Of course, I'm pretty rich. That may have helped.'

'Blair has hardly any money.'

'But they tell me that everybody whose opinion matters regards him as one of the leaders of the younger school of novelists.'

'So he is. But he writes the sort of books that most people don't read. He's above their heads, I mean. As a matter of fact, he makes practically nothing out of his novels.'

'How does he eat?'

'He's got a job with the British Broadcasting Company.'

Packy was interested. He liked his radio of an evening.

'Is he the fellow who says "Good night, everybody, *good* night!"?'

'No. He ...'

'I've got him placed. He's the one who lectures on Fat Stock prices.'

'No. He does the noises off.'

'How do you mean, the noises off?'

'Well, when they have a sketch or something where they have to have noises, Blair makes them.'

'I get you. You mean, somebody says "Hurrah, girls, here comes the Royal Bodyguard!" and Blair goes tramp, tramp, tramp.'

'Yes. And all sorts of other noises. He's awfully clever at it.'

Packy nodded.

'I can quite see why you want to marry him. The home can never be dull if at any moment the husband is able to imitate a motor horn or the mating-cry of the boll-weevil. But you don't think your father will take that view?'

'Father is very material. He seems to think so much of money.'

'And just about now Eggleston is breaking it to him that he hasn't any. Tell me, what is the greatest number of wild cats your father has ever killed with his teeth in a given time?'

The question seemed to displease the girl.

'I wish you wouldn't talk like that.'

'I'm sorry.'

'They may get along splendidly.'

'They may.'

'What I'm hoping is that, even if Father doesn't agree to our marrying at once, at least he will like Blair well enough to give him some good job.'

'Imitating boll-weevils?'

In the bearing of Jane Opal as she hitched herself round in her chair and gazed at Packy there was something of the old fire.

'I see you have a cauliflower ear.'

'An old football wound.'

'Want another?'

'No, thanks.'

'Then don't talk like that. Blair is a very wonderful man, and he only makes noises off because his books are so clever that the public won't buy them. The critics say he is the coming novelist.'

'And here he comes.'

Blair Eggleston had suddenly appeared in the lobby and was standing peering hither and thither in search of his vanished lady. Even at this distance it was evident that he was somewhat dazed. His face wore a bewildered, stunned look.

'Well, he's still in one piece,' said Packy, 'and there don't seem to be any tooth-marks on him. Can Dad be losing his pep?'

'He looks goofy,' said Jane. 'I wonder what the matter is.'

She called loudly, and the coming novelist, at last sighting her, advanced totteringly, as one who has either suffered some severe spiritual shock or received a punch in the wind.

'Well?' said Jane. 'Well?'

Blair Eggleston blinked.

'I say...'

'What happened?'

'Well, I went in...'

'And what happened?'

'I saw your father...'

'He could hardly help doing that,' explained Packy, 'in an ordinary-sized apartment. I saw your father, too – distinctly. How was he coming along with that sheet?'

'Will you please be quiet,' said Jane. 'Blair!' Her voice took on a Senatorial vehemence. It would have interested a student of heredity. 'Stop dithering and tell me what happened.'

Blair Eggleston seemed to pull himself together with a strong effort.

'Well, I went in, and he was standing there, and before I could get a word out he said, "Are you honest and sober?"'

'Honest and sober?' squeaked Jane.

'The first thing fathers ask prospective sons-in-law,' Packy assured her. 'Pure routine.'

'And what did you say?'

'I said I was.'

'That sounds like the right answer,' said Packy critically.

'And then he asked me if I knew how to take care of clothes. And I said I did. And then he said, "Well, you don't look like much, but I suppose I've got to give you a trial." And I suddenly discovered that he had engaged me as his valet.'

'What!'

'Just what you were hoping,' said Packy. 'You said you wished your father would give him a job. The dream come true. Local Boy Makes Good.'

Jane was wrestling with her chagrin.

'But, Blair! . . . Didn't you explain?'

'I hadn't time. The telephone rang, and he told me to answer it, and it was this Mrs Gedge you are going to stay with. She was downstairs and wanted to see him. So he told me to get out, and I got out.'

This information diverted Jane momentarily from the matter in hand.

'Mrs Gedge? Are you sure?'

'Quite.'

'I wonder what she's doing over here. I must go and ask Father.'

She dismissed the subject of Mrs Gedge.

'Then you really mean you left it at that?'

'Your father's last words were that I should meet him at the boat-train at Waterloo to-morrow.'

'Well, that's fine,' said Packy. He turned to Jane, who seemed in need of a kindly word of encouragement. 'Don't you see how everything has worked for the best? You would like him to be at St Rocque with you, wouldn't you? Well, now he will be, and actually in the same house. You can snatch secret meetings with him and bill and coo across the Senator's Sunday pants while he's brushing them.'

'Why, of course! I never thought of that.'

Despite what he had been through, the haughty spirit of the

66

Egglestons was still alive in Blair. He started incredulously and with not a little indignation.

'Are you under the impression that I really intend to come to St Rocque as your father's valet?'

Jane's eyes were shining. The chin which she inherited from the Opal side of the family was tilted and resolute.

'I am,' she said definitely. 'Why, Blair, it's wonderful. You'll be always with Father, making him get fond of you. So that, when we think the time is ripe and I go to him and say, "You know that valet of yours, Father? Well, that's the man I want to marry," he will say "Fine! I liked him from the start," and everything will be lovely.'

'But, really...'

'Blair,' said Jane Opal, 'I'm not arguing with you. I'm telling you.'

Packy rose. It seemed to him that the delicate thing would be to withdraw. Blair Eggleston was looking as like a younger English novelist who has just stopped a sandbag with the back of his head as any younger English novelist had ever looked since first young Englishmen began to write novels, and what he needed, in Packy's opinion, was the opportunity of threshing things out quietly with his loved one with no third party present.

'I congratulate you both,' he said, 'on the happy way in which everything has come out. You will let me know any further developments, won't you? You see, I naturally feel a paternal interest in you young folks. Devonshire House will find me.'

'Must you go?'

'I fear I must. I have got to get my hair cut. My *fiancée* says it is too long. Her last words to me as the train pulled out drew a rather poetic comparison between me and a chrysanthemum.'

'I think you look lovely.'

'I do look lovely. But you know what women are. I regard getting it cut as a sort of sacred trust.'

Blair Eggleston rose bubblingly to the surface of the Slough of Despond which had engulfed him.

'But I don't know how to be a valet!'

'It's quite easy,' Packy assured him. 'A fellow with a brain like yours will pick it up in a minute. Just fold and brush and brush and fold and remember to say "yes, sir" and "no, sir" and "indeed, sir?" and "very good, sir". Oh, and one thing. Be very careful how you remove spots from the clothing. I knew a man who was fired for removing a spot from his employer's clothing.'

'What a shame!' said Jane. 'Why?'

'It was a ten-spot,' explained Packy.

6

It was the opinion of Mr Gordon Carlisle – and Soup Slattery, it will be remembered, had agreed with him – that women are tough. Packy, returning to his rooms after visiting the barber, found himself forced to the same conclusion.

That edict of Beatrice's that he should remain in London was weighing on him heavily. He was aware of a disquieting restlessness. He had picked up his yachting magazine and was re-reading the advertisement of which he had spoken to her at Waterloo. It virtually amounted to a prose poem.

FOR CHARTER. – Auxiliary Yawl, *Flying Cloud*, 45 feet over all, 39 feet on water line, 13 foot beam, Marconi rig, powered with 40 h.p. Universal motor, speed under power 8 m.p.h. Sleeping accommodation for four, large cockpit, good head room, sails and rigging in excellent shape, boat fully found including cooking utensils, silver, etc.

He sighed wistfully. An advertisement like that, he felt, was not the sort of thing to dangle before the eyes of a young man whose *fiancée* had told him to stay in London and go to concerts.

It was as he threw away the magazine so that he should be tortured no more by all those pictures of ketches and sloops and combination keel and centre-board schooners that the telephone rang. He went to it, prepared to work off his depression by being very terse with whoever it was that intruded on his sorrow, but became instantly cordial on recognizing the voice of Jane Opal.

A gregarious young man, Packy liked most people at sight, but he could not remember ever having been so completely attracted to anyone at a first meeting as he had been attracted to this Jane Opal.

There was something about her – he had noticed it even when she had been very properly ticking him off – which had seemed to speak – perfectly platonically – to the depths of his soul. A kindred spirit, if there ever was one, and the thought that she was madly throwing herself away on a fellow like Blair Eggleston rather saddened him. Not that it mattered to him, personally, of course, but he felt it was a pity.

'Hello!' he said with marked good-will.

'Oh, Mr Franklyn!'

It became evident to Packy that something had occurred to induce in this girl an overwhelming excitement. She was gurgling and bubbling and squeaking. So much so that he felt impelled to utter a kindly protest.

'Pull yourself together, chump,' he urged. 'I can't hear a word.'

'But I'm telling you.'

'I dare say. But do it slower.'

'Can you hear now?'

'Yes.'

'Well, listen.'

There was a gulp at the other end of the wire. Jane was apparently going through some process of self-mastery.

'Are you listening?'

'I am.'

'Well – oh, darn it, where shall I begin? Do you remember, when you were cutting Father's hair, something he said about a letter?'

'I didn't miss a word. He had decided not to make Mr Gedge Ambassador to France, and he had written to Mrs Gedge telling her so.'

'That's right.' There was a pause. 'Gosh, I'm all jellied with excitement.'

An idea occurred to Packy. He remembered that Mrs Gedge had interrupted Blair Eggleston's interview with the Senator by announcing herself on the telephone.

'Did she call and sock your father with her umbrella?'

'No, no, no! Nothing like that. Listen! I'd better go back to the beginning. Father wrote this letter to Mrs Gedge.'

'Right.'

'But – this is the point – he didn't. I mean – by the same mail he happened to be writing to his bootlegger in New York, kicking about the overcharges in his last bill. . . . Yes, his *bootlegger*. . . . And what did he do but get the envelopes mixed up, so that Mrs Gedge got the bootlegger's letter and Mrs Gedge's letter is now on its way to New York.'

'Good heavens! Not really?'

Packy was stunned. There came upon him a feeling of respectful awe as he contemplated Senator Ambrose Opal, that intrepid man who, with a million Drys on his voting-list, dared to order his private life so moistly. It was, he felt, the spirit of . . . well, he could not say exactly what it was the spirit of, but it was most certainly the spirit of something. He would have liked to pat Senator Opal on the back and tell him he had misjudged him.

'Have you got all that?' enquired Jane anxiously.

'Every syllable.'

'Well, listen. When I got to the suite, Mrs Gedge had just left, and I've never seen Father a brighter purple. And I must say, poor darling, he had every right to look as purple as he liked. Because, I mean, picture his embarrassment.'

'I do.'

'He told me the whole thing. Mrs Gedge says she is going to hold him up. If he doesn't make Mr Gedge Ambassador to France, she swears she will give his letter to the papers and the whole nation will know that he employs a bootlegger. And that will be his absolute finish politically, because, you see, his whole position rests on the fact that he is a Dry leader, and if this letter is printed in the papers he will be sunk. There are millions of people who have always voted for Father because they believed he was strict lemonade, and if they knew of this they would simply tie a can to him. So that's what Father's up against, and maybe you'll say it isn't plenty.'

'It's quite enough,' agreed Packy. 'Yes, I should say "plenty" is about the right word.'

Squeakings broke out once more at the other end of the wire.

'Stop it!' said Packy.

'Stop what?'

'Stop going on like a basketful of puppies.'

'Was I?'

'You were.'

'Well, I'm excited.'

'So am I. But hark how beautifully I articulate.'

'Well, listen.'

There was a pause. Stern self-discipline seemed to be in progress once more.

'This is the interesting part,' said Jane, becoming calmer.

'It can't be more interesting than Act One.'

'Yes, it is. You see, when Father told me all this, I suddenly saw that here was where I got the chance to put in a little smooth work. It took a bit of doing, as you would understand if you had seen Father standing there with his face bright mauve and telling me all the things he would like to do to Mrs Gedge, which included skinning and poisoning her soup. I mean, you sort of got the impression that he'd had already about as much as he could endure. But I thought of Blair and how much I loved him and I shut my eyes and came through. I told him that I was secretly engaged to a wonderful man, only he hadn't any money.'

'Did you mention that he was at present acting as your father's valet?'

'No. I thought it wouldn't be wise.'

'Quite right.'

'That sort of thing wants breaking gently.'

'Very gently.'

'So I simply told him I was engaged to a wonderful man, and I said, "Suppose I manage somehow to get back this letter from Mrs Gedge will you consent to our marriage?" And Father said that if I got that letter back I could marry the iceman if I wanted to and he would come and dance at the wedding.'

'Fair enough.'

'So that's how things stand at present. Mrs Gedge won't be back at St Rocque for a few days, but we're all going over to-morrow, as arranged. When she arrives, we can start doing something.'

'What?'

'Well, whatever we can think of.'

'Have you thought of anything yet?'

'No.'

'Have you told all this to Eggleston?'

'Of course.'

'What does he think of it?'

There was a shade of hesitation in Jane's voice.

'Well, he seems interested. But the trouble with Blair is that, having this great brain of his, he's rather a little too much the artistic, dreamy type, and what one really needs in a situation like this is a man of action and resource. I mean, when I asked Blair if he had any proposition to put forward that might lead to bringing home the bacon, he just tugged at his moustache and looked goofy and said he hadn't. However, he's going to start thinking, so something may break any moment. And I hope to goodness it does, because apart from being sorry for poor Father and wanting to get him out of a spot, how splendid it would be if Blair and I did this wonderful thing for him and Father said "Bless you, my children!" Gosh darn it, I should be the happiest girl in the world. Well, good-bye, Mr Franklyn, I must rush. I'm supposed to be dressing for dinner. Only I thought you would like to know all about what's happened. Good-bye.'

There was a click. Jane had hung up.

For several minutes after he had finished listening to this story, so vibrant with a young girl's hopes and fears, Packy remained standing at the telephone, staring before him.

73

His appearance was that of a man in a trance. Pins could have been stuck into him and he would scarcely have observed them.

Then, abruptly, a sort of whinnying groan escaped him. If he had chafed before at the prospect of being cooped up in London, he chafed more than ever now. He felt as he had sometimes felt at prize-fights when a wall of uprising citizenry suddenly intruded itself between him and the ring at some sensationally vital moment.

He burned with baffled exasperation. Here he was, tied to this one-horse town, this London, miles away from all this tense human drama, and it made him feel like a caged skylark. The demon of discontent which had been troubling him became of a sudden more vigorous and active than ever. He was a young man who hated to be out of things, and Jane's communication had shown him that the living, pulsating centre of things was the Château Blissac, St Rocque, Brittany.

But Beatrice had told him to stay in London. And Beatrice's word was law.

And yet . . .

Suddenly he emerged from his trance. His bearing was the set, resolute bearing of one who has made a great decision.

Beatrice, when she had told him to remain in London and go to concerts, could not, he felt, have foreseen that a situation like this would arise. Briefly, what it amounted to was that he had been offered the chance of helping to bring happiness to two young hearts. Would she have him refuse it?

Absurd.

Besides, hadn't she given him strict instructions to stick around Blair Eggleston like a poultice? Undoubtedly. And the only way to hitch up with Blair Eggleston was to go to St Rocque.

The whole tone of Jane's remarks had shown him how sorely his presence would be needed there. Even Jane, who loved him, had not failed to realize what a total bust her betrothed was going to be in the crisis which had arisen. All that was chivalrous in Packy revolted at the thought of the poor child having to lean on so weak a reed.

Blair Eggleston might be highly skilled at imitating horses' hoofs and the like, but of what avail would this accomplishment be in a situation like the present one? It was ridiculous to suppose that the determination of a woman like Mrs Gedge could ever be broken down by such means. If Blair Eggleston were to stand in front of Mrs Gedge by the hour, doing imitation glass-crashes or rubbing two coco-nuts together to create the illusion of distant thunder, she would simply laugh at him.

No! What was required, as Jane had pointed out, was a man of action and resource.

He took up the magazine and read once more the advertisement of the Auxiliary Yawl, *Flying Cloud*. He noted the address of the agents responsible for her chartering. He went to the writing-table and began to compose a careful letter to Beatrice, informing her that, feeling a little run down and in need of a change, he had decided after all to take a short vacation. He proposed, accordingly, to start at once for the quaint Breton town of St Rocque, because there he would have a chance of learning a little French, and you never knew when French might not come in useful. Every man, wrote Packy, ought to know at least one language besides his own.

He opened the letter again to add a postscript to the effect that there was probably a picture gallery in St Rocque. Then, sealing and stamping the envelope, he wrote to the agents for the Auxiliary Yawl, *Flying Cloud*, announcing his intention of calling upon them first thing in the morning.

CHAPTER 3

In the days when St Rocque was merely a fishing village, there was built in its harbour a small stone jetty. To it the fishermen tied their boats and on it they spread their nets to dry in the sun. You do not see many nets there nowadays, for the descendants of those fishermen have for the most part given up their ancient trade, finding it more profitable to hire their craft out to summer visitors. Two days after Packy Franklyn had set out on his voyage, a willowy young man with a pleasant face marred at the moment by a slight pallor was standing on the jetty steps endeavouring with the assistance of a voluble son of the sea in high boots and a blue jersey to climb into a small and unsafe-looking row-boat.

The Vicomte de Blissac, on arriving in his native town, had immediately registered at the Hotel des Etrangers. This, seeing that he was expected as a guest at the Château, may seem curious, but he had his reasons. To-day was the day of the Festival of the Saint, and he did not propose to miss it. It was his plan to revel to-night in a manner befitting this important occasion and only on the morrow to present himself at the home of his ancestors – and even then only if he felt considerably better than he expected to feel.

And if his host and hostess, the Monsieur and Madame

Gedge, should grow concerned at his absence – why, that, felt the Vicomte who, as this chronicle has already hinted, took a light-hearted view of life and its problems, was unfortunate but could not be helped.

His motives for embarking on this water jaunt may be explained quite simply. Although Mr Gedge's statement that the Vicomte de Blissac was never sober had been an exaggeration – for he was frequently sober, sometimes for hours at a time – it is undoubtedly true that he had a distinct bias towards the festive. And, becoming acquainted with some agreeable strangers at the hotel on the previous evening, he had found one thing leading to another and so on far into the night. This morning he had woken feeling a little under the weather, and it had seemed to him that a row in the fresh air might act as a pick-me-up.

And the theory was proving itself correct. As he splashed his way vigorously about the harbour, he was growing conscious of a marked improvement.

It was a lovely morning, with a keen breeze whipping the water and turning the little bay to a lagoon of jewels in the sun. White boats lay at anchor everywhere, and gulls wheeled and cried under the blue sky. And so restored was the Vicomte by this time that the uproar of these birds, which at first had given him a shooting pain across the temples, began now to seem almost musical.

Exhilarated, he rested on his oars and looked about him. And, looking, he perceived that he had come within a few feet of ramming an Auxiliary Yawl, bearing on its side the name *Flying Cloud*. He backed a yard or two, and it was at this moment that he observed, leaning over the side of the vessel, a man who smoked a pipe. And with the utmost pleasure and surprise he recognized his old friend, Packy Franklyn.

He waved effusively. Packy took no notice. He waved again. Packy appeared not to be aware of his existence.

The fact was, Packy had come on deck to think, and he was doing it with such intensity that he had no eye for wavers.

The bright, crusading spirit which had taken Packy Franklyn to the shores of Brittany had become, by the time he dropped anchor in the harbour of St Rocque, a little dimmed. He was still as full of zeal as ever, but as he washed up the dishes after his simple morning meal he had to admit to himself that if anyone were to ask him just what he proposed to do now that he had got here they would stump him badly.

As far as he could figure things out at even date, he would be able to offer Jane Opal at this critical point in her life little but brotherly sympathy and understanding. In order to accomplish anything practical on her behalf, it was obvious that he would somehow have to get into the Châeau, and not even eggs and bacon and coffee had given him the slightest hint as to how this was to be done. Unless some pretty striking ideas on the subject were to present themselves shortly, his ranking as a helper of damsels in distress would, he perceived, be even lower than that of Blair Eggleston.

However, there was still a hope. He had not yet smoked the after-breakfast pipe which, as everybody knows, can often prove a source of the subtlest inspiration. Lighting this pipe, he went on deck and, leaning over the side, told his brain to go to it and see what it had got.

It had got nothing whatever. He urged it to try again. And it was at this point that he received the first intimation that his friend the Vicomte had come back into his life. Unable to attract Packy's attention in a sitting posture it had occurred to the

Vicomte that better results might be obtained were he to stand up.

It was a most unfortunate move. A professional acrobat might have stood and waved in a St Rocque pleasure-boat without disaster, but the Vicomte had not had the early training necessary for the task. A sudden lurch sent him staggering sideways, and from there to the water was an easy step. He went in like a performing seal.

From a dozen neighbouring boats there rose immediately a babble of alarm. The French are an emotional race. When they see drama unfolding itself before their eyes, they do not treat it with well-bred silence. They scream and shout and jump and hop. The interpretation which Packy first placed on the uproar was that quite a number of murders must have broken out simultaneously in the vicinity. It was only a few moments later that, happening to glance down at the water, he observed floating in it a human form. And, scanning this form more closely, he recognized it as that of the Vicomte de Blissac.

'Hello, there,' he said.

He found nothing to surprise him in the spectacle. He had known that the Vicomte was in St Rocque, and as for his being in the middle of the harbour in a double-breasted suit of mauve cloth cut snugly about the shoulders, there was nothing particularly odd about that. Eighteen months ago, Packy had only just restrained him from taking a dip in one of New York's better-known fountains in full dress clothes.

It was with gratification, accordingly, rather than astonishment that he leaned over the side and greeted him.

'Hello, there, Veek,' he said. 'How's the boy?'

The boy at the moment of the enquiry was not doing any too well. A wave had caught him unawares, and he now disappeared beneath the surface with a slight gargling sound. When he rose again, it was so evident that he was a poor swimmer that Packy realized that he had got to do something immediately.

Many men in Packy's position would have shrunk from diving in to the rescue, fully clad. Packy was one of them. He was fond of the Vicomte, but not to the extent of ruining a nearly new flannel suit in his interests. However, the spirit of Auld Lang Syne was sufficiently strong in him to cause him to climb into the dinghy, and in a few minutes he had gaffed the poor bit of flotsam and brought it safely aboard.

The affecting reunion which should have taken place at this point had to be deferred owing to the necessity of retrieving the wrecked boat. Boats cost money in St Rocque. It was some little time before Packy returned. When he did so, he found that the Vicomte had not been idle in his absence. He had removed his wet clothes and donned a raincoat, had tracked down the whisky bottle, apparently purely by scent, and was now drinking a medicinal dram against a possible cold in the head.

To his host's enquiries he replied reassuringly.

'I'm all right, my old Packy. Quite O.C. Absolutely O.C.'

An education at Eton and subsequent travel in both Great Britain and the United States had given the Vicomte de Blissac a considerable fluency in the English tongue but not a perfect command of it. He belonged to the school of thought which holds that if you talk quick the words will take care of themselves. This was one of his simpler efforts, and Packy interpreted his meaning without difficulty. He regarded him fondly, as men will a friend dramatically restored to them, and they fell into pleasant conversation.

'I didn't know you were coming to St Rocque, Packy. You said nothing when we meet at Waterloo.'

'I didn't know myself then.'

'What do you do here?'

Packy was guarded. There are some missions too secret to reveal even to an old friend.

'Oh, I'm just pottering around. Tell me, Veek, what happened to you?'

'I fell overboard.'

'No, I mean eighteen months ago. You suddenly disappeared from New York without a word. Did they deport you?'

'Oh, no. My mamma send a cable that I should go out West to Colorado. I left New York to arrive there. It was a great wrench.'

'You were sorry to go?'

'No, I liked going. I had fun.'

'Then why was it a great wrench?'

'Because it was. A great cattle-wrench.'

'I get you,' said Packy. 'Your habit of dropping into Yiddish is a little confusing at times, but I get you. What made your mamma send you there?'

'She hear that I have been making whoopee, and she think I needing a rest-cure. Always my mamma is think I needing rest-cures. That is why I go now to stay with these Gedges at the Château. They are rich Americans who have taken the Château, and I bet you, my Packy, my mamma has make them pay through the nostrils.'

Packy, who had been sitting on the side of the boat, rose as if he had just discovered the woodwork to be red-hot. A thrill of elation passed through him, coupled with a strong vote of censure on that inefficient brain of his. Odd, he felt, that the human brain when tackling a problem always has that curious tendency to overlook the obvious solution.

Until now, this matter of getting into the Château had seemed to him a straight issue between himself and these unknown Gedges. How, he had asked himself, was he to establish connection with these Gedges and induce them to invite him to the house? And all the while there was the old Veek right on the spot, in a position to get as many of his friends invited as he pleased.

'Are you at the Château now?'

'Not yet. I go soon . . . perhaps.'

'Perhaps?'

'Well, you never know, my Packy. If the Festival is so good as always it has been, maybe I do not arrive for days and days.'

'What Festival?'

The Vicomte waved a hand shorewards. The little town was gay with flags and bunting, and even at this early hour care-free noises had begun to make themselves heard.

'To-day is the Festival of the Saint. St Rocque, you understand. It is his anniversary which is being celebrated. Just one of those dam' silly binges where the populace cuts loose and steps on the gas,' explained the Vicomte, genially tolerant of the recreations of the lower orders, 'but not bad. Quite good fun. I broke almost my neck last year, jumping over a table.'

Packy was not interested in the Festival of the Saint.

'Look here, Veek,' he said urgently. 'Be a sport. Get me invited to the Château, will you? I can't explain, but I have a particular reason for wanting to spend a few days there.'

The Vicomte smiled indulgently.

'Aha! The beautiful Miss Opal, yes?'

Packy was annoyed. Jane Opal, except as a mere acquaintance to whom he wished to do a good turn, was nothing to him. It was intensely irritating to have to listen to such nonsense.

'Nothing of the kind. I happen to be engaged to be married.'

'To Miss Opal?'

'*Not* to Miss Opal. I introduced you to my *fiancée* at Waterloo.'

'Was that your *fiancée*? That very lovely girl?'

'Yes.'

'And yet you come all this way to see Miss Opal?'

Reluctantly, Packy abandoned the idea of beating his friend over the head with a belaying-pin. He must, he felt, be tactful.

'Well, never mind, never mind. The point is, can you get me into the Château?'

'Alas, no.'

'Why not?'

'My old Packy, what you ask is impossible. By the time I arrive at the Château, I shall be in very wrong with these Gedges and what I say will not go. They expect me arriving yesterday, and most likely I do not turn upwards till the day after to-morrow, if even then. This will annoy these Gedges confoundedly. They will be sicker than mud. You understand?'

Packy was unwilling to accept defeat.

'All the same . . .'

'No,' said the Vicomte definitely, 'it cannot be done. So far from inviting my friends to the Château, I shall be extremely fortunate if I do not myself become kicked out. I have met these Gedges never, but my mamma tells me they are very upright, respectable *bourgeois*, and you would not believe, my Packy, how much not liked by upright, respectable *bourgeois* I can grow in quite a short space of time. It will be a case of "'allo, Monsieur le Vicomte, come in. Good-bye, Monsieur le Vicomte, get out," and I shall be back once more in my good little hotel.'

Packy argued no further. He was depressed, but he could see the force of the other's reasoning. The Vicomte might be good company, but he was not a good social sponsor. Search, he realized, must be made elsewhere for means of entry to the Château Blissac.

'And now,' said the Vicomte, dismissing the unprofitable theme, 'let us forget these Gedges and the Château, and we will speak of the Festival. This Festival is good fun, Packy. Do you remember how in New York once you take me to a fête of artists at Webster 'All?'

Packy nodded austerely. He recalled the episode, but it was one which in his capacity of a steady young fellow engaged to a girl of ideals he preferred to forget.

'Well, it is like that, something, only bigger much. It is our great fancy costume carnival, you understand. The whole town goes cuckoo. Everybody puts on funny clothes and becomes pie-eyed.'

Packy shivered prudishly. He was aware, of course, that there were still people in the world who disgraced themselves in the manner described, but it was not nice to have to hear about them.

'What great good fortune that you should arriving on this particular day, my Packy, and that we should so happily have met. We will whoop it up.'

St Anthony might have equalled Packy's stare, but only on one of his best days.

'You don't suppose I'm coming, do you?'

'Why, what else?'

Packy rubbed his chin pensively. He had suddenly discovered that this was opening up a new line of thought.

Anything in the nature of rowdy revelry was, of course,

intensely distasteful to him nowadays. He had put all that sort of thing far behind him. But in the case of this Festival of the Saint there was Beatrice to be considered. Beatrice, recognizing the great educative value of the experience, would probably be much annoyed were he to miss such a colourful, characteristic affair. And he would not like to do anything to displease Beatrice.

'It's pretty full of historic interest, this Festival, I should imagine, is it not? Might broaden the mind a good deal, I take it?'

'Just a lot of dam' fools hotting it up and getting so tight as owls.'

Packy frowned. It seemed to him that his friend was wilfully missing the point.

'Naturally on such an occasion,' he said, 'there would be a certain amount of hearty, old-world jollity. That is only to be expected. But what I mean is, suppose a fellow wanted to study the Soul of France . . .?'

'Oh, undoubtedly.'

'Count me in,' said Packy. 'But there's just one thing. If you think you or anybody else are going to get me into fancy dress, you're very much mistaken.'

'Not even a simple pierrot?'

'No, sir!'

'A pierrot is not much.'

'No.'

'Myself,' said the Vicomte, 'I attend the carnival as a . . . how do you call those little green things that run about and lie in the sun?'

'You don't mean to tell me,' said Packy, shocked, 'that you are going to this jamboree as a lizard?'

'Lizard! That is it. Yes, I go as a lizard.'

'I hope somebody steps on you.'

'Everyone steps on everyone everywhere at the Festival of the Saint. It is part of the good fun. We shall meet, then, to dine, at eight o'clock at the Hotel des Etrangers. That is that big great building you see there beside the Casino. You will find me in the cocktail bar.'

'You don't need to tell me that,' said Packy.

CHAPTER 4

It was at ten minutes to eight that night that Mr Soup Slattery entered the cocktail bar of the Hotel des Etrangers and, breathing heavily, placed his foot on the rail and ordered a dry Martini. He was panting like a stag pursued by hounds.

The Festival of the Saint had found in Mr Slattery an unappreciative audience. He was not *en rapport* and would have preferred to ignore it. But when you are in St Rocque on the fifteenth of July the Festival of the Saint rather thrusts itself upon you.

It had begun under Mr Slattery's window at 7 a.m., a fact which in itself would have been enough to create a prejudice, for, when not engaged in his profession, he was one of those health-loving sleepers who like to get their full eight hours. It had continued in the shape of a waiter in complete peasant costume, who sang some old Breton folk-song in an undertone as he brought him his coffee. It had haunted him all day in the crowded, vocal streets. And now it had driven him into what seemed the only sane spot in town, the cocktail bar of the Hotel des Etrangers.

Soup Slattery shared Packy Franklyn's austere distaste for fancy dress. Men who donned it he considered sissies, and, as for the other sex, he held that Lovely Woman forfeited all claim to reverent devotion when she put on baggy check trousers and went about blowing a squeaker. And when positive dowagers, who should have been setting an example, suddenly assaulted perfect strangers with those long, curly things which shoot out like serpents when you puff into them, he felt that the limit had been overstepped.

It was a distressing occurrence of this nature which had finally sent him hurrying for sanctuary. His thoughts, like drifting thistledown, had been floating about the Château Blissac and the jewellery in its interior, when the beastly thing caught him squarely on the tip of the nose, utterly disorganizing his whole nervous system.

And it was with a strong sense of being unfairly persecuted by Fate that he now perceived that even in the quiet, almost ecclesiastical atmosphere of the Hotel des Etrangers' cocktail bar he was not safe. Leaning against the counter not three feet away from him was a young man in apparel so curious and exotic that it smote Mr Slattery like a blow.

The Vicomte de Blissac's costumier's conception of a lizard had been planned on broad and impressionistic lines. The finished product suggested more some sort of parrot. The Vicomte, as he leaned on the counter exchanging civilities with the man behind it, was covered from head to foot in bright green scales and his shapely nose was concealed beneath a long crimson beak. And Mr Slattery, having shied like a horse and blinked violently, became conscious of an overwhelming urge to get to the bottom of this sad affair. It made him ill to contemplate the Vicomte, but, mingled with the nausea, there was this feeling of intense curiosity. He felt he would not be able to sleep that night if he did not ascertain what on earth the other supposed he was representing.

Finishing his Martini accordingly, he sidled along the bar and tapped him on the arm.

'Hey!' he said.

The Vicomte turned. And it was evident from his demeanour that he was in a spacious, friendly mood.

''Allo-'allo!' he replied genially. 'Have a drink, my old dear sir. Something for the gentleman, Gustave.'

Mr Slattery was a little mollified by this cordiality. Looking a shade less grim, he ordered another dry Martini.

'Say, what are you made up for?' he asked.

'I'm a blizzard.'

'Oh?' said Mr Slattery, still unenlightened. 'Well, pleased to meet you.'

He produced a card. The Vicomte eyed it owlishly, tucked it under a convenient scale, and after some complicated groping brought out his own card-case.

'Have one of mine.'

'Thanks.'

'Have two.'

'Sure.'

'Take the whole lot,' said the Vicomte, overflowing with generosity. There was nothing small about the De Blissacs.

Mr Slattery regarded the collection with a wooden stare. He seemed to be wondering how many of these he had to collect before becoming entitled to a cut-glass tobacco jar. Then he started. The name had impressed itself upon him.

'Say! Are you Veecount D. Blissac?'

His companion considered this question with the gravity it deserved. It was not one to be answered off-hand. He studied the nearest of the cards, then the one next to that.

'Yes,' he said, convinced.

'From that Chatty-o place up the hill?'

'Completely.'

All Mr Slattery's moroseness had left him. If there was one person he had been wanting to meet, it was somebody with an inside knowledge of the Château Blissac, somebody who would give him the low-down on its *personnel*. More than anything else, he desired to know how well off for dogs the place was. On one occasion in his career his most careful plans had been wrecked by a wholly unforeseen Pekingese.

He pressed genially upon the Vicomte, therefore, going so far as to place a friendly arm about his shoulders. And it was thus that Packy, coming in on the stroke of the hour, discovered them.

By this time, Mr Slattery's whole outlook on the Festival of the Saint had undergone a radical change. A very different man from the frowning recluse who had fled to the cocktail bar to seek refuge from it, he was now undisguisedly pro-Festival. And it was with something of a shock, democratic mixer with his fellow-men though he was, that Packy learned that this exceedingly tough-looking citizen was to be his companion at dinner and that after dinner all three of them were to go on and dance in the Public Amusement Gardens. For an instant, a vision of Beatrice rose before him, and he could not see any soft light of approval in her eyes.

Then there came to him the restorative reflection that Beatrice was a long way away. It cheered him immensely. There are few things which so spruce up a *fiancé* on these occasions as the realization that a good, broad strip of water separates the loved one and himself. Shaking hands with Mr Slattery, he prepared to be – if not the life and soul of the party, for the Vicomte was obviously going to be that, at any rate a willing celebrant.

And he was giving uniform satisfaction in this respect when their little gathering of three kindred souls suddenly turned into a gathering of four. Bustling through the doorway there came a small, stout man in what appeared to be an Oriental costume of some kind. He paused for a moment on the threshold, as if savouring the delights within, then circled towards the bar like a homing pigeon.

And as he caught sight of Mr Slattery a look of intense pleasure came into his face and he broke into a sort of primitive step-dance.

'Ee-yah!' he cried. 'Ee-yah! Ee-yah!'

In the days which had passed since his wife's departure for England, J. Wellington Gedge had not faltered in his resolve to take advantage of her absence and attend the Festival of the Saint. The passage of time, indeed, had cemented rather than weakened that determination. Senator Opal's obvious unfriend-liness from the very moment of his arrival had seemed to indicate to him that there was little anxiety to be felt regarding that Ambassador project. The fact that the Senator could not look at him without snorting like a buffalo appeared to Mr Gedge proof positive that the other had no intention of supporting his candidature. A great load had rolled off his mind, and in its place had come an intense desire to celebrate his escape. Knowing nothing of the fateful letter, for Mrs Gedge was always slow in taking him into her confidence, he felt care-free and elated.

The future seemed bright, and the manifest duty that lay before him was to make the present brighter still. As he came down the hill from the Château, old memories of Shriners' Conventions were turning Mr Gedge's blood to flame. His only regret, as he entered the cocktail bar, had been that he had no companion to share these golden moments.

And at this particular golden moment whom should he espy but his dear old friend, Mr Slattery, the nicest stick-up man he had ever met. The encounter seemed to him to place the seal of success on the night's proceedings.

'Ee-yah! Ee-yah! Ee-yah!' he whooped, jumping rapidly up and down.

Nor was there any lack of answering cordiality in Mr Slattery's manner. He had had three dry Martinis, an orange-blossom, and something which the man behind the bar called a Gustave Special, and he was feeling like the little brother of all mankind.

'Well, I'm darned!'

'Ee-yah!' said Mr Gedge.

'Ee-yah!' said Mr Slattery.

'Whoops!' said Mr Gedge.

'Whoops!' said Mr Slattery.

'Well, well, well!' said Mr Gedge.

'Lafayette, we are here!' said Mr Slattery.

He turned to the others, to make this added attraction known to them.

'Meet my friend, Mr Gedge.'

The Vicomte uttered a cry that sounded like the howl of a pleased hyena.

'Not Mr Skeleton Gedge?'

'Yessir.'

'Well, well, well!' said the Vicomte. He smote Mr Gedge lustily on the back, then tapped his own chest with an identifying finger. 'Me – the Vicomte de Blissac!'

'You don't say!'

'Completely!'

'Well, well, well!'

Nothing could have exceeded Mr Gedge's astonishment and enthusiasm at this unexpected meeting with his young guest. Well-well-welling once more, he grasped the Vicomte's hand, shook it, clung to it, released it, grasped it again. You could see that this was a big moment in his life.

The Vicomte indicated Packy.

'My friend, Mr Franklyn.'

'Well, well, well! What,' enquired Mr Gedge lyrically, 'is the matter with Franklyn? He's all right.'

'Who's all right?' asked Mr Slattery.

'Franklyn,' said Mr Gedge.

'Yay Franklyn!' said Mr Slattery.

'Yay Franklyn!' said Mr Gedge.

He released the Vicomte's hand once more and gripped Packy's. He gripped it warmly, but not so warmly as Packy gripped his. To Packy, it was as if a miracle had been performed while he waited. All day he had been goading his brain to discover some method by which he could enter the Château Blissac, and lo! here was the lessee of the place in person. So to ingratiate himself that the other would shower invitations upon him would surely be a simple task. By way of starting the treatment, he massaged Mr Gedge's shoulder and told him he looked fine.

'You like the costume?'

'It's great.'

'My own.'

'No!'

'Yessir. Thought it all out myself.'

'Genius!' said Packy.

Mr Gedge, having possessed himself of a small table, was beating rhythmically on the bar with it.

'We're going to have a drink to celebrate this,' he said authoritatively. 'Yessir, that's what we're certainly going to do. To-night, boys, I intend to step high, wide, and plentiful.'

'Try a Gustave Special,' was Mr Slattery's advice. 'Swell for the tonsils.'

'Perfectly,' agreed the Vicomte. 'They are good, those Gustave Specials.'

'They are?'

'They certainly are.'

Mr Gedge was convinced.

'Three cheers,' he cried buoyantly, 'for the Gustave Specials!'

The Vicomte went further.

'Four cheers for the Gustave Specials!' And Mr Slattery further still.

'Five cheers for the Gustave Specials!'

'Six!'

'Seven!'

'Eight!'

'Nine!'

'Ten!' vociferated Mr Gedge, topping the bidding. 'All together now, boys. Ten cheers for the Gustave Specials!'

It became increasingly evident to Packy that this was going to be one of those evenings.

CHAPTER 5

Fairy lanterns, assisted by a rudimentary moon, lit up the
Public Amusement Gardens of St Rocque, of which one may
safely say that their best friend would not have known them now.
Normally, they are quiet and decorous, these Public Amusement
Gardens, even to the point of dullness. Children walk in
them with their nurses. Circumspect lovers whisper in them.
Elderly gentlemen sit in them, reading the *Figaro* or *Le Petit
St Rocqueois*. Their whole aspect lulls the observer to a stodgy
calm: and, hearing their name, you cannot help feeling that
St Rocque must be easily amused.

To-night, all was changed. Tables and waiters and bottles had
broken out on every side like a rash. A silver band – and for sheer
licentiousness you can't beat a silver band – was playing on the
little platform in the centre, and round this platform, in many
cases far too closely linked, pirouetted the merrymaking citizenry of St Rocque. The Festival of the Saint was in full swing.

So, also, were Mr Soup Slattery and the Vicomte de Blissac.
The former, in intimate communion with a chance-met lady
friend, was tearing off a few of those fancy steps which had made
his name a byword at bootleggers' social evenings in Cicero. The
latter, who preferred to be untrammelled by a partner, was
performing some intricate gyrations by himself in the very

middle of the fairway, a source of no small inconvenience to one and all.

Packy was not dancing. Nor was Mr Gedge. Mr Gedge had taken a turn or two earlier in the evening, but, chancing to trip over his feet and fall a little heavily against the bandstand, he had retired to a table on the edge of the arena and was now sitting there with a dark scowl on his face, regarding the revellers with every evidence of disapproval and dislike. He had, indeed, conceived a very deep-rooted loathing for his fellow-human beings. Spiritually, he was in the depths.

Much has been written against the practice of over-indulging in alcoholic stimulants: but to the thinking man the real objection to such over-indulgence must always be the fact that, beyond a certain point, the wine-cup ceases to stimulate and, instead, depresses. The result, as Packy was shortly to discover, being that, with a companion well under the influence, you never know where you are. You start the evening gaily with a sunny-minded Jekyll, and suddenly and without any warning he turns on your hands into a brooding Hyde.

During dinner and for an hour or two after it, J. Wellington Gedge had had all the earmarks of one who on honeydew has fed and drunk the milk of Paradise. He had overflowed with amiability and good-will. A child could have played with him, and, what is more, he would probably have given it a franc to buy sweets with. And Packy, having no reason to suppose that he was not still in this Cheeryble-like frame of mind, felt encouraged and optimistic.

That Mr Gedge's mood had changed completely and was now like something Schopenhauer might have had after a bad night, he did not begin to suspect. True, the Seigneur of the Château Blissac had become a little quiet. But, then, if only to restore the average, it was about time that he stopped howling and singing for a moment or two.

It was with bright confidence, therefore, and without any inkling of the truth, that Packy, at last finding himself alone with Mr Gedge, started to bring the talk around to the subject nearest his heart.

'So you live at the Château Blissac?' he said.

Mr Gedge did not appear to have heard the remark. He was still staring with a kindling eye at the dancers. His lower jaw protruded a little, and he breathed heavily through his nose.

'So you live at the Château Blissac, Mr Gedge?'

'Eh?'

Packy repeated the observation for the third time, and his companion sat in silence for a while, turning it over in his mind. A close observer would have seen that it did not please him.

'At the Shattlebissack?'

'Yes.'

'I live there?'

'Yes.'

'Who says I don't?'

'I said you do, don't you?'

Mr Gedge frowned.

'If any man says I don't live at the Shattlebissack, I'll poke him in the nose. Yessir! They can't talk that way to Wellington Gedge.'

'No, no. Everybody says you do.'

'They better,' said Mr Gedge, quietly but none the less menacingly for that quietness.

He relapsed into a dark silence again, and for the first time it began to be borne in upon Packy that the other was not his former winsome self. He felt a little disquieted. So much, however, hung upon this thing that he tried again.

'It must be a wonderful place.'

'Eh?'

'I say it must be a wonderful place.'

'What must?'

'The Château.'

'What Château?'

'The Château Blissac.'

'Never heard of it,' said Mr Gedge.

Packy was now definitely discouraged. It was plain to him that it was going to be difficult to extract a formal invitation from this sozzled man. He wished now that he had broached the all-important topic during dinner. There had been a point, just after the first bottle of champagne and just before the second, when Mr Gedge had been in the mood to invite anyone anywhere.

He was roused from his meditations by a choking sound at his side. Mr Gedge was glaring out at the dancing floor with open hatred.

'Frenchmen!' said Mr Gedge.

'I beg your pardon?'

'If you ask me what's wrong with the world,' proceeded Mr Gedge, gritting his teeth, 'there's too many Frenchmen in it. Never liked them and never shall. Alblassador to France? I won't do it. No, sir! Not even if they come to me on bended knees. You know what I'll say to 'em? I'll say "No, sir! Certainly not!" Who's that horrible tomato over there in green?'

'That's the Vicomte.'

'What Vicomte?'

'The Vicomte de Blissac.'

'He wants a good poke in the nose.'

'Would you say that?'

'I'd say a lot. Leaky cisterns!'

'I beg your pardon?'

'Granted.'

There was a pause, during which Mr Gedge threw a moody champagne cork at a passing couple.

'You said something about leaky cisterns,' prompted Packy.

His companion swung round with sudden passion.

'And why wouldn't I? Lookut! Suppose a Vicomte's mother told you the plumbing of a Shattlebissack was in good repair, and it wasn't? Suppose this Vicomte's mother kept a leaky cistern under her hat...never mentioned a word of it...practically swore there wasn't such a thing in the place...wouldn't you poke him in the nose?'

'Too bad,' said Packy diplomatically.

'Eh?'

'I said it was too bad.'

'It couldn't be worse,' said Mr Gedge severely.

Packy waited a few moments, but the other had apparently said his say. He had found half a roll and was balancing it in his hand. He seemed undecided whether to throw it at the leader of the orchestra or at an obese, middle-aged Gaul with a long spade-shaped beard who, though his best friends should have advised him against it, had come to the Festival dressed as a Swiss mountaineer.

'This cistern leaks, does it?'

'What do you mean, does it? I've seen it. Seen it with my own eyes.'

'I wish you would show it to me.'

'Eh?'

'I say I would love to see your leaky cistern.'

'How the devil can you see my leaky cistern? It's up at the Shattlebissack.'

Packy would have preferred to postpone the question to another and more propitious moment, but the cue was so pat that it seemed a pity to refuse it.

'Why don't you invite me there?'

'Invite you where?'

'To the Château.'

'What Château?'

'To the Château Blissac.'

Mr Gedge hammered the table with extraordinary violence. The request appeared in some mysterious way to have acted as the last straw.

'I won't invite you to the Shattlebissack. I wouldn't do it. No, sir, I wouldn't do it even if I could. I don't like you. Never have. And don't you snort at me!'

'I was sighing.'

'Sighing's just as bad.'

Packy compromised by throwing silent reproach into his gaze.

'I didn't know you disliked me.'

'Of course I dislike you,' replied Mr Gedge with spirit. 'Who wouldn't?'

'I thought at dinner that ours was going to be one of those great friendships.'

Mr Gedge frowned thoughtfully. He seemed to be trying to direct his mind back to the dinner hour.

'I pictured you then falling on my neck and insisting that I should come and stay at the Château for ever.'

'What Château?'

'I am still referring to the Château Blissac.'

'I live there,' said Mr Gedge with the air of a discoverer.

'I know you do.'

'You better know I do. No fresh young mutt with a cauliflower ear is going to tell me where I live and where I don't live.' He stared at Packy disgustedly.

'Where did you get that ear?'

Packy explained that it was a souvenir of a certain November afternoon when he had been attempting to die for dear old Yale and – with the assistance of eleven sympathetic Princeton men – nearly succeeding in doing so.

'Yale?'

'I played football at Yale.'

Mr Gedge gave a hard laugh.

'They don't play football at Yale,' he said. 'Bean-bag, that's what they play at Yale.'

Packy started, wounded to the quick. Abruptly, the desire to conciliate this tubby little inebriate had vanished, swamped by a fury of injured patriotic pride. A man with an end to gain may suffer much from a cock-eyed acquaintance, but not aspersions on the quality of the football played by his old University.

'Bean-bag,' repeated Mr Gedge firmly. 'You want to see football, you come to California. Yale don't play University of Southern California. No, sir! They know too much.'

Packy was sorry for Jane Opal and regretted that he would be unable to further her interests by coming to the Château Blissac and breaking open safes for her, but he could no longer humble himself before a man who held these monstrous views. He rose, and Mr Gedge regarded him with a glazed eye.

'Where you going?'

'Home.'

'You better, before you get a poke in the nose.'

Packy preserved a proud silence.

'Order another shottle-o'-champagne,' said Mr Gedge.

'Order it yourself,' said Packy.

The brusqueness of the reply seemed to induce in Mr Gedge a swift change of mood. His eyes filled with tears and he leaned his head dejectedly on a plate of ice-cream.

'Nobody loves me,' he whispered.

'Shows their sense,' said Packy.

CHAPTER 6

I

THE moon which had collaborated with the fairy lanterns in the illumination of the Public Amusement Gardens had the lighting of the sand-dunes by the harbour to look after alone, and was making a half-hearted job of it. Packy, who had strolled on to the dunes for a pipe before returning to his boat, found himself in a world of shadows, and after one or two stumbles on the uncertain pathway he decided to sit down and stroll no more.

In the matter of alcoholic stimulants, Packy had lagged behind his fellow-revellers both during dinner and after it, wishing to keep his head clear for the fascinating of Mr Gedge. He reaped the reward of his abstinence now in a heightened appreciation of the beauties of the night.

It was a warm, soft, silky night, restfully silent. From time to time there came from the direction of the Amusement Gardens the noise of Gallic mirth, but it was too faint to compete with the musical splash of the waves on the shore below. Little breezes whispered about his ears. Shy moths fluttered to and fro. In short, taken by and large, the setting and surroundings were ideal for a good, long lover's reverie.

But Packy, oddly enough, was not thinking of Beatrice. It was the picture of the girl Jane Opal which filled his mind. And as he thought of Jane Opal remorse began to grip him.

He could not conceal it from himself that he had failed the poor child. In the hour of her need, when a little tact might have put him in a position to serve her, he had let her down with a bump. Stung by the other's sneers, he had definitely parted brass-rags with Mr Gedge, with the result that however large and varied the house-party at the Château Blissac might be it could never now include Packy Franklyn in its ranks. He should have persevered with Mr Gedge, he realized too late. He should have been patient and long-suffering with him. He should not have permitted a few derogatory observations on the quality of the football played at Yale to divert him from his purpose.

He had just arrived at this conclusion and had risen, intending to make for the jetty where he had moored the *Flying Cloud*'s dinghy, when abruptly through the night there came to him the sound of running footsteps. Somebody in a hurry was heading his way.

The next moment the moon, peeping from behind a cloud, shone weakly down on the well-remembered form of Mr Soup Slattery.

Mr Slattery was cutting out a good pace, but it was apparent as he reached the little knoll where Packy stood that sprinting was not his forte. He was panting heavily. He came galloping along, sighted Packy, recognized him, waved an agitated arm in the direction from which he had come, shot at him one brief, concentrated look of appeal, then, leaping to the left with the last remnants of energy in him, sank with a gurgle behind the knoll. And for some moments nothing was to be heard but his muffled gasping.

And then once more running feet became audible, and almost immediately there burst in view a posse of St Rocque's able *gendarmerie*. They, too, appeared a little touched in the wind, and it was plainly with a certain relief that they accepted Packy as an excuse to stop and ask questions.

Packy was not a French scholar, and even if he had been, he would certainly have been unable to follow the constabulary remarks, sounding as they did like water rushing over a weir. But his special knowledge enabled him to make a guess at what they wanted to know and he pointed with animation along the path beyond him.

The pursuit rolled off in that direction. Only when the last footstep had died away did the head of Mr Slattery emerge from behind the knoll like that of a diffident turtle.

'Zowie!' was Mr Slattery's comment on the affair, and the fact that he had regained sufficient breath to say even as much as that told Packy that he was once more in a condition to travel. Not pausing to ask for explanations, he seized his arm and hurried him down the slope. A few minutes' earnest cross-country work brought them to the jetty. He thrust the hunted man into the dinghy and pulled out.

The distance to the *Flying Cloud* was not great, and during the journey Mr Slattery made only two remarks. One was 'Boy!' the other 'Give me Chicago!' Arriving on the deck of the yawl, he became more expansive.

'Brother,' said Mr Slattery, sinking on a pile of rope and taking off his shoes, 'if I live a hundred years, I'll never forget this night and what you done for me!'

Packy waved away his gratitude modestly.

'What happened? Did you murder somebody?'

'No, sir. I didn't murder nobody. But . . .'

'I'll get you a drink,' said Packy, remembering his obligations as a host.

'Boy!' said Mr Slattery, passing a long tongue over his lips.

Returning with the materials for a night-cap, Packy found his guest a good deal restored. He had put his shoes on again, and his breathing was easier. He accepted the proffered glass and drained it with relish.

'Boy, could I write a book!' he said.

He was so evidently convalescent that Packy felt there would now be nothing inhuman in asking for details of the affair.

'Tell me all,' he said. 'What were the events leading up to the tragedy? Why the gendarmes?'

'The what?'

'The cops. What had you done to annoy them?'

'Me singing – that was the start of it.'

'Can they arrest you for singing in France?'

'Well, what I mean, I was breaking the table, too.'

'I see. That may have been partly the trouble. Why were you breaking the table?'

'Why not?' said Mr Slattery reasonably.

'Of course,' said Packy, seeing his point.

Mr Slattery refreshed himself again.

'Well, anyways, there I am, cutting up and having a good time, and all of a sudden a bunch of fellows dressed as French cops come up and start pushing me around. Well, hell!' said Mr Slattery with feeling, 'nobody can say I'm not a good sport. You don't find me beefing if a party gets a little bright. Give and take, that's me. So when they push me, I push them. And so on back and forth.'

'Quite right.'

'Wait!' said Mr Slattery. 'You don't know nothin' yet. It wasn't more than about half a minute when one of these palookas suddenly pulls out a young carving-knife and sticks me in the wish-bone with it. Good and hard he sticks me, and it got me plenty sore. And I say to myself, "Well, here, come now, what the hell?"'

'You could hardly have said less.'

'"Well, what the hell?" I say to myself. "Fun's fun, but there's a limit." I warn him first, mind you. I say, "Brother, don't go letting that party spirit run away with you, brother," I say. "You get rough, me I can get rough, too." But no, he has to stick me again, and that burns me up and I cut loose. Two, three of those guys I must of poked in the schnozzle, and I'm just beginning to go nice when all of a sudden ... Ever been struck by lightning?'

Packy said he had not.

'Well, it was like that. Because right in a sort of flash it dawns on me that these fellows ain't just party hounds made up for cops. They're real cops. And, what's more, French cops. And one thing you learn over on this side is that France ain't America. Back home, what I mean, a cop knows how to take a joke and don't hardly even notice it if you sock him on the beezer. But gee! in this darned country a man might get sent to Devil's Island or somewheres for hitting a what-was-it-you-said. So I don't wait to apologize. I beat it, with the whole bunch after me. And where I'd of ended up if I hadn't of run into you and you steered them off of me, I wouldn't like to say. You're aces, boy, and you can write home and tell the folks Soup Slattery said so.'

'Soup?' said Packy. 'Is that your name?'

'It's what they call me back in Chi. On account me being an expoit safe-blower,' explained Mr Slattery modestly.

Packy started.

'A safe-blower? Do you mean you know how to open safes?'

'Do I know how to open safes? Do *I* know how to open *safes*? Ask the boys back home if Soup Slattery knows how to open safes! Why, is there any little job in that line you want doing?' asked Mr Slattery, noting the oddness of his companion's expression. 'If there is, say the word.'

Packy groaned in spirit. Life's dreadful irony was saddening him. What he had wanted from the very start of this expedition of his was a kindly friend who knew how to open safes, and now that he had found him it was too late. He mourned once more over that foolish pride which had caused him to sever relations with Mr Gedge and so render an invitation to the Château impossible.

'No,' he sighed. 'Not at the moment, I'm afraid.'

He crushed down these fruitless repinings over what might have been.

'Tell me,' he said. 'What happened to the others?'

'Gedge and D. Blissac?'

'Yes. I left early.'

Mr Slattery rumbled like a semi-extinct volcano. It seemed to be his way of expressing amusement.

'Boy, you missed somethin'! A circus. No less.'

He indulged in another deep rumble.

'Get this,' he said. 'Me, back at the table, see? And here's this Gedge bird, acting kind of ugly.'

'He was that way when I left.'

'Well, he hadn't gotten no sunnier, believe me. He was muttering to himself, what I mean, and throwing things. And after a while he turns to me and starts in rolling the fat about the plumbing at this Chatty-o place which he's rented. Claimed it was terrible.'

'Leaky cisterns?'

'That and a raft of other things. And he's just beginnin' to go good when this D. Blissac guy, that's been dancing by himself out in the middle somewheres, gets tired of it and comes back to the table for a snootful. And just as he pulls in, here's this Gedge bird shoutin' about the plumbing of this Chatty-o and not saying it with flowers, neither.'

'Good situation,' agreed Packy. 'Dramatic.'

'Well, sir, this here now Blissac he sort of draws himself up and calls him. "What's that?" he says. "What's what?" says the Gedge bird. "What's that you're saying about our plumbing?" says this Blissac, very high-hat. "It's rotten," says the Gedge bird. "Say that again," says D. Blissac. And this Gedge he says it again, and the next thing you know they're rolling on the floor, and me acting as referee and telling them to break. Boy, it was a couple of minutes before I could get 'em unstuck.'

Packy's sympathies were entirely pro-Vicomte. No man of spirit will lightly endure strictures on the plumbing of his boy-hood home. He said as much.

'Me, too,' agreed Mr Slattery. 'And that's what I tell this Gedge when I'd unsorted him. "Is it nice," I say, "giving the razz to a fellow's home plumbing? Is that a system?" He seen it, too, because he started crying into some fruit salad. And then I argue with this Blissac, trying to make him take the big, broad view. And presently we're all hotsy-totsy again, and from then till they suddenly passed out cold on me you wouldn't have wanted to see a happier little bunch than the three of us.'

Pausing at this point, Mr Slattery regarded Packy with surprise and not a little pique. He considered that he had been telling a good story well. Yet here was his companion apparently in a trance, not listening. He was standing rigid, gazing out into the night.

'Of course, if you ain't interested....'

Packy turned. His eyes gleamed strangely.

'You say they passed out?'

'Stiff. Just turned up their toes and lay there.'

'What became of the bodies?'

'I attended to that. I put D. Blissac in a cab and shipped him off to the hotel.'

'And Gedge?'

'I put him in another and sent him up to the Chatty-o. I told the chauffeur to ring the front door bell and go on ringing till somebody answered it and then hand in the corpse and tell them to put it on ice and come away.'

Mr Slattery paused a little complacently. He seemed to be feeling that, left *in loco parentis* to two fellow-human beings in circumstances of some embarrassment, he had acquitted himself well.

Once more he perceived that his audience's attention had wandered.

'Maybe you don't think that was smooth?' he said, aggrieved.

Packy started apologetically.

'I'm sorry. I was thinking. I've just had an idea, and I don't often get them. When I do, they knock me endways.'

'Idea?'

'A sort of idea.'

'What?'

'Oh, just an idea. Just something that had been bothering me a good deal, and now I think I see my way. A bright light has shone upon me. Look here, are you feeling equal to making the trip ashore? Because, if so, I'll row you in. I would rather like to have a word with the Veek.'

'Who's he?'

'Your old friend, V. D. Blissac. You sent him back to the hotel, you said. Would there be any chance of his having come to life yet?'

'Maybe. What do you want to see him about?'

'Oh, just something. Just something that happened to occur to me while you were talking.'

'Well, I don't know as I'm not about ready to hit the hay.'

'Fine. Then we'll start at once. By the way, that offer of yours to crack a safe for me, if desired, still holds good?'

'Brother,' said Mr Slattery with fervour, 'after what you done for me to-night, I'd bust the National City Bank for you.'

2

There was good stuff in the Vicomte de Blissac. Many men in his condition would have remained where they had been dumped, inert, till the following morning. But it was scarcely an hour after the pall-bearers had laid him on the bed in his room at the Hotel des Etrangers before he was, in a manner of speaking, up and about. That is to say, he had so far regained the mastery of his faculties as to be able to totter to the wash-hand stand, drink perhaps a pint and a half of water out of the pitcher which stood thereon, and fill a sponge and press it to his burning head.

He had just renewed the contents of this sponge and was passing it gently across his brow once more when he became aware of a knocking on the door, and, limping to open it, discovered on the threshold his friend Packy Franklyn.

''Allo,' said the Vicomte in a weak voice. He was not sure if he was quite pleased at the other's arrival. For some reason there had stolen over him an odd, languid feeling and a desire for repose and solitude.

Packy did not reply. He had come into the room and was now closing the door with every circumstance of wariness and caution. It was as if he had been the janitor at an emergency meeting of the Black Hand to whom had been assigned the task of making sure that the coast was clear.

The Vicomte watched him with growing distaste.

'What do you doing?' he asked.

''St!' said Packy.

The Vicomte sat down on the bed and put his head between his hands. He was in no mood for this sort of thing.

Looking up a moment later, he found that Packy was regarding him with a kind of anxious concern.

'Veek!'

''Allo?'

'Brace yourself up, old man.'

'Why?'

'Because I've some rather bad news for you.'

A shooting pain passed through the Vicomte's head. All this was making him exercise his brain, and it was imperative that for some little time to come he should think as sparingly as possible.

'Bad news.'

'About poor Gedge.'

'Gedge? What about Gedge?'

'It seems very doubtful if he will recover.'

The Vicomte blinked.

'He has obtained an accident, then?'

'Veek,' said Packy reproachfully, 'I'm your friend. What on earth is the sense of bluffing with me? I'm not the police.'

'Police?'

Packy went to the door and opened it quickly. Apparently reassured, he returned to the bed and put a brotherly hand on his companion's shoulder.

'There's only one thing to be done,' he said. 'You must lie low here till the hue and cry has died down.'

'But I do not understand.'

Packy's eyebrows rose.

'You're kidding.'

'I have not understood at all what you are saying.'

'But you surely can't have forgotten having the fight with Gedge?'

'What about it?'

'What *about* it? Well, you practically killed the man.'

The Vicomte had leaped from the bed, and was staring wide-eyed.

'But, my Packy, it was nothing but a tiny little turn-up on the floor such as almost always occurs. You cannot mean this what you say that I injured seriously this Gedge? Why, we sat together and had some drinks after and he was as well as a violin.'

'You are speaking now of the first fight?'

'Do not tell me we had another?'

Packy patted his shoulder and turned away.

'What happened?' demanded the Vicomte pallidly.

'Don't ask me.'

'But when . . . ?'

'No, don't ask. If you've forgotten, it is much better that you shouldn't know. Otherwise, you might worry.'

'Worry!'

'There is just a chance that you will be all right if you lie low. It was darned good luck that you happened to be wearing that lizard costume. The beak hid your face. I don't suppose really that anybody would be able actually to identify you. But it's no good taking chances. You mustn't stir from this room for several days. You understand that, of course?'

'But, my Packy, I am engaged to arrive at the Château!'

He gazed at Packy in deep agitation. It was plain to him from the expression on his face that his friend had forgotten this.

'That's true,' said Packy thoughtfully. 'Yes, of course.'

'I do not arrive, suppose, and what occurs? These Gedges telegraph to my mamma....'

'Mr Gedge, I'm afraid, will hardly be in a condition to telegraph to anyone for a long while. If ever. He's written his last telegram, poor chap, I very much fear.'

Packy remained plunged in thought.

'Veek,' he said suddenly, 'there's only one way out. Obviously you can't go to the Château. A nice thing that would be – you arriving and being shown to your room and stopping suddenly on the stairs and saying to the butler: "What was that curious sound I just heard? Is somebody playing the castanets?" and him replying: "That was Mr Gedge's death-rattle, sir, thank you, sir." It wouldn't do. You can see that for yourself. No, the only thing to be done is for me to go in your place. I wouldn't do it for everybody, but you're a pal and I'd like to help you in this jam. *I* will go to the Château.'

'But ...'

'Mrs Gedge has never seen you. Mr Gedge has seen you, but is in no condition to meet company. I could get away with it nicely.'

A moment's reflection, and the Vicomte was convinced. It hurt his head to do so, but he burst into a torrent of broken thanks. Packy waved his gratitude aside.

'There isn't much I wouldn't do to help a pal like you, Veek,' he said with emotion. 'Now, you go to bed and have a nice long sleep, and in the morning you tell them that you've got a slight chill and will require your meals sent up till further notice.'

'Yes, Packy.'

'Don't stir from this room on any account.'

'No, Packy.'

'And you'd better give me that beastly costume of yours. The cops are probably scouring the town for its owner at this very moment. I'll take it back to my boat and drop it overboard. And I hope,' said Packy, a little priggishly, perhaps, but the subject was one on which he felt deeply, 'that this will be a lesson to you not to go to fancy-dress balls as a lizard. If fewer people went about the place pretending to be lizards,' said Packy, 'this would be a better and a sweeter world.'

3

Mr Gedge, as he lay on the sofa in the drawing-room of the Château Blissac at two o'clock on the following afternoon, was not at the peak of his form. He was conscious of a dark sepia taste in his mouth and a general disinclination for any kind of thought or action. Outside, the birds were singing merrily, and he wished they wouldn't.

His recollections of the previous night were hazy in the extreme. He could remember broadly passing through an experience such as he had not had since the Shriners met in Los Angeles, but as regards the details he was shaky. His only outstanding recollection was of having had a fight with someone.

And then suddenly the picture grew clearer, and he sat up with an anguished start. He had just remembered that his adversary in that combat had been a young man brightly dressed as a lizard, and as the only celebrant at the festivities so costumed had been the Vicomte de Blissac, the battler consequently must have been he. Mr Gedge was not at his most nimble-witted this afternoon, but he could reason out a simple thing like that.

He was appalled. The Vicomte was due to arrive at the Château to-day for an indeterminate visit, and the problem of what is the correct attitude for a host to adopt towards a guest of honour whom on the previous night he has earnestly endeavoured to throttle was more than he could solve.

He was still wrestling with it when the door opened and the butler's voice, announcing the Vicomte de Blissac, brought him to his feet as if the sofa had exploded under him.

A moment later, in walked Packy with outstretched hand.

'Good afternoon, good afternoon, good afternoon!' said Packy. 'What a day, what a day! The lark's on the wing; the snail's on the thorn; God's in his heaven; all's right with the world; and how are *you*, Mr Gedge?'

Mr Gedge regarded him with a cold, shuddering hostility. To a man who disliked snails and was not any too sold on larks, such jovial effusiveness at such a moment, even if exhibited by a personal friend, must inevitably have proved distasteful. And Packy was not a personal friend. Mr Gedge could not remember exactly why, but he knew that he objected to him strongly.

And, in addition to reciting poetry at him at a time when even the lightest prose would scarcely have been endurable, this offensive young fellow was frivolously claiming to be the

Vicomte de Blissac. Foggy though Mr Gedge might be about some of the minutiæ of the proceedings of the previous night, he did know who had been the Vicomte de Blissac and who hadn't. He decided to take a very short way with this sort of thing.

'What the devil are you doing here?'

'I've come to stay.'

Mr Gedge gave him one look and moved to the bell.

'I wouldn't,' said Packy.

'What do you mean?'

'I just wouldn't.'

'I'm going to ring for my butler and have you thrown out.'

'I wouldn't.'

'You muscle in here, pretending to be the Vicomte de Blissac....'

'I have a very good reason for pretending to be the late Vicomte de Blissac. Ah, Gedge, Gedge,' said Packy, 'you don't know your own strength.'

Mr Gedge stared.

'What on earth are you talking about?'

'Surely you have not forgotten the fight you had with the Vicomte?'

Mr Gedge seemed to be trying to swallow his Adam's apple. He did not succeed, for it was still plainly to be seen bobbing up and down.

'But I never touched the fellow.'

'That is not the view the police take. They have put out a drag-net and are combing the countryside for a small but burly assassin last seen wearing a sort of Oriental costume with a scarf-turban round his head.'

Mr Gedge quivered.

'I mean, I hardly laid a hand on him.'

'You are speaking now of the first encounter – what I might call the preliminary skirmish?'

'First?'

'Then you have forgotten the second one?'

'Holy mackerel!' said Mr Gedge.

He searched desperately in the recesses of a maddeningly defective memory for even the smallest detail of the affair. He found nothing.

'You don't mean we had another battle?'

'And how!'

'And you say this bird is in bad shape?'

'You could hardly say he was in any shape. And I thought the only thing to do was to come here in his place. Of course, looking at it in a narrow, technical way, I am not the Vicomte de Blissac. But I think you will be making a great mistake if you don't accept me as such. If Mrs Gedge returns and finds no Vicomte at the Château, don't you think she will start making enquiries?'

Mr Gedge had sunk into a chair and was kneading his forehead. To believe or not to believe?

One portion of his mind was telling him that it was simply absurd to suppose that a man could have a desperate fight round about supper time and not remember anything about it on the following afternoon. And then, stealing back, there came the unnerving thought that Packy might be speaking the truth. In which case, to expel him from the Château would be disaster.

And thus the native hue of resolution – Mr Gedge's resolution – was sicklied o'er with the pale cast of thought (Mr Gedge's), and enterprises of great pith and moment – such as ringing the bell and telling the butler to show Packy the door – with this regard their currents turned awry and lost the name of action. Few men in alpaca coats and striped flannel trousers had ever so closely resembled Hamlet as did Mr Gedge at this moment.

'Well, it beats me,' he groaned. 'I don't see how I could have forgotten. Why, the time the Shriners met at Los Angeles I remembered everything the next day. I distinctly recalled having socked a fellow of the name of Weinstein. Red-haired man in the Real Estate business. He made a crack about the Californian climate. It all came back to me.'

'I hadn't the pleasure of being with you when the Shriners met at Los Angeles, but I don't think you can have been quite so boiled then as you were last night. I don't know when I've seen a man so boiled. I dare say you've forgotten socking me?'

Mr Gedge's eyes bulged.

'Did I?'

'You certainly did. Just one dirty look and then – *zingo!*'

Mr Gedge was convinced at last. If he could have forgotten committing assault and battery on a man of Packy's physique, he could have forgotten, he argued, anything.

'So where do we go from here?' asked Packy. 'All I am trying to do is to save you unpleasantness. If you wish me to leave, of course I'll leave at once. But in that case how about Mrs Gedge? Won't she write to the Vicomtesse asking what has become of her son? Of course she will. The whole story will then come out, and I don't see how the police can fail to track you down. And after that . . . Well, you can say what you like about the guillotine – the only known cure for dandruff and so on – but nobody's going to persuade me that you will enjoy it. So how about it? Do I stay or go?'

Mr Gedge shot from his chair. He clutched feverishly at Packy's coat.

'Don't you dream of going!'

'On reflection, you wish me to remain?'

'You're dern tooting I wish you to remain!'

'I think you're wise.'

Mr Gedge mopped his forehead. He looked at Packy ador-ingly. It amazed him to think that there could ever have been a time when he had not liked – nay, worshipped – this sterling young man.

'I don't know how to thank you, honestly I don't.'

'Quite all right. A pleasure.'

'It's white of you. That's what it is. White.'

'No, no, really. The merest trifle.'

A belated memory of the night before returned to Mr Gedge.

'Say, listen,' he said. 'I seem to recall saying something at that Festival about Yale couldn't play football.'

'Oh, never mind that.'

'But I do mind that,' said Mr Gedge earnestly. 'I admire Yale football. I think it's swell.' He hesitated a moment, then, as if feeling that the supreme sacrifice must be made, went on. 'Ask me, I should say Yale was better than University of Southern California by around three touch-downs.'

'Not three?'

'Yessir. Three.'

'One at the most.'

'Well, call it two,' said Mr Gedge, making a concession.

CHAPTER 7

In every chronicle of the rather intricate nature of the one which is here being related, there occurs a point where the conscientious historian finds it expedient to hold a sort of parade or inspection of the various actors in the drama which he is unfolding. It serves to keep the records straight, and is a convenience to a public to whom he wants to do the square thing – affording as it does a bird's-eye view of the position of affairs to those of his readers who, through no fault of their own, are not birds.

Here, then, is where everybody was at the moment of Packy Franklyn's arrival at the Château Blissac. And this is what, being there, they were doing.

Mrs Gedge was in the office of her lawyer in London. His operations on her behalf in the matter of evasion of English Income Tax had dissatisfied her, and she was talking pretty straight to him.

Lady Beatrice Bracken was in the garden of her father's seat, Worbles, in Dorsetshire. She was reading for the third time Packy's letter announcing his departure for St Rocque. Well knowing that resort to be a hot-bed of gambling and full of the most undesirable characters, notably the Vicomte de Blissac, she thoroughly disapproved of his choice of destination. As she read, she frowned. As she frowned, she tapped her foot. And as she tapped she said 'H'm!' And she meant it, too. At lunch that day her aunt Gwendolyn had once more expressed the opinion that Packy was a flippertygibbet, and Beatrice found herself in complete agreement with the old fossil.

Mr Gordon Carlisle, looking more gentlemanly than ever in a new hat, new shoes, a new suit, and a gardenia, was standing on the deck of the steam-packet *Antelope*, watching the red roofs of St Rocque grow more and more distinct as the vessel approached them in the afternoon sunlight. The new suit-case which lay beside him bore a label on which a keen-sighted bystander might have read the legend 'M. le Duc de Pont-Andemer'.

Soup Slattery was at the Casino. His overnight experiences had made his head a little heavy first thing in the morning, but a pick-me-up of his own invention had soon put that right and he was now feeling fine. He was punting cautiously at one of the *chemin-de-fer* tables and, if the matter is of any interest, was slightly ahead of the game.

The Vicomte de Blissac was not in quite such good shape. As he lay in bed in his room at the Hotel des Etrangers, staring at the ceiling and starting convulsively whenever a footstep approached his door, he was suffering a good deal of discomfort through the activities of some unseen person who would persist in running white-hot skewers through his eyeballs. This, taken in conjunction with the fact that at any moment he was expecting the door to burst open and the Arm of the Law to reach in and haul him off to prison on a capital charge, was having rather a depressing effect on the unfortunate young man.

Mr Gedge had returned to the drawing-room sofa. He was groaning a little.

Senator Opal was taking a brisk walk in the grounds.

Blair Eggleston was in the servants' quarters of the Château, broodingly brushing the spacious seat of the Senator's dress trousers. He was not happy. But then Senator Opal's valets never were. The first thing a valet in the employment of the Senator had to learn was that life is stern and earnest and that we are not sent into this world merely to enjoy ourselves.

Miss Putnam, Mrs Gedge's social secretary, was in the library doing a crossword puzzle, a form of mental exercise to which she was much addicted.

The cook was asleep.

The butler was writing to his mother.

Medway, Mrs Gedge's maid, was busy about her duties. When these were concluded, she proposed to go and relax down by the lake with the mystery novel which she had begun reading on the previous evening.

Packy was looking for Jane.

And Jane was standing on the rustic path which wound its way along the hillside on which the Château was situated, gazing thoughtfully down at the harbour.

It was not, as has already been hinted, a big day for larks and snails. The fact that the former were on the wing and the latter on the thorn had brought little comfort to Mr Gedge. Equally small was the solace it conveyed to Jane Opal. As she stood scanning the view beneath her, her heart was troubled. To-day, for the first time since sudden love had thrown them into each other's arms, she had found herself beginning to wonder if her Blair was quite the godlike superman she had supposed. There even flashed through her mind a sinister speculation as to whether, when you came right down to it, he wasn't something of a pill.

The thought did no more than pop out of her subconsciousness and back again in an instant, but it had been there and it left her vaguely uneasy. Its lightning entrance and exit had tarnished the sunshine and taken at least forty per cent off the entertainment value of the blue sky and the carolling birds.

In these last few days, Blair Eggleston had undoubtedly not been showing himself at his best. Constant association with Senator Opal had induced in him a rather unattractive peevishness. Querulousness and self-pity had marked him for their own. At their stolen meetings, when Jane would have preferred to talk of love, he showed a disposition to turn the conversation to the subject of his personal misfortunes and keep it there. And it is trying for a sensitive and romantic girl, when she comes flitting through the laurels in the quiet evenfall to join her lover, to find that all he proposes to discuss is her father's habit of throwing oatmeal at him in the bedroom.

All this, however, Jane could have forgiven, had he but come through with a red-hot scheme for retrieving the fateful letter from Mrs Gedge. But if it is true that the Hour produces the Man, it is also true that it remorselessly reveals the wash-out. As a schemer, Blair Eggleston had proved entirely negligible. He had no constructive policy of any kind to put forward. He might just as well not have been there.

Reluctantly, Jane came to the conclusion that what she needed in a predicament like this was somebody more on the lines of Packy Franklyn. There, she felt, was a man of action, a man who could be relied on at least to try to start something instead of just loafing about and wasting his time complaining because somebody had thrown a little oatmeal at him. She thought wistfully of Packy. With a sudden whole-hearted intensity she wished that he were here now, and, looking up, saw that he was. He was at that very moment coming down the path towards her. Quick service, decided Jane, and jumped perhaps two inches and a quarter in her astonishment at this miracle. She felt a little as Aladdin might have done if he had rubbed his lamp by accident.

'You!'

She had said the same word to him on a previous occasion. Then it had had something of the effect of a Mills bomb. Now it brought to his face a gratified smile. A connoisseur of 'You's!' Packy had recognized this one for what it was, a welcoming, even an ecstatically welcoming 'You!', the sort of 'You!' it did a fellow good to hear.

'What . . . Why . . . What . . .'

Packy was pressing her little hand. A purist might have said that for an engaged man he was pressing it perhaps just the slightest shade too fondly.

'It's quite all right.'

In a few simple words he explained the situation. He related the interview with the Vicomte de Blissac, the more recent interview with Mr Gedge. Forestalling any possible question as to how, now that he was in the Château, he proposed to open a locked safe, he spoke of Mr Slattery and Mr Slattery's gratitude, showing that he had a skilled assistant who would do all that sort of thing for him. All that had to be done, he pointed out, was to wait till Mrs Gedge returned and then leave a handy window open, and Mr Slattery would do the rest.

'So there you are,' said Packy.

Jane Opal breathed deeply. If she had not been an exceptionally pretty girl, one might have said that she snorted. There was a light in her eyes which Packy had not seen there before. It was a light he liked, and once more he was aware of a feeling of regret that a girl like this was throwing herself away on a man so obviously one of Nature's prunes as Blair Eggleston.

'But how splendid of you!'

'Oh, no, really.'

There was no necessity for him to have taken her hand again and pressed it, but he did so.

'But why should you be doing this for me?'

She had touched on a point which from time to time had a little perplexed Packy himself. It was, of course, absurd to suppose that any slight physical attraction which this girl might possess could have had any influence on a man who was engaged to Lady Beatrice Bracken. He was compelled to put it down to some innately noble quality in his character. You came across fellows like that occasionally – fine, big-hearted, selfless altruists, men who with no motive of personal gain simply raced about the place doing good to all and sundry. He supposed he was one of them.

Too modest to advance this theory, he waved a deprecating hand.

'Well, it struck me that you might be needing a little help. I rather gathered from what you said over the telephone that evening that you weren't expecting very solid results from Eggleston.'

Jane sighed.

'Blair's been no good at all.'

'I feared as much.'

'He can't seem to take his mind off that oatmeal.'

'What oatmeal?'

'Well, it was like this. It happened the first morning we were here. Father wanted his breakfast in bed, so Blair brought him his breakfast in bed, and naturally the cook, knowing Father was

American, took it for granted he would want oatmeal, so she fixed oatmeal. And then it turned out that oatmeal was a thing Father doesn't like.'

'Many people don't.'

'Yes, but he didn't just say so. That wouldn't be Father. No! He waited till Blair had put the tray down by his bed, and then he lifted the cover off the dish and said, "What is this? Oatmeal?" and Blair said, "Yes, oatmeal," and Father said in quite a mild, gentle sort of way, "Ah! Oatmeal?" and Blair started to leave the room and suddenly something hot and squashy hit him on the back of the head, and there was Father sitting up in bed, digging the spoon in the oatmeal; and Blair was just wondering what it was all about, because the back of his head was all covered with oatmeal, when Father dug the spoon out again and it was full of oatmeal, and Father held it at the bottom with his left hand and at the top with two fingers, and then he let fly rather like one of those old catapults you read about in stories where ancient towns are besieged, and Blair got it all – in the face this time.'

A slight shudder shook Packy's wiry frame. He was recalling that incident of the hair-cutting and realizing the risks which he, a gay, heedless boy, had so recklessly taken with this oatmeal-jerking Senator. He shivered to think what Ambrose Opal could have done on that occasion had he had a blanc-mange or a couple of bowls of soup handy.

'So there was Blair with oatmeal on the back of his head and oatmeal all over his face, practically a mass of oatmeal, you might say, and then Father smiled a quiet, affectionate kind of smile and said, "I don't like oatmeal." And the whole thing has rather preyed on Blair's mind. He's a little cross about it, I'm afraid. He says I ought to have warned him what he was letting himself in for when he became Father's valet.'

'I don't see how you could have known.'

'Well, Father did tell me his valets never stayed with him more than a week or so, but he said he thought it must be due to this Bolshevist spirit that you see springing up on all sides. It's a great pity, of course, because it has made Blair a little peevish, and I don't think he's very happy.'

'I can quite see how he might not be. Personally, I'd sooner be somebody living in Chicago that Al Capone didn't much like than your father's valet.'

He would have gone on to develop this theme, but at this moment there was a puffing noise and round the corner came Senator Opal in person.

On seeing Packy, the Senator halted abruptly. A look of concern came into his face. He had been much worried of late, and worry, he knew, breeds hallucinations. Then he saw that this phantasm was holding his daughter's hand and that she appeared to be aware of his presence, and he felt a little reassured. And when the girl turned to him and said, 'Oh, hullo, Father. Here's Mr Franklyn!' his last doubts disappeared and what had been the chill of apprehension turned into righteous wrath.

'Only,' proceeded Jane, as his colour began gradually to deepen and memories of old hair-cuts lit the flame in the eyes which he was fixing on Packy, 'you must remember to call him the Vicomte de Blissac.'

Nothing, as Shakespeare appreciated, is more tedious than a twice-told tale, but in Jane's demeanour as Packy for the second time related the events which had led up to his being at the Château in another's name there was no suggestion of boredom. She stood there with sparkling eyes, interjecting an occasional 'Isn't that great!' and from time to time a 'Get this, Father, it's good!'

Nor was the Senator an unemotional audience. Gradually, as he listened, the purple flush faded from his face and into it came that awed, reverential look which had come a short while before into the face of his daughter and a short while before that into the face of Mr Gedge. As the story drew to its conclusion, he stood for a while puffing. Then he gave tongue with the air of one who now saw all things clearly.

'So this is the fellow!'

'What, Father?'

'This is the fellow you were telling me about in London. Fellow you want to marry.'

A little gasp escaped Jane. The mistake was a natural, even an inevitable one, but this made it none the less disconcerting. She looked at Packy, her face reddening.

In Packy's gaze, also, there was a certain embarrassment. But he winked quickly, a wink that said, 'Humour him. It is better so.' To explain, he realized, would merely be to introduce the Blair Eggleston *motif*, and his intuition told him, as Jane's had told her on an earlier occasion, that to do this would not be wise.

'Yessir,' he said, with a faint echo of Mr Gedge. 'That's right.'

Senator Opal was all genial cordiality. He patted Packy's shoulder in the heartiest possible manner.

'You get that letter back, and you won't find any kick coming from me. Franklyn? . . . Franklyn? . . . You aren't the football Franklyn, are you?'

'I did play football at Yale.'

'Played football at Yale! You made the All-American.'

'Yes, I did, as a matter of fact.'

'I'm a Yale man myself. Why, dammit, I know all about you. Somebody left you two or three million a few years ago.'

'My uncle.'

Senator Opal regarded his daughter in a manner that suggested that he was uneasy about her sanity.

'A Yale man ... An All-American half-back ... A fellow with three million dollars ... Why you wanted to have all this secrecy and hole-in-the-corner business is more than I can imagine. Why you couldn't have told me straight out ...' He turned to Packy, and the severity of his demeanour softened to a sort of mellow unction. He looked like a Victorian father about to bestow a blessing. 'You're simply exactly the very son-in-law I've always been hoping for. Kiss her!'

If there had been a touch of embarrassment in Packy's manner before, there was more than a touch now. He was not a young man who blushed readily. Indeed, many of his friends looked upon him as one who had forgotten how to blush at the age of six or thereabouts. Nevertheless, there undoubtedly stole into the healthy tan of his face at this point a faint pink, turning it to a rather pretty crushed strawberry.

'Oh, that's all right, sir,' he said, backing a little and averting his gaze from the now incandescent Jane.

Senator Opal was a man who, when he issued instructions, liked to see them obeyed with a snap. He had, moreover, wholesome, old-fashioned views on how young lovers should behave towards one another. The geniality in his face waned.

'You hear what I said? You kiss her.'

'But ...'

'Come on, come on, come on!'

It is not easy to bestow a kiss with a warmth sufficient to satisfy a father who likes his kisses emotional and at the same time to convey to the party of the second part a suggestion of deep and respectful apology. But Packy did his best.

'Right!' said Senator Opal briskly, apparently passing the salute as adequate. 'And you can do that as often as you like. And now about this letter. Do you know where I'm off to?' he asked, staring impressively from beneath his bushy eyebrows.

'You aren't going, Father?' said Jane, with some concern.

'Yes, I am going, and I'll tell you where I'm going. Now that this young man has come, we can get action. And the first thing to do is to find out where that infernal woman will put that letter of mine. She's sure to bring it back with her. Women are like that. If a man had a thing of that sort, he'd put it in a safe-deposit box. But women, poor fools, like to keep their valuables by them, so that they can take them out every two minutes and gloat over them.'

'Quite true,' said Packy.

'Of course it's quite true. And that's what this Gedge woman will do. I know that from the way she's always acted about her jewellery. I used to tell her to keep it at the bank, but she never would. This letter is going to be put in a safe, and I'm ready to bet that safe is in her bedroom. I'll go and see. Meet me on the terrace in twenty minutes.'

He stumped off, and Jane and Packy started to walk back to the Château. They walked in silence, each a little pensive.

Packy was feeling mildly surprised that, considering how deeply in love he was with Beatrice, the recent embrace had not revolted him more. He had not enjoyed it, of course. He could scarcely have been expected to do that. But it had not really revolted him. He was, however, conscious of a feeling of relief that Beatrice had not been an eyewitness of the episode.

Jane was thinking rather along the same lines. It would be too much, naturally, to say that she had derived any pleasure from Packy's kiss. On the other hand, it had not jarred every fibre of her being. But she was glad that Blair had not happened to be looking on at the moment.

They came meditatively in view of the house.

'How funny these old French Châteaux are,' said Jane.

'Very funny,' said Packy.

'All those turrets and things.'

'Yes, all those turrets.'

They began to discuss mediæval French architecture in a guarded way.

CHAPTER 8

I

I⊤ was some fifteen minutes later that the garden door of the Château was flung exuberantly open and Senator Opal came bounding out with quite a juvenile jauntiness in his step. His quest had been completely successful. The briefest of explorations of the Venetian Suite had shown him the safe, let into the wall beside the bed. He was feeling pleased with himself and his manner showed it.

During these last days, Senator Opal had been dwelling in the shadows. There are few less agreeable experiences for a man of proud and autocratic temperament than to find himself tied hand and foot and at the mercy of a woman for whom he has always felt a definite dislike. And what had added to Senator Opal's bitterness was the fact that there was absolutely nobody else to blame. To his carelessness, and to his carelessness alone, the disaster had been due.

But now everything was splendid once more. Mrs Gedge, when she returned to the Château, would bring the letter with her. She would put it in the safe. He had located the safe. And that excellent young fellow, Franklyn, of whom he was beginning to approve more highly every moment, knew a man who could open safes and had promised to open one for him any time he gave the word.

Rendered quite lissom with relief, Senator Opal began positively to frisk up and down the terrace. And as he frisked he suddenly became aware of a young woman approaching him. It was Medway, Mrs Gedge's maid. In one hand she carried a book, in the other a half-smoked cigar.

This surprised the Senator. He was far from being an anti-tobacconist, nor had he any prejudice against the fashionable modern addiction of women to the weed. But he could not remember ever having seen a woman with a cigar.

Medway drew closer. Halting, she fixed him with a respectful eye and extended the cigar-stump between dainty fingers.

'Would you be requiring this any further, sir?'

'Eh?'

'You left it in moddom's room, and I thought perhaps you would be needing it.'

2

A good deal of Senator Opal's effervescence evaporated. An almost automatic and unconscious smoker, he had forgotten that he had been half-way through a cigar when he embarked on that search of his. A well-defined feeling of constriction in the muscles of his throat caused him to utter a faint sound like the gurgle of a dying duck.

'You weren't there!'

'Yes, sir.'

'I didn't see you.'

'No, sir.'

The Senator cleared his throat noisily. There were several

questions he would have liked to ask this calm-browed girl, but he felt that the asking would be injudicious. The salient fact, the one that must be dealt with immediately, was that she had seen him nosing about in the Venetian Suite. Where she had been concealed was a side issue.

'H'r'r'mph!' he said awkwardly.

Medway awaited his confidences with quiet respect. And yet, the Senator asked himself as he gazed into it, was that eye of hers quite so respectful as he had supposed? A demure girl. Difficult to know just what she was thinking.

'I dare say,' he said, 'it seemed a little strange to you that I should be in Mrs Gedge's room?'

Medway did not speak.

'The fact is, I am a man with a hobby. I am much interested in antiques.'

Medway remained quiescent.

'An old place like this . . . a historic old house like this . . . a real old-world Château like this, full of interesting objects, is – er – interesting to me. It interests me. I am interested in it. Most interested. It – er – interests me to – ah – potter around. I find it interesting.'

A fly settled on his snowy hair. Medway eyed it in silence. He cleared his throat again. He was feeling that he would have to do a little better than this.

'But I can quite see,' he proceeded, contriving now to achieve a faint suggestion of the orotundity which so impressed visiting delegates at Washington, 'I can quite understand that Mrs Gedge might not like . . . might object . . . might view with concern the fact that in her absence I have been visiting her – ah – *sanctum sanctorum*. It might strike her as . . . in fact, just so. I should be greatly obliged to you, therefore, my good girl, if you would say nothing to her about the matter. Here,' said Senator Opal, getting down to business and bringing paper money out of his pocket. He hoped it was not a *mille*, but he did not dare to stop and look. 'You take this and say nothing about it.'

'Thank you, sir.'

'You understand? Not a word.'

'Yes, sir.'

'It is not that ... It is not that I feel ... On the other hand, there is no doubt that I ought to have waited until Mrs Gedge returned and was able to conduct me in person about the Château. ... But as ... er ... seeing that ... Well, in short, I think it will be best if you ... ah ... h'r'r'mph ... just so.'

'Very good, sir.'

The girl's docility charmed the Senator. Her tactful behaviour in what might have been a situation of some embarrassment had completely restored his sense of well-being. He did not mind now if it had been a *mille*. He felt thoroughly kindly-disposed towards her, and it seemed to him that a little affability of a strictly paternal nature would now not be out of place.

'Got a book there, I see.'

'Yes, sir.'

'Fond of reading?'

'Yes, sir.'

'I suppose you have a good deal of leisure with Mrs Gedge away?'

'Yes, sir.'

The Senator began to like this girl more and more. Most attractive, her nice deferential manner.

'And what are we reading?' he asked, in a voice which was practically tantamount to a pat on the hand. 'Some love story?'

'No, sir.'

'Don't you like love stories?'

'No, sir. I don't believe in them. Men,' said Medway, with the first touch of feeling she had shown, 'aren't sincere. Them and their love!' said Medway, now quite bitterly.

The Senator shrank from probing the tragedy at which her words and manner hinted.

'A mystery story, eh?' he said, catching a glimpse of the book's jacket, which revealed a muscular gentleman with a mask on his face apparently engaged in jiu-jitsu with a large-eyed girl, the pair of them seemingly unaware that a hand holding a revolver was protruding from behind a curtain in the background. 'One of those thrillers?'

'Yes, sir.'

'Well, don't let me keep you. I dare say you've just got to the most exciting part?'

'Yes, sir. It's where these criminals are trying to burgle a safe in a country house, little knowing that the girl they think is a maid is really Janice Devereux, the detective. Good afternoon, sir.'

She passed on her way, moving gracefully over the turf. But it was not mere æsthetic pleasure at her gracefulness that caused Senator Opal to stand gazing after her until she was out of sight. A sudden monstrous suspicion had come to him.

'Goosh!' he soliloquized.

A gay clatter of voices broke in on his fevered meditation. His daughter Jane had come on to the terrace, accompanied by that young fellow Franklyn.

3

The slight feeling of embarrassment which at first had militated against an easy flow of conversation between Jane and

Packy had not lasted long. They were now on excellent terms, and Senator Opal, listening to their carefree chatter, thought he had never heard a more revolting sound.

'Hey!' he called sharply. He resented cheerfulness at such a moment.

Their voices died away. The fact that he was undergoing some upheaval of the soul was one which nobody, at such close range, could fail to observe. Jane was concerned, for she loved her father. Packy was surprised, because it was a revelation to him that the Senator could look like that. He had always supposed him a man of blood and iron, impervious to the weaker emotions.

'Whatever is the matter, Father?'

The Senator glanced about him conspiratorially. Except for a frog which had come out of the bushes and was sitting staring in that odd, apoplectic way frogs have, as if wondering what to do next, they were alone. Nevertheless, he lowered his voice to a hoarse whisper.

'Listen! We've got to watch out.'

'I'm watching,' said Packy airily. 'Leave everything to me, everything to me. Old P. ("Reliable") Franklyn. I have the situation well in hand.'

'Don't talk like a damned fool.'

'Father!'

'And don't you say "Father!" Do you know what's just happened?'

And, still speaking in that low, bronchial voice, Senator Opal proceeded to relate his story. He told of the purposeful dash for the Venetian Suite, the successful discovery of the safe, the subsequent sensation of triumph and exhilaration, the walk on the terrace with chest out and chin up.

Then the recital passed into a minor key. He spoke of Medway and cigars, of Medway and enigmatic looks, of Medway and mystery novels, of Medway and parting words, which if they weren't sinister – well, what were they?

'It's where these criminals try to burgle a safe in a country house, little knowing that the blasted maid is a detective in disguise. Those were her very words, and I wish you could have seen the sort of flick of the eye she gave me when she said them. If she had told me straight out that she was a private detective, she couldn't have made it any plainer. I went all cold.'

Jane was an optimist.

'Oh, she can't be.'

The Senator was a pessimist.

'She is, I tell you.'

Packy held the scales between the two.

'It is quite possible, of course, that Mrs Gedge may have engaged a detective to look after her belongings,' he conceded. 'But what this girl said was nothing but a coincidence, if you ask me.'

'I don't ask you.'

Jane said it was no use being a gump and losing your temper. The Senator said he was not a gump and had not lost his temper.

'I am quite calm, perfectly unruffled. I am merely placing the facts before you, so that we may debate upon them and explore every avenue. All I am trying to get at is what we are going to do if this woman is a detective, and when I was a young man girls did not speak to their fathers like that.'

Resisting an impulse to ask him to tell them all about when he was a young man, Packy frowned thoughtfully.

'I agree with you that it is a thing which we ought to know for certain before starting operations,' he said. 'This colleague of mine, of whom I have spoken, is a tough bozo, but I suppose even tough bozos prefer not to work in the dark. It would scarcely be fair to ask him to do his stuff in a state of uncertainty as to whether or not a female dick was likely to pop up out of a trap and make a flying tackle the moment he got action. Grateful though he is to me, it might pique him if we let him in for anything like that.'

'He means the man might find it awkward if there was a detective in the house,' explained Jane.

The Senator said he was aware that that was what Packy had meant. He also threw the butt of his cigar at the frog, hitting it on the nose and removing all its dubiousness as to what it proposed to do next. It made the bushes in two jumps, and Packy, who had employed the interval in tense thought, advanced a suggestion.

'Our first move,' he said, 'must be to find out about this girl. We must institute a probe or quiz and make her come clean.'

The Senator asked how the devil they were to do that.

'The problem,' said Packy, ignoring his slight brusqueness, 'is not so much "How?" That part of it is simple. Obviously, somebody has got to ingratiate himself with her – not to mince matters, flirt with her – make love to her – worm his way into her confidence and get the truth from her. The question is – Who?'

He looked at the Senator so meaningly that the latter asked if Packy seriously intended to suggest that he, a pillar of the United States Government, should go about organizing petting-parties with ladies' maids.

'You wouldn't have to do much,' urged Packy.

'Of course you wouldn't,' said Jane.

'Just a kindly word or two and an occasional squeeze of the hand.'

'He could kiss her.'

'He might kiss her. Yes, that would help.'

'I don't believe he would have any trouble at all. Father's got quite a lot of *It*. You'd be surprised.'

'I am,' said Packy.

The Senator uttered a sharp cry. For an instant, Packy supposed it to indicate the advent of one of those fits of Berserk rage to which he was so unfortunately subject, and he backed a little to be ready for the rush. With a man like Senator Opal, you could never be quite sure when you might not be compelled to put in some shifty footwork.

But it was not fury that had caused the other's emotion. The cry had denoted inspiration.

'Eggleston!'

'Eh?'

'Eggleston,' said Senator Opal, 'is the man to do it. That infernal, ugly, idle, lop-eared valet of mine. Everything points to Eggleston.'

4

If he had expected this ingenious solution of the problem to meet with unanimous approval, he was disappointed. Packy, it is true, saw its merits immediately. Apart from the fact that it was high time he started doing something constructive for the Cause, Blair Eggleston was ideally situated for the purpose they had in mind. He had endless opportunities of foregathering with this Medway, and what could be more suitable than that a valet should pass the time flirting with a lady's-maid? There was a sort of artistic inevitability about it. It seemed somehow to round off the picture. As far as Packy was concerned, the Senator had got one vote.

Jane was less enthusiastic. During her sojourn at the Château she had had plenty of time to observe Medway, and the thought of Blair on chummy terms with one so attractive jarred on her sensibilities.

'Oh, but, Father!'

'Now what?'

'He wouldn't do it.'

'Of course he would do it. If he has any fidelity or sense of duty in his system, he will jump at the chance. I've always treated the man with unremitting kindness, and if he won't do a little thing like this for me, I'll kick his spine up through his hat.'

And in accordance with his customary method of summoning his personal attendant Senator Opal threw his head back and began to howl like a timber-wolf, and continued to howl until Blair Eggleston came running round the corner of the house with a clothes-brush in his hand. He had been some little distance away, but his master's voice was a carrying one.

'Come on! Come on! Come on!'

The sharp dash which he had just taken had left Blair Eggleston short of breath. He stood panting like a Marathon runner at the winning-post until the Senator, who liked his valets alert, took him by the shoulders and gave him a hearty shake to stimulate his faculties. It nearly removed the young novelist's head from its moorings, but it had the effect of securing his attention.

'Now listen, you pop-eyed defective,' said the Senator.

The task of explaining to your valet that you wish him to make love to your hostess's lady's-maid with a view to ascertaining whether she is a detective in disguise is not an easy one. It might have baffled an ordinary man. Senator Opal was not an ordinary man. He did it in about sixty-five words.

'So there you are,' he concluded. 'Go to it.'

'But...'

'Did you say "But"?' asked the Senator dangerously.

Jane felt compelled to intervene.

'I'm sure,' she said with an apologetic smile, 'you must think it an odd request....'

The Senator would have none of this truckling.

'Never mind what he thinks. Let him go and do it. And what do you mean, "request"?'

'But, Father...'

'Can't waste the whole day talking. If there's anything the poor half-wit doesn't understand, explain it to him.' He turned to Packy. 'I want a word with you,' he said. 'Kiss Jane and come along.'

There are few things which call for so nice an exhibition of tact as the kissing of a girl in the presence of her *fiancé*. Packy did his best to perform the feat in a manner calculated to cause the minimum of disapproval, but he was haunted by a suspicion that he had not quite got the sympathy of his audience.

Abstaining from glancing at young Mr Eggleston, for, after all, he knew what he looked like, he followed the Senator off the terrace.

5

In suspecting that Blair Eggleston might find matter for criticism in his recent performance, Packy had not erred. In the novelist's manner, as he now gazed at Jane, there was a quite definite suggestion of Othello. He breathed heavily and was, indeed, so overcome by emotion that he even passed the clothes-brush absently through his hair.

'What,' he asked throatily, 'is all this?'

Jane was soothing.

'I know it must have sounded odd, darling. But Father has got it into his head that Mrs Gedge's maid . . .'

Blair Eggleston waved the clothes-brush impatiently.

'I am not referring to that. This fellow Franklyn.'

'Oh, that. Well, that's a long story. He has come here pretending to be the Vicomte de Blissac. . . .'

'Never mind what he's pretending to be. He kissed you!'

If Jane had been soothing before, she was oil and honey now.

'Yes, I wanted to explain that. It's most unfortunate, but Father seems to think he is the man I'm in love with.'

'I am not surprised, if you are in the habit of behaving towards him as you did just now.'

'But, Blair, don't you see . . .?'

'He kissed you!'

'Yes. Father insisted. You don't suppose I enjoyed it, do you?'

'I am not so sure.'

'Blair!'

'I certainly did not receive the impression that you had any strong objection.'

'Well, what could I do, with Father looking on? Did you expect me to scream for help? Or perhaps you would have liked me to tell Father that it's really you. . . .'

The remark had a sedative effect. The stern, accusing look in Blair Eggleston's eye, which would have recalled to a reader of the poetry of the late Lord Tennyson the celebrated scene of King Arthur's interview with Guinevere in the convent, gave place to one of positive alarm. An able student of psychology, like all Bloomsbury novelists, Blair had long since read his employer's character like a book. And what he had seen in that book did not encourage him to support any such suggestion.

'On no account!' he said hastily, turning a little green at the mere idea. His relations with Senator Opal had not been of such a nature as to lead him to suppose that the latter would receive with gratification the news that he was engaged to his daughter. 'Do nothing of the kind!'

'Well, then!'

'All the same . . .' said Blair Eggleston.

He twirled the clothes-brush thoughtfully. With his other hand he endeavoured also to twirl his moustache, his invariable policy when in a dilemma. But there was no moustache to be twirled. In deference to his employer's outspoken statement that he did not propose to have a valet hanging around him festooned with fungus and snorting at him all the time from behind a great beastly soupstrainer (for thus coarsely had the Senator alluded to that neatest of little lip-ornaments), he had regretfully shaved the treasured possession.

Its loss had cost him a good deal of mental pain, but it seemed to amuse his betrothed.

'Oh, Blair!' said Jane. 'You do look a scream without it.'

And yet, even as she spoke, she was aware subconsciously that the matter went deeper than that. The world is full of men who ought never to shave their upper lip, and Blair Eggleston was one of them. Coming out into the open, as it were, like this, he had revealed himself the possessor of a not very good mouth. A peevish mouth. The sort of mouth that bred doubts in a girl.

He stiffened. He had enough to endure these days without having to listen to girlish persiflage.

'I am glad that you are amused!'

'I was only kidding.'

'I see.'

'Can't you take a joke?'

'I have never,' began Blair weightily, 'been accused of being deficient in a sense of humour. . . .'

'Oh, all right. Let it go. It was only a remark, anyway. Just a random crack. For goodness' sake, let's not quarrel.'

'I have no desire to quarrel. . . .'

'Nor have I. So that's fine.'

There was a pause. Then, abruptly, it became apparent to Blair Eggleston that without any desire on his part to change the subject the main topic of debate had been adroitly sidetracked.

'All the same,' he said, 'I strongly object to this kissing.'

'Well, what can I do?'

'There can be no necessity for it whatever.'

'Can't there? You should have been there the first time. Father was all set to strike Packy with some blunt instrument if he had jibbed.'

'So you have got to Christian names?'

'Oh, Blair!'

Blair Eggleston was not to be checked by any exhibition of feminine irritability. He swelled a little, and waved the clothes-brush with a certain cold dignity.

'I do not think I can be said to be unduly exacting when I complain of this – er – of what is going on. And on one thing I must insist, that you see as little of this man Franklyn as possible. Personally, I am at a loss to understand what he is doing here at all.'

'He has come to try to help me.'

'Why?'

'Because he feels I need help, I suppose.'

'Oddly altruistic behaviour in one who is virtually a complete stranger.'

Pinkness, like the first faint flush of a summer dawn, had come upon Jane Opal.

'You needn't suggest...'

'I am suggesting nothing.'

'What on earth is the sense of saying you're suggesting nothing when you're suggesting it with every word you say?' demanded Jane heatedly. She was a straightforward girl, who disliked evasions. 'That's just the sort of silly, idiotic thing people are always saying in your books.'

'I am sorry if the characters in my books appear to you to be lacking in intelligence.'

'Anyway, you're all wrong. I don't mean a thing to Packy... oh, all right, to Mr Franklyn. Can't you understand that he's the sort of man who comes into a business like this just for the fun of the thing? Besides, he's engaged. You were there when he was telling us about it.'

Blair Eggleston had forgotten this. He looked a little taken aback. He recognized that the fact weakened his position.

'So you see! Now perhaps you realize what a chump you've been.'

Blair could not go as far as this.

'It is possible that I may have allowed myself to become unnecessarily...'

'Anyway, I should have thought you could have trusted me. I'm trusting you.'

'In what way?'

'Letting you go off and flirt with this Medway girl.' The greater urgency of ventilating his grievance in the matter of

Packy had caused Blair Eggleston momentarily to forget that he was a man with a mission.

'What *is* all that?' he asked, with agitation.

'It's quite simple. We think Medway may be a detective. And Mr Franklyn said the only way to find out was for someone to make love to her and win her confidence.'

'It would be Franklyn!'

'It was Father's idea that you should be the one to do it.'

Blair Eggleston choked. He had his personal views on Senator Opal and would have enjoyed giving them at some length.

'Well, I won't do it.'

'You must!'

'I positively and definitely refuse.'

'You've got to do it, Blair. You simply must. It's absolutely vital that we should find out about this girl. I do think you might do something to help. You've been about as much good so far as a sick headache.'

What retort Blair Eggleston would have made to this thrust will never be known. It would probably have been something fraught with dignified rebuke, but it must remain among the good things that were never spoken. For at this moment Jane put forward a suggestion that wiped the words from his lips.

'Do you want me to tell Father that you refuse?'

That faint shade of green came into Blair Eggleston's face once more. Whatever his long line of valets might feel about Senator Opal, none of them had ever looked upon him as a man whose wishes might lightly be ignored. Blair, the latest of the dynasty, would as readily have defied a charging rhinoceros.

He swallowed unhappily.

'Oh, I suppose I'll have to do it.'

'That's the way to talk!'

'But let me tell you that there are moments when I think what I have been – er – let in for, when I ask myself...'

He had no time to reveal what he asked himself, for Packy had come hurrying on to the terrace.

Packy seemed amused.

'I've been having rather a trying time with that poor fish...I beg your pardon – I mean with your respected father. He had three separate schemes to put forward, and each was loonier than the last. It took me quite a while to persuade him that he had better leave all the active work to me.'

Blair Eggleston barked sharply.

'Why the mirthless laugh?' asked Packy, surprised.

'Correct me if I am wrong, but it appears to me that I, though insignificant and of scarcely less use to you all than a sick headache, am about to do a certain share of what you describe as the active work.'

Packy stared.

'What! Holding Medway's hand? You don't call that work? Child's play. And most enjoyable, to boot. Besides, an experience like that will be useful to you in your business. I shouldn't be surprised if you didn't get a plot for a novel out of Medway.'

'Blair's novels haven't any plots.'

'No? Why's that?'

'He thinks they're crude.'

'I must read Blair's novels some day. Not just now. Later.'

'The critics say they have a strange fearless quality.'

'Well, that's always something, isn't it?'

The literary discussion was interrupted by the abrupt departure of the author. With a dark frown on his face, Blair Eggleston was stumping off towards the house.

Packy watched him with concern.

'A little peeved?'

'A little.'

'Did he . . . I forget what I was going to say.'

'Yes, he did.'

'I was afraid he might.'

Jane sighed.

'Blair can be very difficult.'

'I should imagine so.'

'It's the artistic temperament, I suppose.'

'Probably. Tricky devils, these novelists. The ink gets into their heads.'

'I sometimes wonder . . .'

'What?'

'Oh, nothing.'

'Pardon me,' said a deprecating voice behind them, 'but are you doing anything just now, Vicomte?'

They turned. It was Miss Putnam who had spoken. She was standing there beaming benevolently through her horn-rimmed glasses.

'Mrs Gedge was very anxious that I should show you our leaky cistern.'

It had not been Packy's intention to pass the summer afternoon inspecting leaky cisterns. The suggestion, which would have enchanted a plumber, left him cold. However, he was courteous.

'It will be a real treat,' he said. He turned to Jane. 'Will you join us?'

'I don't think I will, thanks.'

'Girls,' said Packy to Miss Putnam with a regretful shake of the head, 'are very *blasée* nowadays.'

'I thought of going and sitting in the hammock on the lawn.'

'You are probably missing something good, but do just as you please. I will stroll round there later.'

'It will only take a few minutes,' said Miss Putnam apologetically.

'In a few minutes, then,' Packy informed Jane, 'I will be with you.'

Despite the fact that he had been reluctant to start upon this sight-seeing expedition concerning which Miss Putnam seemed so enthusiastic, Packy became conscious of a certain pleasurable excitement as he followed the secretary to the upper regions of the house. This cistern, after all, had played an important part in his life. If there had been no leaky cistern, there would have been no falling out between Mr Gedge and the Vicomte de Blissac; and if there had been no such falling out he would not have been here in the Château now. It was as one visiting a historic monument that he came at length to the dark and narrow flight of stairs which seemed to lead to Journey's End.

At the head of these, Miss Putnam paused.

'Be careful, Vicomte. The ceiling is a little low. Though I guess,' she went on, simpering respectfully, 'you don't need to be told that.'

'Not now,' said Packy, rubbing his head.

'I mean, I suppose you have often hidden up here, playing hide-and-go-seek when you were a little kiddy.'

'No,' said Packy. He hoped his companion was not going to dwell too much on the dear old days at the Château. 'This is my first visit. Rather like Hell, isn't it?'

The secretary smirked, as Virgil might have done had Dante essayed a mild pleasantry while he was conducting him through the Inferno.

'It is not very pleasant,' she agreed. 'I suppose as a little kiddy you might have been scared to come up here.'

'I was never a very little kiddy,' said Packy, to correct an apparent misapprehension. 'Always rather an out-size kiddy. Big bones. Lots of firm flesh.'

Miss Putnam appeared to think this over, for she was silent for a while. Then she waved her hand in the direction of the asthmatic gurgle which was punctuating their conversation.

'This,' she said, 'is the cistern.'

It was the first time Packy had been formally introduced to a cistern, and he was not quite sure of the correct etiquette. He bowed slightly and eyed the repellent object with interest.

'It leaks,' said Miss Putnam.

'You are sure of this?'

'It leaks all the time.'

'Not on Sundays?'

'Mrs Gedge wanted you to see it before she sent for the plumber. Naturally she is a little annoyed. The Vicomtesse assured her that everything was in perfect order.'

'She's like that. A great kidder.'

'Well, if you are satisfied . . . '

'Oh, quite. I consider that Mrs Gedge has a cast-iron case. She has caught Mother bending and will, I trust, soak it to her good.'

They descended the stairs. Packy would have been quite content to descend them in silence, but Miss Putnam became chatty again.

'I do so envy you having been in this lovely home as a kiddy, Vicomte. What memories you must have!'

'Oh, yes.'

'You don't speak very enthusiastically.'

'I am never fond of talking of those days,' said Packy, who felt that this sort of thing must be firmly dealt with at the outset. 'Mine, you see, was not a happy kiddyhood. Lonely. Neglected. I prefer to forget it.'

'How very sad.'

'Oh, I'm all right now. I've perked up a lot recently.'

'How idiomatically you speak English, Vicomte.'

'Yes?'

'I am sure nobody would take you for a Frenchman.'

Here, again, in Packy's opinion, was a trend of thought that called for prompt measures.

'I was educated at an English school.'

'Where was that?'

'Aytong.'

'Aytong?'

'E-t-o-n.'

'Oh, Eton? That accounts for it, doesn't it?'

Packy hoped so.

'But what seems so odd to me is that you speak English so like an American.'

Packy was beginning to dislike this woman. At first, she had seemed to him a fragile, timid little thing whom it was a pleasure to put at her ease and generally behave like a great, big, strong – but kindly – man to. Now, she began to give evidences of possessing many of the less attractive qualities of a Class A gumboil.

'I have travelled in America much. Ah, mademoiselle,' said Packy, with Gallic fervour, 'how great a country!'

'I am glad to hear you say so, being American myself.'

'You are from Les Etats Unis?'

'I have lived there all my life.'

'Ah? You were a little kiddy there?'

'Did you find it very difficult, Vicomte, learning English?'

'Oh, no.'

'I have never been able to manage foreign tongues. I found it a great handicap when I was in Mexico a year or two ago.'

'Yes?'

'Oh, yes. I would have given anything to meet somebody I could have talked to in my own language.'

'I know the feeling.'

'You have it yourself sometimes, I guess, even though you speak English so well?'

'Oh, frequently.'

They passed through the hall and came out on to the steps which led to the gravel drive in front of the Château.

'Oh!' said Miss Putnam.

What had caused the exclamation was the sudden appearance of an ancient taxi-cab. It had rounded the corner of the drive and was bowling briskly towards them.

'This must be the Duc.'

'The who?'

'The Duc de Pont-Andemer,' explained Miss Putnam. 'A telegram arrived from Mrs Gedge saying that he would be arriving to-day.'

Her woman's instinct had not deceived her. The cab came to a grinding halt at the steps. Its door opened. And from it, hopping in an aristocratic way, there emerged a gentleman of distinguished mien.

'Good afternoon,' said the new-comer, advancing with a sunny but dignified smile. 'Permit me, shall it not, to introduce myself. I am the Duc de Pont-Andemer.'

CHAPTER 10

I

GORDON CARLISLE was a man who in his time had played many parts. Starting at the bottom of the ladder as the genial young fellow who had found a ruby ring in the street and was anxious, as the bally thing was of no use to him, to sell it for what it would fetch, he had worked his way up by sheer talent and application to the top of his profession. To impersonate even a South American hidalgo with title deeds to lands rich in oil and minerals was nowadays a mere nothing to him.

It is not to be supposed, therefore, that the task of depicting a member of the French aristocracy would occasion him any concern. He was glowing with careless confidence. He felt that these people, whoever they were, were seeing him at his best.

Packy, on the other hand, though a young man not easily put out of countenance, was experiencing an attack of something akin to panic. He had not anticipated that he would be called upon to forgather with Ducs. And if this encounter had to take place, he wished fervently that it had not occurred in the presence of Miss Putnam. He knew his Putnam. Unless forcibly prevented, she was very shortly going to say how nice it would be for a Vicomte and a Duc to have somebody with whom they could converse in their own language.

At the moment, she was occupied with greeting the handsome guest.

'How do you do, Duke? I am Mrs Gedge's secretary.'

'Mademoiselle!' said Mr Carlisle, bowing.

Miss Putnam beamed upon this worthy upholder of the *politesse* of the *ancien régime*.

'I hope you had a pleasant journey?'

'Most, thank you. The sea was like a . . .'

'Mill-pond?' said Miss Putnam. A student of crossword puzzles, she was seldom at a loss.

'A meal-pont. Exactly. And this gentleman?'

'This is the Vicomte de Blissac. How nice it will be . . .'

It seemed to Packy that at the mention of the Vicomte's name some kind of fleeting emotion had shown itself for an instant in the visitor's face, but he was too preoccupied with his own predicament to give it attention. He plunged desperately into small-talk.

'How do you do? Nice to see you.'

'It is to me,' replied Mr Carlisle with his unfailing politeness, 'a great privilege to visit your historic Château. The Château Blissac has figured much in our country's history.'

'You are not from these parts?'

'Ah, no. My estates are in Touraine.'

'Have you come from Paris?'

'From England.'

'By boat?'

'Yais.'

'How nice . . .' said Miss Putnam.

'So many people,' said Packy quickly, 'fly nowadays.'

'Ah, yais.'

'I am very fond of flying.'

'I also.'

'There is something about flying.'

'Yais.'

'So much quicker.'

'Yais.'

'How nice . . .'

'Think,' said Packy, 'what a lot of time one wastes on the train and then on the boat, coming to a place like this.'

'Yais.'

'In a 'plane it would have taken you only an hour or two to get here.'

'Yais.'

'Still, you did get here, didn't you, Duke?' said Miss Putnam, smiling in a roguish sort of way. 'And how nice it will be for you, having somebody to talk to in your own language. I was saying to the Vicomte only just now that, however well you speak a foreign language, it is never quite the same.'

A somewhat strained pause followed the delivery of this dictum. For the space of perhaps a quarter of a minute the French aristocrats stared at one another dumbly. Here, you would have said, watching them, were two strong, silent Frenchmen.

Mr Carlisle was the first to rally from the shock.

'*Parfaitement*,' he said.

'*Alors*,' said Packy.

'*Parbleu!*'

'*Nom d'une pipe!*'

There was another pause. It was as if some theme of deep interest had been exhausted.

Packy indicated the sky, as something to which he felt the visitor's attention should be directed.

'*Le soleil!*'

'*Mais oui!*'

'*Beau!*'

'*Parbleu!*' said Mr Carlisle, rather meanly falling back on old stuff.

They paused again. Packy, except for '*Oo là là!*' which he did not quite know how to bring in, had now shot his bolt.

But Mr Carlisle was made of sterner stuff. If there is much to be said from a moral standpoint against Confidence Trickery as a profession, there is this to be urged in its favour, looking at it from a purely utilitarian point of view – that it undoubtedly breeds in its initiates a certain enviable coolheadedness and enables them to behave with an easy grace in circumstances where the layman would be nonplussed. Mr Carlisle, after what he would have been the first to confess a bad two minutes, was his resourceful self once more.

'But really, my dear fellow,' he said, with a light laugh, 'all this is vairy delightful, but you must not tempt me, no. My English it is not good, and I promise my *instructeur* that always I would speak it only. You understand?'

The interval of silence had enabled Packy to dig up a really hot one.

'*C'est vrai,*' he said, with a glance at Miss Putnam which suggested that that, in his opinion, would hold her for awhile. '*Mais, c'est vrai, mon vieux. Oo là là, c'est vrai!* I, also, study the English and do not wish to speak the French.'

He regarded the descendant of the proud Pont-Andemers with an almost doglike devotion. He felt he had never met a more charming, delightful man. A Frenchman, yes – but how nobly he had lived it down by this sturdy refusal to speak or listen to his native tongue. Let him but carry on along these lines, never swerving from his determination, and Packy saw no reason why their mutual visit to the Château Blissac should not result in one of those great friendships you read about.

The departure of Miss Putnam, which occurred at this point, gave him an excuse for tearing himself away. The secretary, apparently losing interest now that the torrent of idiomatic French had dried up, had made one of her silent exits. Packy, well pleased, felt that the time had come for him to proceed to the hammock, where, he considered, he had already kept Jane Opal waiting too long.

'Well, Duc, I'll be seeing you,' he said cheerily. 'I have a date. Good-bye.'

'*Au revoir*,' said the Duc de Pont-Andemer.

He watched Packy disappear across the lawn. Then, turning, he strode briskly off down the drive. He wished to have a word with his friend and colleague, Mr Soup Slattery.

2

He found Mr Slattery, as he had expected to find him, in the cocktail bar of the Hotel des Etrangers.

The safe-blower, his modest day's gambling concluded, was refreshing himself with a Gustave Special.

He looked up as Mr Carlisle approached.

'Hello! you back?'

'Yes, I'm back.'

'How did you make out?'

'Oke. I'm in the Château.'

Respectful admiration shone in Mr Slattery's eyes. He was a man who could give homage where homage was due.

'Nice work, Oily. You're certainly smooth.'

As a rule, Mr Carlisle liked compliments, but he cut these short.

'Listen, Soup. Things aren't so good as you think.'

'How's that?'

'There's another bird in this Château, on the same lay as us.'

'What!'

'That's right. I found him there when I arrived. He says he's the Vicomte de Blissac.'

'I know D. Blissac.'

'So do I. It isn't more than a year since I took a couple of thousand bucks off him one night in London. That's how I know this bird isn't him. It made me jump, I tell you, when that woman points at this guy and says to me: "Shake hands with the Vicomte de Blissac." Right there I was on to him. I've never seen him before. He's a husky guy that looks like a prize-fighter.'

'Was he on to you?'

'No. He thinks I'm a French Duc. We've got to get rid of him.'

Mr Slattery's massive jaw protruded.

'You betcha we've got to get rid of him. And quick. I'm not going to have anyone muscling in on our territory.'

Mr Carlisle nodded, well pleased. Negligible though he considered him as an intellectual force, he had known that he could count on Soup when it came to crude physical action.

'He's too big for me to handle, so it's up to you. What you've got to do is go have a talk with him, and it better be to-night.'

'I'll talk to him. But how,' asked Mr Slattery, the difficulties of the undertaking beginning to impress themselves on his somewhat slow mind, 'do I locate him?'

'I don't know yet where he's sleeping, but I'll find out, and I'll leave a plan of the house under a stone on the right side of the front door steps, so you can get it when you come. And somewhere there'll be a window open for you. Okay?'

'Kayo,' said Mr Slattery shortly.

'You go to this guy, then, and knock the daylights out of him. Make him see it isn't healthy for him around these parts.'

Mr Slattery, without speaking, extended a massive arm and clenched and unclenched the ham-like fist at the end of it. Mr Carlisle, smiling approvingly, bade him farewell and set out for the Château with an easy mind. He felt he had left the matter in good hands.

3

Mental activity generally expresses itself in correspondingly rapid physical action. Mr Carlisle had started to walk back to the Château at a brisk pace, and as the afternoon sun was now beating down with considerable force it was not long before he became conscious of feeling extremely warm. As he passed up the drive, he was thinking how remarkably pleasant a cold bath would be. And it was just as he had begun to toy with this thought that his eye was attracted by the silver gleam of water through the trees to his left.

It drew him like a magnet. He left the drive and took a cross-country route in its direction. And presently he found himself on the edge of what was known locally as the lake, but which was in reality a sort of salt-water lagoon connected with the harbour of St Rocque by a narrow channel.

It looked extraordinarily inviting. He glanced modestly to right and left. Thick bushes screened this portion of the lake, almost meeting across the path down which he had come. There appeared to be no eye that could observe him. With a sigh of satisfaction, he removed his coat and tie, and he was just about to slide out of his trousers when there spoke in his immediate rear an austere, maidenly voice.

'Hey!' said the voice.

It seemed to rip through Mr Carlisle like a bullet.

4

Medway, the maid, on leaving Senator Opal, had taken her book down to the lake. It was a favourite haunt of hers. Here, lying on the soft turf in the pleasant shade, she proceeded to resume the adventures of Janice Devereux, Detective, at the point where she had left off on the previous night. But barely had she had time to read the opening murder of Chapter Eleven when the sound of footsteps told her that her sanctuary had been invaded. Legs passed her and halted on the brink of the water.

Parting the bushes, she peered out. And it was the sight she saw that drew from her the shocked exclamation just recorded.

All the woman in Medway was stirred to its depths.

'Hey!' she cried, and it might have been Mrs Grundy herself speaking. 'What do you think this place is? A bath-house?'

Mr Carlisle was still tottering where he stood. He looked like a gentlemanly poplar swaying in the breeze. The lake and the trees about it had not yet ceased to perform the complicated *adagio* dance into which they had broken. He gasped painfully, and with good reason.

Any feminine voice speaking at such a moment would have startled Mr Carlisle. What rendered this one so peculiarly disintegrating was the fact that he recognized it. Indeed, one might say that it had been ringing in his ears ever since the day, twelve months ago, when it had called him a two-timing piece of cheese – a remark which had been followed almost immediately by the descent on his frontal orbital bone of a large china vase.

It was the voice of his lost Gertie.

The next moment, she had come out of the bushes and was facing him.

'Gertie!' cried Mr Carlisle.

We who have been privileged to peep into Gordon Carlisle's soul can understand his emotion. Although at their parting this girl had beaned him with a vase, and rather a good vase, too, all the old love still remained. The first shock of astonishment over, it was ecstasy that predominated in the bosom which he was now hastily covering with his coat. His trousers, it need scarcely be said, for the code of the Carlisles was rigid, he had hitched up at the first intimation that he was not alone.

'Gertie! At last! After all these long, weary months!'

The girl was looking cold and hard and proud. Ancient grievances still rankled in her bosom, for women do not lightly forget.

'Well, Mr Carlisle,' she said.

It was plain that such icy aloofness at what should have been a lovers' meeting wounded her companion.

'Gertie,' he said, and there was the quiver in his voice which had once extracted a ten-pound subscription to the Home for Brave Ailing Mothers from a man named MacPherson, 'aren't you going to let bygones be bygones?'

'No, I'm not.'

Mr Carlisle gulped. He sought for words that would soften this obduracy.

'You don't know how I've missed you, Gertie.'

'Says you.'

'I've been searching for you everywhere.'

'Says you.'

'Yes, says me!' cried Mr Carlisle passionately. 'What would I be doing over in Europe if I hadn't heard that you had gone there?'

Medway laughed scornfully.

'And I suppose you came to this Château as the Duke de something because you heard I was here? I know all about you. I was there when Miss Putnam was talking to the butler. She was saying put you in the Yellow Room. Personally,' said Medway, speaking with a sort of queenly disdain, 'I'd put you in the ash-can.'

'No,' admitted Mr Carlisle, 'I did not come to the Château because I heard you were here. I'm on a job. And I'll bet it's the same job you're on. You've hired yourself out as a maid to get a chance of grabbing Mrs Gedge's ice.'

'Well, have you any objection?'

'Certainly, I've an objection. Just pushing your head into trouble, that's what you're doing. You haven't a chance, working alone.'

Medway bit her lip reflectively. She had started on this enterprise with a gay optimism, feeling that surely the time must come when Mrs Gedge would forget just once to lock up her trinkets. She had learned now that she was in the employment of a woman who never forgot a thing like that, and hope had begun to die.

'What's the idea?' she said. 'Do you want to team up with me?'

'Well, why not?'

'I don't know why not. I've nothing against a fifty-fifty strictly business proposition. But what good would you be? This thing isn't in your line. You can't bust a safe.'

'I can, too, bust a safe. Soup doesn't know it, and I didn't tell him, but if it's the ordinary sort of safe these women have, I can do it easy.'

'Who's Soup?'

'You remember Soup Slattery. We're in this thing together. The idea is that I let him into the house and he does the blowing. But that's all wet. Now I've found you, we'll double-cross him and keep the stuff for ourselves.'

Medway was impressed.

'Where did you ever learn to bust safes?'

'Plug Donahue taught me. It was just after you went away. He saw I was all shot to pieces and needed something to take me out of myself...'

'Never mind all that apple-gravy. Talk business. If you want us to work together on this job – fifty-fifty – I'm willing. I've seen for quite a while it was too big for me.'

Mr Carlisle breathed emotionally.

'If you knew what it meant to me, Gertie, to feel that you and I are once more...'

'Say, listen,' said Medway, breaking in on what promised to be a speech of no small audience-appeal, 'here's something that's on my mind. Could a sap that says he's Senator Opal not really be Senator Opal?'

'Nobody would say he was Senator Opal unless he knew it could be proved against him,' said Mr Carlisle, who was not a supporter of the great law-maker's views on the suppression of the Demon Rum. 'Why, is that old pest here?'

'Him or somebody that claims to be him. And I found him

just now snooping around in Mrs Gedge's room, where the safe is. And when I put it up to him, he had some story about being interested in antiques.'

Mr Carlisle reflected.

'I guess that's all there was to it,' he said, at length. 'Anyway, he can't be a ringer. These Gedges know Senator Opal. Mrs Gedge told me so. Nobody could slide in here made up for old Opal and get away with it. He was probably just rubbering around. But I'll tell you who is a ringer, and that's the fellow who says he's the Vicomte de Blissac.'

'What!'

'You see,' said Mr Carlisle, tenderly pointing the moral. 'You didn't know that, did you? How long has he been here?'

'He blew in this afternoon. I saw the butler showing him into the drawing-room, and he told me who he was.'

'Well, he isn't.'

'How do you know?'

'I've met the real one. I took a couple of thousand dollars off him once. You could have had half of that, Gertie, if you hadn't run off the way you did.'

'Never mind that. So that bird's a ringer, is he? And I suppose he's after the ice, same as we are.'

'Of course he is.'

'Well, what do we do about it? We can't have him messing around. We've got to push him out.'

'And how would you set about it?'

Medway frowned.

'I'm darned if I know.'

'Exactly,' said Mr Carlisle, once more pointing the moral. 'Maybe you begin to see now how much you need me.'

'What can you do?'

'What can I do?' Mr Carlisle's manner was airy. 'Why, simply go to his room to-night and hammer the stuffing out of him. If he's here to-morrow, it'll be on crutches.'

The little gasp which his companion gave at these brave words was the sweetest sound that Gordon Carlisle had heard in many a day. For it was the gasp of reluctant admiration. Her cold reserve seemed to have melted.

'You couldn't do that?'

'You see if I can't do it.'

'But the guy's as big as a house.'

'Tchah!' said Mr Carlisle carelessly.

'Well, this is new stuff to me,' said Medway. Her eyes, as they rested on his face, were shining with a light that had not been there before. 'I didn't know you were like this.'

'You've never got me right, Gertie,' said Mr Carlisle with affectionate reproach, 'never.'

'You'll really go and beat this great, husky guy up?'

'For your sake, Gertie, I'd beat up a dozen like him.'

Medway drew a deep breath.

'Well,' she said, 'if you put that through, maybe I might overlook all what happened a year ago. I'm not saying I will, mind you, but I don't say I won't. You do it, and then we'll chat things over and see where we stand.'

''At-a-girl!' said Mr Carlisle devoutly.

No qualms disturbed him. He knew that he could rely on Soup Slattery.

CHAPTER 11

I

NIGHT, sable goddess, from her ebon throne in rayless majesty stretched forth her leaden sceptre o'er a slumbering world. Down at the Casino Municipale brisk business was still being done, but up at the Château Blissac all was dark and silent. The hour was nearly one, and the Château Blissac had put the cat out and tucked itself in at about eleven-thirty. In all its broad grounds there was not a sound to be heard.

If there had been, it would not have been Soup Slattery who made it. Despite his impressive bulk, there were few men who could move with a softer tread when the occasion demanded it. He had found Mr Carlisle's rough chart of the house and was now consulting it with the aid of an electric torch outside the window which the other had left open for him.

The chart was clear. He switched off the torch and climbed silently in.

To those who, like the Vicomte de Blissac and Gustave, the cocktail blender at the Hotel des Etrangers, had seen Soup Slattery only in his moments of conviviality, it would have been a revelation to behold the stern purposefulness of his face as he mounted the stairs. He was about to confront a trade rival, and towards trade rivals his attitude had ever been one of dourness and austerity. He did not like them, and he let them see that he did not like them. This particular one he intended to cause to jump out of the window in his slumber-wear and not stop running till he reached Paris.

The door of Packy's room was locked, but locked doors meant nothing to Mr Slattery. A few seconds' expert manipulation of a small steel implement and the obstacle gave way.

The noise of this operation, though slight, woke Packy. He was not aware, however, that a visitor had arrived until there came the click of the electric switch and light flooded the room.

Even then, he did not immediately discover the intruder's identity. But recognizing sleepily that here was something hostile, he sprang from the bed and alighting on the heel of an upturned shoe spoiled any impressiveness the demonstration might have had by hopping vigorously.

Mr Slattery was a plain, practical man, not at all inclined to waste time watching classical dances when on a business trip.

'Stick 'em up!' he said.

The implied suggestion that he was covering Packy with a gun was not based on truth. He never carried a gun on these expeditions, holding very sensibly that if you had one you might use it and that if you used it all sorts of unpleasantness might ensue. What he was pointing at Packy was the small steel implement.

But Packy was not concerned with the other's armoury. He had recognized him now and was greeting him as an old friend.

'Mr Slattery – or may I say Soup, how nice of you to drop in. Neighbourly, I call it.'

Mr Slattery was all confusion and apology.

'You! Say, I didn't know you were in here.'

'Oh, yes, this is my little nest. Come right on in and take a seat. You're just the man I wanted to see. I was planning to come to the hotel and have a talk with you.'

'I wouldn't of bust up your beauty-sleep for the world,' said Mr Slattery contritely. 'I've been given a wrong steer. I'm looking for the bird who's here calling himself Veecount D. Blissac.'

'That's me. It's a long story...'

'It's really you?'

'Yes. You see...'

'Say, listen,' said Mr Slattery, once more nipping the narrative in the bud.

He had seated himself on the bed, and was regarding Packy with a grave reproach. A moment before, he had been all remorse at the thought of having disturbed the night's rest of one who had saved him from the fate, so to speak, that was worse than death. But now other emotions had crept in. Personal friend though Packy might be, he was none the less a rival, and we have seen how Mr Slattery felt about rivals.

'Say, listen,' he said, 'I hate to throw a spanner into a guy's game that's been as swell to me as you have, but you and me have got to have a little talk.'

'Nothing I should enjoy more. You don't mind if I climb between the sheets again?'

'You steered those cops off of me, and I owe you a lot for that. Still and all, when it comes to you horning into this joint and aiming to gum the works for me and my business associate, well, that's something else again.'

Packy looked puzzled.

'I don't quite follow this.'

Mr Slattery shook his head in disapproval of this trifling.

'You can't kid me. I know why you're in this Chatty-o.'

'I'll bet you don't.'

'Come clean,' said Mr Slattery, like a rebuking aunt. 'Quit fooling. You're after that ice.'

'What ice?'

'Mrs Gedge's ice.'

'Mrs Gedge's jewels?'

'Ah.'

'Nothing of the kind.'

'Brother!'

'Nothing,' repeated Packy, 'of the kind. I want to get back a letter.'

'A letter?'

'A compromising letter which a friend of mine wrote to Mrs Gedge and which, when she returns, will be in her safe. That is the safe I want you, if you will be so good, to open for me.'

Many men in Mr Slattery's place would have rejected this story as thin. But Mr Slattery was a movie-fan and he knew all about compromising letters. Anything to do with them or with the missing papers or the stolen plans he was prepared to accept without question, especially when told to him by one whom he esteemed as highly as he esteemed Packy. He softened visibly.

'Is that the straight up-and-up?'

'It is.'

'You're not stringing me?'

'Certainly not.'

'Why, then everything's fine. I naturally thought you was after that ice.'

'You can have the ice.'

'Boy, I'm going to do just that little thing. And when I collect it, I won't forget the important documents.'

'"t". Not "ts". One only. A single letter.'

'I'll get it for you. You shall have it.'

Packy patted his shoulder warmly.

'Your words are music. I knew I could rely on you. I don't mind telling you that if you had failed me I should have been pretty badly stymied. You see, owing to a defective education, I couldn't even begin to open a safe myself. How do you, by the way? I've often wondered.'

Mr Slattery was delighted to lecture on his favourite theme.

'Well, first,' he said weightily, 'you get your soup.'

'What's soup?'

'Why, it's soup. Stuff you make out of dynamite. Get your dynamite, crumble it up, put it in a sack, fill a can half full of water, and boil. The grease sinks to the bottom, you drain off the water, and what's left is the soup. Put it in a bottle and there you are.'

'In how many pieces?'

Mr Slattery smiled tolerantly.

'It won't explode. 'Course, you don't want to play football with it.'

'I see. No, that might be a mistake. All right, we're through with the soup course. What then? We are now approaching the safe. What does our hero do?'

'Well, there's two kinds of safe. The tough kind is the sort that's got a keester in it.'

'And a keester is—?'

Mr Slattery was no Thesaurus.

'Well, hell, it's a keester. I don't know what else you'd call it. A sort of extra pete built inside the real pete.'

'A kind of inner compartment?'

'That's right. When it's one of those you're up against something. First, you've got to blow the door open to get at the keester. Then you've got to knock off the pressure bolt. Then you've got to wedge something into the top edge of the keester door. Then you've got to push in something thicker. Then you've got to plug in gauze. Then you wet the gauze with the soup and touch it off. It's no cinch, whatever way you look at it.'

'So I should imagine. Let's hope Mrs Gedge's safe is not that kind.'

'Couldn't be. Not in a house. You find those in banks and that. The kind of pete a dame would have in her house would be one of the ones you borrow a hairpin to open. Or, if nobody's got a hairpin, just eat some garlic and breathe on the lock. Or, if you don't want to do that, find the combination. Where is this pete?'

'In the Venetian Suite on the floor below.'

'Anybody there?'

'Not at the moment.'

'Then let's go down take a look at it,' said Mr Slattery. 'Now's a good time to find out if it's one of those easy ones. Sure to be, though. You don't get keesters in a joint like this. Ask me, it'll be one of those four-letter combinations, and opening those is like shelling peas.'

2

There is something about Milady's bedroom, even when unoccupied, which tends to cast a certain awe upon the intruder. So Packy, at least, found. The Venetian Room was a large, ornate apartment on the first floor of the Château, with french windows which opened on a balcony looking down upon the drive. Packy, as he accompanied Mr Slattery across the threshold, was strongly conscious of a desire to be elsewhere. He had never met Mrs Gedge, but the picture he had formed of her in his mind was that of a tough baby. And, unreasoning though he knew it to be, he could not altogether repress a fear lest at any moment this formidable woman might suddenly bound out at them from behind the heavy curtains that draped the windows.

Fortunately, for such an occurrence could not have failed to prove a source of embarrassment, his apprehensions were not fulfilled. Great woman though she was, Mrs Gedge could not be simultaneously at the Carlton Hotel in London and in the Venetian Suite of the Château Blissac. No sudden roar, as of a tigress defending her cubs, came to break the stillness. Mr Slattery was enabled to conduct his investigations undisturbed.

The result of these evidently gratified him. He inspected the safe and smiled amiably. It was, it appeared, as he had foreseen, one of the easier, more likeable types of safe. He also spoke with cordial approval of the french windows and the balcony, which, he pointed out in the devout voice in which men call attention to the benevolent acts of Providence, might have been placed there expressly to afford the cracksman a nice, smooth getaway.

And it was at this point, just when everything was going so capitally and the whole atmosphere was so redolent of quiet contentment, that the jarring note intruded itself. For some moments, Mr Slattery had been glancing idly about the room, and now, abruptly, something in its aspect seemed to wipe the genial satisfaction from his face. He stiffened, and his eyes grew wider. It was as if he had seen a serpent in the way.

'But this is a woman's room!'

He spoke in a hoarse, agitated whisper, lowering his powerful voice to such an extent that it sounded like gas escaping from a leaky pipe. But neither this peculiar mode of address nor his care-stricken aspect for the moment conveyed to Packy a sense of anything untoward. He replied calmly, paying no attention to these portents.

'That's right. Mrs Gedge's.'

Mr Slattery shivered.

'Brother,' he said, much moved, 'I hate to break it to you, but if that's so the proposition's cold.'

Packy stared.

'Cold?'

'It's off. You'll have to let me out. I can't do it.'

'What!'

'No, sir,' said Mr Slattery, apologetically but with the utmost firmness, 'I just can't do it. You don't get me busting no woman's room.'

Packy gasped, aghast at this unforeseen exhibition of temperament in one on whom he had looked till now as the most level-headed of his sex.

'Why not?'

'Because,' said Mr Slattery, 'you bust a woman's room and what happens? She wakes up and gets set to scream. And what happens then? You either have to do a dive out of the window and prob'ly break your dam' neck, or else you've got to go and choke her. I never choked no woman yet, boy, and I don't aim to begin.'

The sentiment was one which would have caused Sir Galahad or the Chevalier Bayard to shake hands warmly with Mr Slattery, so instinct was it with the best spirit of chivalry. One dislikes to have to state, therefore, that it awoke in Packy only a disgusted exasperation.

'But, good Lord, you must have had to burgle a woman's room occasionally in the course of your distinguished career. How long have you been cracking safes?'

'Years and years.'

'Well, then.'

'No,' said Mr Slattery. 'You see, brother, up till a few years back I've always worked with a partner. The best inside worker a safe-blower ever had. Julia, her name was, and she's quit me now, but in the old days we were a team.'

'I don't see what Julia has to do with it.'

'She used to get herself invited to these swell homes,' explained Mr Slattery. 'Having class. And if the pete was in a dame's room she'd slip in before I got there and put a sponge of chloroform under her nose, so that by the time I arrived everything was hotsy-totsy. Boy, you don't know how I've missed Julia since she walked out on me. I've felt like a little child without its mother.'

He was plainly suffering from the wild regret, of which the poet speaks, for the days that are no more, but Packy was in no frame of mind to offer condolences. His mood was regrettably self-centred. He brooded morosely.

'Then you won't get that letter for me?'

'I can't. Say, whose letter is it, anyway?'

'Senator Opal's.'

'No.' Mr Slattery shook his head regretfully. 'If it had been yours, maybe I might have stretched a point. But I don't go busting no beazels' rooms for any Senator Opal.'

'And those jewels? You're really going to pass them up?'

'Don't talk of them,' begged Mr Slattery. 'Just to think of them gives me a pain. But there it is. I'm sorry.' His face lightened. 'But, say, listen. You fix it so's Gedge sleeps in here, and the deal's on again.'

The implication that he was in a position to dictate their sleeping arrangements to his host and hostess increased Packy's annoyance.

'And how do you suggest that I do that?'

'Well, hell,' said Mr Slattery, 'I don't see where it's so difficult. Here's this pete, full of ice. Just being there, it makes it dangerous for a dame to sleep in the room. You tell this Gedge dame she's apt to get her head pushed in one of these nights if she goes on laying with it up against a pete full of stuff, and she'll see it. If she's like most dames.'

'From what I hear, she isn't.'

'Well, I guess she's like enough to make her feel that if there's going to be a murder in the home she'd rather it was the old man than her. You put it to her, boy. You go to her and say, "Lookut, Mrs Gedge, it ain't safe for you, sleeping in that room with all that ice. First thing you know, some heist-guy'll be busting the joint and then where'll you be? Getting your head pushed in or lying there with your throat cut, that's where you'll be. You snap out of that room, Mrs Gedge," you say, "and let your old man sleep there, or before you know where you are X'll be marking the spot." That'll shift her.'

Packy weighed the advice thoughtfully. There seemed a good deal in it. Such a speech might well have the desired effect. The trouble was that it would be rather difficult to lead up to in general conversation. It was not the sort of thing you could spring on a woman you had only just met, in the middle of a chat about beautiful Brittany or the weather.

'Well, I'll think it over,' he said.

'You do,' said Mr Slattery. 'You go back to bed and think it over. Me, I rather guess, now I'm in the joint, I'll take a look around. Folks sometimes leave gold clocks and that on the dressing-table. What I mean, you never know. And you don't want to miss a trick these days. Say, did you ever see the Stock Market in such a state? Everything down to nothing, you might say, and me with all my capital locked up. Got to make what you can when you can, what I mean.'

It was not for Packy to stand in the way of a fellow-man pluckily trying to make good losses incurred through the fluctuations of the world's markets. It was plain to him, moreover, that no arguments would move Mr Slattery from the position he had outlined. So long as this room continued to be that of a beazel, the man would remain adamant. He bade him good night and passed on his way upstairs.

It seemed to him after he had been in bed some ten minutes that the silence of the Château was broken by a distant shout or cry, but he was too sleepy to give it his attention. He closed his eyes again and dropped off.

3

One of the things one always wants to know about a house party is what sort of a night everybody had. As regards the Château Blissac, the slumbers of the great majority of its inmates had been entirely satisfactory. Mr Gedge had slept well. Packy had slept well. Senator Opal had slept well. Jane had slept well. Miss Putnam had slept well. Medway had slept well. Blair Eggleston had slept well.

Only Mr Gordon Carlisle had failed to rest adequately. Much thinking, rendering him feverish, had caused him to turn and toss till an advanced hour, and when he did succeed in achieving a doze he was jerked out of it by that same shout or cry which had momentarily disturbed Packy. Speculation on this had made him wakeful again. It was not till dawn that he finally fell asleep, and it was scarcely two hours later when sunlight, streaming in through the window across which he had forgotten to draw the curtain, brought him to life once more.

His idea on getting out of bed had been to exclude this sunlight. But, finding himself at the open window, he leaned out, like everybody else who ever approached an open window in the early morning, to see what kind of a day it was.

From where he stood, on the second floor of the house, the view was spreading and attractive. His window did not command that distant prospect of the harbour which was the Château's pride: but there were plenty of good things to make up for this deprivation. Gardens, gay with flowers, lay before Mr Carlisle, and beyond them woods and the Breton quaintness of the home farm: while above him, as he raised his eyes, there was a blue sky, flecked with little clouds; a few of the local birds going about their business; an insect or two; a couple of butterflies; and a pair of legs encased in grey trousers and terminating in two shoes of generous dimensions.

It was these last that enchained his attention. The spectacle of legs where no legs should be is always an arresting one. Mr Carlisle, drinking them in, was frankly nonplussed. Rapidly running over in his mind the topography of the house, he discovered that their owner, if they had an owner and were not simply a stray pair of legs which had just been left about, must be sitting on the window-sill of the bedroom occupied by Senator Opal.

There surged over Mr Carlisle an intense desire for further data. He was not accustomed to be up and about so early as this, but if ever a man had a good excuse for brushing with hasty steps the dew away to meet the sun upon the upland lawn, that man was he. Only by going out and looking up from a less acute angle could he hope to probe this mystery.

Taking a snap judgement on the evidence at present to hand, he presumed that the sitter must be the Senator himself. Only a man of established eccentricity would roost on window-sills first thing in the morning – or, indeed, at any hour of the day, and what he had seen of Senator Opal had been enough to convince him that the latter was eccentric enough for any form of self-expression.

Only when he reached the garden did he discover that his reasoning had been faulty. Senator Opal might be temperamentally of window-sill-sitting timbre. Quite possibly the day would come when he would take to sitting on window-sills. But he had not done so yet. The man on whom Mr Carlisle's astonished gaze rested was his old friend, Soup Slattery. And as he espied Mr Slattery, simultaneously Mr Slattery espied him.

There followed one of those awkward periods which occur when a man who is compelled to confine himself entirely to grimaces is endeavouring to convey his thoughts to a second party who is so overcome with amazement that he would scarcely be in a position to understand the plainest speech. Mr Slattery contorted his features. Mr Carlisle continued to gape. It was only at the end of about five minutes, just after Mr Slattery had nearly dislocated his lower jaw in a particularly eloquent passage, that the marvelling Confidence Trick artist realized that what his friend was silently appealing for was a ladder.

Raising his hand in a sort of Fascist salute and nodding vigorously several times, he proceeded in quest of the desired object.

A ladder is not one of those things you can just reach out and lay your hand on. Mr Carlisle had to search thoroughly and well. Eventually, he discovered one outside a distant shed, only to find that it was too heavy for him to carry. Returning with the distasteful task before him of explaining this misfortune in dumb show, he received another shock.

The window-sill, which ten minutes before had featured Mr Slattery so prominently, was now empty.

Gordon Carlisle paused on the brink of believing in miracles. The only theory that seemed to fit the facts was that his friend had suddenly soared through the air like a bird. He could not have fallen, for the only corpse on the ground below was that of a small snail.

Then, just in time to save his reason from collapse, Mr Carlisle observed the stout water-pipe which ran down the wall near the window. And, putting two and two together, he deduced that in the interval of his absence Mr Slattery must have discovered this pipe. The fact that he had not done so earlier appeared to indicate that he had taken to the window-sill while the world was still in darkness. And that was perplexing, too, when you came to look into it. Mr Carlisle's reason, saved once from disintegration, began to wobble again.

Fortunately for his professional future, for a Confidence Trick artist cannot hope to continue in a keenly competitive business if his brain has come unstuck, something now occurred which threw a light on the matter. The window opened, and Senator Opal appeared. He was wearing orange-coloured pyjamas and a revolver, and on his face was a look of wonder and bafflement.

Sighting Mr Carlisle below, he sought information in a voice of thunder.

'Where's my burglar?'

Mr Carlisle had nothing to reply to this. The Senator's tone grew more peevish.

'You down below there…. You Duke…. Have you seen my burglar?'

Mr Carlisle perceived that it behoved him to pull himself together.

'*Ah, non,*' he replied, in that musical accent which went with his portrayal of the Duc de Pont-Andemer.

'Ah, what?'

'Ah, no.'

'How long have you been down there?'

'I have this moment only arrived.'

'Did you see anyone sitting on my window-sill?'

'No. No. On the window-sill, no-one.'

'Hell!' cried the Senator.

You cannot conduct a full-throated long-distance conversation in the early morning and finish up by ejaculating 'Hell!' in a voice like the bursting of an ammunition-dump without rousing such sleepers as may be in your vicinity. From a window to the left the head of Mr Gedge appeared.

'What's the matter?'

'I've lost a burglar.'

'Where did you see him last?' asked Mr Gedge.

Before the Senator could reply to this pertinent question, a window on the right revealed the wondering face of Jane. She looked charming in a blue negligee.

'Whatever is the matter, Father?'

'I left a burglar on the window-sill, and he's gone,' said the Senator, rather in the manner of a householder complaining of the loss of a bottle of milk.

'How do you mean, you left a burglar on the window-sill?'

'I mean precisely what I say. I found the fellow in my room last night and I wasn't going to lose my sleep calling up the police, so I made him sit on the window-sill, intending to collect him in the morning.'

'You must have been dreaming.'

'I was not dreaming.'

'Say, listen,' said Mr Gedge chattily. 'I had the strangest dream last night. I dreamed I was at the Biltmore, Los Angeles, and the waiter came up to take my order, and do you know what he was? A skeleton. Yessir, a skeleton in a pink middy-blouse.'

The disposition to be impatient towards the recital of other people's dreams is almost universal. Senator Opal was not one of those exceptional men who made good listeners on such occasions.

'Stop gabbling, you Gedge!'

'Father!'

'And you stop saying "Father!" What's become of the fellow, that's what I want to know.'

'I never heard of such a thing,' said Jane primly. 'Putting burglars on window-sills.'

'Well, you've heard of it now.'

'Why didn't you simply...?'

'I've told you why I didn't simply. Do you think I was going to lose my night's rest just because a blasted burglar came into my room?'

Mr Carlisle intruded on this family jar.

'I think the man must have made his descent by the water-pipe.'

'Water-pipe?' The Senator gaped, aghast. 'You don't mean there's a ... My God! There is. It was so dark I didn't see it.'

'Serves you right,' observed Jane, who, womanlike, intended to have the last word if it took all summer, 'for being such a smarty.'

'A what?' boomed the Senator, quivering at the offensive term.

'A smarty,' repeated Jane firmly. 'Putting burglars on window-sills. Much too clever to do anything like anybody else, aren't you? I'm very glad he has gone. It will be a lesson to you.'

She gave him a severe look and withdrew, closing the window behind her. She was a kind-hearted girl, but, like every modern girl, she did not believe in being foolishly indulgent with parents. When they behaved like cuckoos, you had to tell them so – quite quietly – not angrily – just pointing it out to them and leaving their intelligence to do the rest.

But even with her departure Senator Opal did not find himself free from criticism. Even as he puffed and exercised his eyebrows, it broke out unexpectedly in another quarter.

'She's quite right,' said Mr Gedge, protruding from his window like a snail out of its shell. 'Yessir, the girl's absolutely right. Should have thought a man would have had more sense.'

Mr Gedge, as has been indicated earlier in this narrative, was not without a certain native shrewdness, and it had just occurred to him that here, sent by Providence, was a most admirable opportunity for intensifying and consolidating the hostility which this snorting man already felt towards him. The madder, he argued, he made Senator Opal, the firmer would become the latter's already firm resolve to do all that lay in his power to see that he, J. Wellington Gedge, was not appointed to the post of Ambassador to France.

Pleasantly aware that they were a long distance apart and that there was no chance of the other getting at him, he proceeded to give his views at considerable length. It was like ticking a man off over the telephone, and Mr Gedge had always been a very lion over the telephone.

He spoke, accordingly, forcefully and well. And the debate was at its height when Packy, disturbed by these voices, put on his dressing-gown and came down to see what it was all about.

He could make nothing of the affair. An argument of some kind appeared to be in progress between his host and Senator Opal, but as they were talking simultaneously at the extreme limit of their lungs it was not easy to follow thrust and counter-thrust. He turned to the Duc de Pont-Andemer as an intelligent bystander.

'What seems to be the trouble?' he asked.

He was surprised to note that his companion, on whom a moment before he had been looking as the one safe and sane unit in what had all the appearance of being a rally of lunatics, was staring at him in a manner that struck his critical sense as definitely goofy. Packy knew that he was not beautiful – he never was till he had shaved – but he could not understand what there was about him to cause this normally unruffled aristocrat to goggle at him with this odd expression of horror.

Mr Carlisle could have explained, but he did not do so. Instead, he turned sharply and hurried without a word on the long trail which went winding to the Hotel des Etrangers. It seemed to him imperative that he should have immediate speech with Soup Slattery.

4

What had startled Mr Carlisle in Packy's appearance was the fact that it was unblemished. That cry in the night had convinced him that Mr Slattery, carrying on according to plan, had invaded the other's boudoir and put it across him in his own inimitable manner. And here the fellow was, as good as new. Not so much as a black eye.

It stunned Mr Carlisle. At their parting on the previous day, Mr Slattery had been all fire and generous wrath. He had hinted unmistakably at a punitive expedition on lines of the most gratifying severity. And apparently he had done nothing.

It was with the utmost consternation that Gordon Carlisle charged into the hotel. He finally succeeded in running his quarry to earth in the main dining-room, where Mr Slattery, peckish after his night in the open, was restoring himself with a bite of breakfast.

The Continental breakfast, as a rule, consists of a pot of what the French smilingly call coffee, three smallish dabs of butter, a roll shaped like a roll, and another roll shaped like a horseshoe. Mr Slattery had introduced some variations of his own invention. He had just finished an *omelette fines herbes*, a double order of ham and eggs, and a small sirloin steak, and as Mr Carlisle burst into the room he looked up at him questioningly with his mouth full of toast and marmalade.

'Ah,' he said, swallowing the consignment.

He turned to a hovering waiter.

'*Encore de coffee,*' he added.

Mr Carlisle regarded the human python feverishly. Questions rained from him. But when the other finally spoke, which was only when the coffee had arrived and he had drained his fifth cup, it was not to reply to any of these but merely to put into words a dream, a sort of opalescent vision, which had come to him in the silent watches of the night.

'All I ask,' said Mr Slattery with feeling, 'is that some day – I don't care when it is – just some day – I meet that white-haired bird down a dark alley with no cops in sight.'

A shudder of reminiscent horror passed through him.

'Putting a fellow out on a window-sill!' he continued with growing vehemence. 'I ask you, is that nice? Cheese! And me scared of heights ever since a girl I knew betted me I wouldn't lean over the edge of the Woolworth Building and spit into Broadway. If I get over this by the time I'm a hundred, it'll be soon.'

'But how…?'

'I'll tell you how. Me, snooping around that Chatty-o seeing wasn't there something I could pick up and there's this door with someone snoring behind it, and I twist the handle and it ain't locked. Swell, I think to myself, and I give it a pull and what do you know? The dam' thing squeals like putting on the brakes in a second-hand flivver, and the next thing, there's this white-haired bird pulling a gun on me and telling me to close the door gently and walk to the window. Well, cheese! If I don't do like he says, I see it's a case of writing my own tombstone. You can't do nothing when a guy's sticking the heat on you. That gun looks like it's due to go off if there's any funny business. So I walk to the window. And the next thing I know, I'm sitting outside of it, and the guy's closing the shutters. And after a while out breaks the snoring again, and I see he's in for the night and I'm out for the night. And after about three thousand years it begins to get daylight, and a coupla centuries after that you come up, and after you're gone I see that pipe and slide down it. And I want to tell you,' said Mr Slattery, 'that I wouldn't have my worst enemy slide down no pipes. If even one of those johndarms was planning to slide down a pipe, I'd take him by the arm and say, "Come away, brother. You wouldn't like it."'

A more sympathetic heart than that of Mr Carlisle would have been moved by this recital. Gordon Carlisle did not even click his tongue.

'But what about the bird who's pretending to be the Vicomte de Blissac?'

Soup Slattery spread marmalade on toast and snapped at it like a rising fish.

'Oh, him? He's all right.'

'All right?'

'Old buddy of mine,' explained Mr Slattery. 'We had a little talk, and he put me wise. You had him pegged wrong. He's not after that ice. All he wants, he tells me, is some letter or other that this Gedge dame's got. One of those copperizing letters.'

To say that Mr Carlisle was aghast would not be to over-state the facts. He had always known that Soup Slattery, stout man of action though he was, had the irreducible mini-mum of intelligence, but surely even Soup could not have swallowed so obviously flimsy a tale. He stared with horrified incredulity.

'And you believed him?'

'Sure I believed him.'

'Well, I'm darned!'

'Certainly I believed him. He's a friend of mine.'

Mr Carlisle gulped. So did Mr Slattery. But whereas the latter gulped because that is the quickest way of getting a sixth cup of coffee into the system, what caused Mr Carlisle to gulp was the extreme of dismay. He realized whither all this was tending.

'Then do you mean,' he quavered, 'that you aren't going to beat this bird up?'

It is not the simplest of tasks to laugh derisively with your mouth full of coffee, but Mr Slattery succeeded in doing so.

'Who, me? Why, say! Him and me are like that.'

He placed two banana-esque fingers together to indicate the closeness of the trust and friendship which linked Packy and himself.

'You don't have to worry about that guy. He told me all about it. This letter is one some fellow named Senator Opal wrote and it'll get him in Dutch, far as I gather, if it comes out. And the Gedge dame has got hold of it. That's all this guy is after. He ain't attracted by the ice. Don't hold no fascination for him at all. He told me so himself.'

Mr Carlisle drew his breath in sharply. He found the tale suddenly plausible. Himself an expert in falsehood, he had almost a sixth sense when it came to detecting what he would have described as the phony. Yes, the story had the ring of truth, and for an instant he forgot his troubles. His eyes gleamed. If Senator Opal had written a letter so indiscreet that he had to employ bravoes to recover it for him, it must be a letter worth acquiring.

For one reason and another, Gordon Carlisle, though a many-sided man, had never yet made any experiments in the direction of blackmail. It was not that he had any moral objection to it, for there were very few things to which he had any moral objection. It was simply that he had never just happened to get around to it.

But now... with this wonderful opportunity opening before his eyes...

The mood of elation did not last long. Chilling it, there came the dismal reflection that he could never hope to convince Gertie of this. She would see Packy going about all hale and hearty, and she would demand an explanation and would certainly refuse to accept the only one he could give.

He bade Mr Slattery a hasty farewell. The safe-blower had observed a melon on a side-table and was now trying to order a slice, and as the waiter's English was weak and he himself did not know the French for melon, the process promised to be a lengthy one. Long before they had got the matter straightened out, Mr Carlisle had left them. He had seen all he wished of his friend breakfasting.

What, he asked himself as he walked towards the Château, would Gertie say when she found that he had not fulfilled those gallant boasts and promises of yesterday?

He was given an early opportunity of ascertaining what she would say. She met him half-way down the drive and said it.

'Hey!' she cried, and there was no mistaking the censure in her voice. 'What's all this? You told me you were going to beat that ringer guy up last night, and I see him just now strutting his stuff without so much as a mark on him. How come?'

Mr Carlisle moistened his lips, and summoned to his aid all his professional skill. Now, if ever, was there need for that magic eloquence of his.

'You'll be surprised when I tell you,' he said, and was dismayed to find how lame and halting his words seemed. At this crisis in his life, eloquence had deserted him. 'The fact is, we've been all wrong about that bird.'

'What do you mean by that?'

'Why, he isn't after the ice at all. What he's come for is a compromising letter. . . .'

'What!'

'Just that. He told me so himself.'

'When?'

'Last night, when I went to his room and . . .'

'When you went to his room! You never went near him. I see it all now. I might have known that you were just bluffing yesterday. You got cold feet.'

'I give you my word . . .'

'And me thinking maybe you weren't such a false alarm after all! Well, good-bye, Mr Carlisle.'

'Where are you going?'

'None of your business. If you really want to know, I'm going back to Mr Eggleston.'

A spasm of anguished alarm shot through Gordon Carlisle. This was the first intimation he had received that his already difficult wooing might be further complicated by a rival.

'Who's he?'

'Senator Opal's valet. I like him very much. So if you will excuse me, Mr Carlisle, I will be going back to him.'

She passed on her way, even her back hair expressing her loathing and contempt.

Mr Carlisle remained where he was. A jealous fury had him in its grip. This Eggleston! . . . As far as his seething mind was capable of formulating any coherent plan, he resolved that he would seize the earliest opportunity of taking a look at this Eggleston.

And if on inspection this Eggleston proved to be of a not too formidable physique, he would know what to do about it.

CHAPTER 12

THE day of Mrs Gedge's return to the Château of which she was the temporary lessee and proprietor was as fine as every other day had been for weeks. St Rocque was certainly having a great summer; and if certain of those residing in and about it were not appreciating it to the full the fault was theirs, not that of the weather.

The sun shone bravely down. And it cannot but assist the readers of this chronicle if, in pursuance of his tested policy of pausing from time to time to offer a bird's-eye view of affairs to his patrons, the historian gives here a brief list of the more interesting objects on which it shone.

We may omit the Vicomte de Blissac, that modern hermit, still languishing in his cell. We need not mention Mr Soup Slattery, confined to his room with a slight cold in the head. But the movements of the rest of our little group deserve each their brief notice.

In a clearing of the shrubbery down by the lake, Gum-Shoe Gertie (*alias* Medway) was listening with considerable pleasure to the compliments of Blair Eggleston – compliments which never fell below a certain high level because the speaker was uncomfortably aware that his employer, Senator Ambrose Opal, was hiding in a bush close by, drinking in every word. It had always been the Senator's belief that subordinates worked better under careful personal supervision.

Gordon Carlisle had gone for a country walk. This was not because he was fond of exercise, but because he hoped that the wearying of the body might a little ease the torment of the spirit. Jealousy was gnawing grievously at Mr Carlisle's soul.

Jane Opal was in her room, writing letters. Packy had argued against this course, but it seemed that there had arrived in Jane's life that moment, which comes to all women, when her correspondence could wait no longer.

Packy, accordingly, had wandered off to the terrace, and was employing this period of solitude in an effort to work out some plan by means of which Mrs Gedge, when she arrived, could be induced to vacate the Venetian Suite and hand it over to Mr Gedge. On this, he perceived, turned the whole success of his venture.

Miss Putnam was in the library, doing a crossword puzzle.

The cook was in the kitchen, baking a pie for her betrothed, a likeable young man of the name of Octave, one of that agile corps of *gendarmerie* who had chased Soup Slattery on the night of the Festival. He was waiting for it in the bushes outside the kitchen door.

Mr Gedge was down at the dock. He had gone there to meet Mrs Gedge.

And Mrs Gedge, standing on the deck of the steam packet *Antelope*, was chatting with a fellow-passenger whose acquaintance she had made on the voyage.

The steam packet *Antelope* slid cautiously towards its moorings. The process, as always, involved a great deal of tooting and shouting and ringing of bells, and Mr Gedge, making himself as inconspicuous as possible in the little group on the dock, found it intolerably slow. Every minute spent out in the open like this was anguish to Mr Gedge. Already he had seen two gendarmes, and there were probably dozens more lurking round the corner. At any moment he expected to hear cries of '*Scélérat!*' and '*Assassin!*' and to find the whole strength of the force piling themselves on his neck.

He mused bitterly on this mess into which Fate had thrust him. Simply because he had taken a few drinks, just as any red-blooded man would have done on an occasion like that of the Festival of the Saint, here he was with murder on his soul, cowering from the police. Why should this have had to happen to him of all people? There had been scores of revellers at the Festival every whit as pickled as he, but they had not gone about destroying Vicomtes. That hideous feat had been reserved for him, J. W. Gedge, and it seemed to him unfair discrimination.

The rattle of the descending gang-plank came to him like music. Returning wanderers stepped down it, to be greeted by their loved ones. Presently Mrs Gedge appeared. She was talk-ing over her shoulder to a girl, and so remarkable was this girl's loveliness that Mr Gedge momentarily forgot his troubles and unconsciously straightened his tie. House-broken husband though he was, he had still an eye for beauty.

The crossing had evidently been a smooth one. Mrs Gedge, who tended on occasions like this to look green and give at the knees, seemed to be in excellent shape. She walked composedly, kissed Mr Gedge composedly, and introduced him to her companion.

'Lady Beatrice Bracken. My husband.'

Now that the girl had come closer, Mr Gedge was able to see that, though beautiful, she was not altogether the sort of girl he would have cared to be left alone with for long. There was that about her which would have rendered any male uneasy. In her lustrous eyes he observed a look which he had sometimes detected in those of his wife – the look that spells trouble. If she had come to St Rocque to meet some member of his own sex, he did not envy that member.

'Lady Beatrice has been so kind to me, Wellington. She lent me her smelling-salts, and they made all the difference.'

Mr Gedge murmured appreciatively with one eye on a gendarme who had strolled up and was twisting his moustache in what seemed to him a sinister way. The unpleasantness of the spectacle diverted his attention and caused him to miss his companion's next few remarks. When he forced himself to listen once more, the girl was talking about hotels.

'I wonder,' she was saying, 'if you could tell me which are the principal hotels in this place?'

Mrs Gedge said that the Hotel des Etrangers was where everyone went.

'They will make you very comfortable. We stayed there for a few days while the Château was being got ready. We have rented the Château Blissac for the summer. It is a large house up the hill, belonging to the Vicomtesse de Blissac. Perhaps you have met her?'

'No. I know her son. Slightly.'

'Really? He is visiting us now. Won't you come and lunch to-morrow? I'm sure he would be delighted to meet you again. Whatever is the matter, Wellington?'

Mrs Gedge regarded her husband with that rather school-teacherine air of censure which his behaviour so frequently evoked in her. His sudden gasp had startled her a good deal.

'I'm all right,' mumbled Mr Gedge. 'Touch of cramp.'

He stood awaiting the doom. Next moment, this girl would be accepting the invitation. Next day, she would come to the Château. And immediately on her arrival she would meet Packy and fail to recognize in him the Vicomte de Blissac whom she knew slightly but presumably well enough to cause her to accept no substitutes. Oh, felt Mr Gedge, as the poet had done before him, what a tangled web we weave when first we practise to deceive.

Then her voice came to his ears, uttering a life-restoring refusal.

'It's awfully kind of you, but I expect to be catching the night boat back to England.'

'You are returning to-night?' It was Mrs Gedge's turn to be taken aback. 'So soon?'

'Yes. I simply came over to... There is a friend of mine staying in St Rocque... When I asked you about hotels, I was just wondering where I would be likely to find... We shall probably go back on the night boat together. I see my porter has got me a cab. Good-bye. It has been so nice meeting you.'

'Can't we drop you at the hotel in the car?'

'No, thank you. Good-bye.'

Mrs Gedge looked after her with the dissatisfied air of a woman from whom confidences have been withheld.

'The English are so reticent,' she said discontentedly. 'Perfect clams.'

They started to walk off the dock, Mr Gedge a little like Daniel threading his way through the den of lions. So far, the constabulary had been inert. But you never knew. They might just be biding their time. He was not going to feel entirely at his ease till he was safe inside the car with the chauffeur stepping on the accelerator.

'Just clams,' said Mrs Gedge, settling herself against the cushions and resuming her remarks on the Island Race. 'Considering how friendly we became on the boat, you would have thought she would have told me all about it.'

'About what?'

The car was making good progress, and Mr Gedge had begun to feel a little better.

'Well, I'm only guessing, of course, but here is what I think must have happened. Lady Beatrice is engaged to an American boy named Franklyn...What *is* the matter with you to-day, Wellington?'

'Matter?'

'Why are you puffing like that?'

'Deep breathing,' whispered Mr Gedge. 'Good for you. Did you say Franklyn?'

'Yes. It was in all the papers. I remember reading about it when I was in a beauty-parlour with Mrs Willoughby Simms. She had got hold of a *Daily Mirror* and was looking at the photograph...'

'Photographs!'

'There was a photograph of Lady Beatrice...'

'And of this fellow Franklyn?'

'No. Only of Lady Beatrice. I was interested, of course, because I knew Mr Franklyn.'

'Knew him!'

'Well, I knew all about him, and I knew people in America who knew him.'

'Have you ever met him?' asked Mr Gedge, speaking in a thin, faint voice like the death-rattle of one of the smaller *infusoria*.

'No, I never actually met him. But I've heard a great many stories about him. Everybody said he was very wild. He is the young man, if you remember, who came into a great deal of money when he left college some years ago. I always say it is a mistake for men to have money.'

The doctrine was one with which Mr Gedge was not in sympathy, and at another time he might have contested it with some warmth. But relief had rendered him incapable of speech. He was leaning back with closed eyes. Mrs Gedge, who always preferred a silent audience when she was talking, proceeded equably:

'Here is what I think must have happened. It looks to me very much as if this young man Franklyn had sneaked off to St Rocque on some escapade, and Lady Beatrice has found it out and has come to take him back. She said "a friend". It would have to be a very close friend to bring her all this way.'

Mr Gedge's relief had been of but brief duration. The question he was now asking himself, a question which made him feel as if snakes were crawling over him was this: What if this infernal girl's search for her errant *fiancé* led her to the Château Blissac? He had never been entirely easy about his heart, though several doctors had assured him of its perfect soundness. A little more of this, and there would, he was convinced, shortly be a lucrative job for the St Rocque undertaker.

He awoke from these reflections to find that Mrs Gedge was asking him a question.

'Eh?'

'I said "How do you like the Vicomte?"'

The sensation of panic which had been gripping Mr Gedge had now to some extent subsided. It would be too much to say that he was at his ease once more, but he was telling himself that he had possibly overestimated the extent of his peril. After all, there was very little chance of the girl trailing Packy to the Château.

'He's fine,' he replied.

'You get on well together?'

'Oh, sure. There's one thing you'll notice about that bird,' said Mr Gedge, feeling that this ought to be made clear at once. 'You'll be surprised that he's a Frenchman.'

'Yes?'

'Very much surprised. You would almost take him for an American.'

'He has travelled quite a good deal in America, I believe.'

'That's right. Sure. That explains it. I just thought I'd mention it in case you wondered when you saw him. He talks like an American, too.'

'How is his appetite?'

Mr Gedge was puzzled.

'His appetite?'

'Yes. Is he eating enough?'

'Sure. Why?'

'Well,' said Mrs Gedge maternally, 'when I was in Paris arranging with his mother about taking the Château and she showed me all those photographs of him, it seemed to me that he was much too thin. Almost delicate, I thought he looked. Dissipation, I suppose.'

Mr Gedge made no comment on the diagnosis. He was leaning limply back in his seat blowing little air-bubbles. If the St Rocque undertaker could have beheld him now, he would have given him a very sharp look and instructed his assistants to get ready for the big rush of business.

CHAPTER 13

I

PACKY, pondering on the terrace, had not yet hit upon that bright idea of which he was in search. It seemed, indeed, further off than ever, and he was on the verge of confessing himself baffled when he saw that Mr Gedge had come out of the house and was hurrying in his direction as if desirous of having speech with him. He went to meet him, rather welcoming the opportunity of relaxing his brain in idle chatter, even with Mr Gedge.

'Hullo. So you're back? Has Mrs Gedge arrived?'

A muscular spasm contorted the little man's face.

'She's arrived!' he said.

Packy eyed him with some concern. It seemed to him that all was not well with Mr Gedge. He looked like one who has passed through the furnace. If a series of spectres had recently appeared to him, he could not have been more agitated.

'Is something the matter?'

One of the hollowest laughs that had ever been heard on the terrace of the Château Blissac broke gratingly upon the afternoon stillness.

'Oh, no. There's nothing the matter. Nothing whatever. Except that when Mrs Gedge was in Paris she saw fifty-seven varieties of photographs of the real Vicomte de Blissac and she looked out of the window just now and saw you and said, "Who's that piece of cheese?" and I said, "That's the Vicomte," and she said, "My left foot it's the Vicomte." And she's sent me out here to fetch you in and explain. Outside of that, everything's fine.'

In transmitting to a third party a *résumé* of a conversation, what it is necessary to convey is not so much the actual words as the spirit of the thing. This Mr Gedge had succeeded in doing. Packy leaped like a startled fawn, and his brain, to which he had hoped to grant a brief rest, began whirring again under the fullest pressure.

'What!'

'You heard.'

'You don't mean that?'

'What do you think I mean?'

'But, my gosh!'

'All right,' said Mr Gedge wanly, 'all right. I've said all that.'

'But what did you tell her?'

'What could I tell her? I just said, "Well, darn it, how was I to know?" I said you blew in, claiming to be the Vicomte, and I naturally thought you were the Vicomte. It went all right, but what,' said Mr Gedge, plying his handkerchief like a bath towel, 'is the use of that? In about two minutes she'll start telegraphing to Paris, asking what's become of the real one. Or maybe she'll just 'phone the police without waiting to telegraph.'

Until this moment, it had seemed to Packy that his brain was incapable of further activity. He supposed that he had tested it to the uttermost. But now it was as if he had changed gears and suddenly discovered a speed superior to that which he had always imagined to be third. He could almost hear it buzzing, and was surprised that sparks were not flying out of his head.

His drawn brow suddenly cleared.

'It's all right.'

'I'm glad you think so.'

'I've had an idea.'

'It better be a good one.'

'It is. It's a pippin.'

Packy looked about him cautiously. The house, where Mrs Gedge lurked, was well out of earshot, but with a woman like that you never knew.

'Tell me, where does Mrs Gedge insure her stuff?'

'What stuff?'

'Her jewels and so on.'

'What do you want to know for?'

'It's vital. If you can't remember, we're sunk.'

'We're sunk already.'

'Not if you know the name of that insurance company.'

'Of course I know it. It's the New York, London and Paris. But where does that get us?'

Packy tapped himself on the chest.

'Meet one of the boys.'

'What boys?'

'One of the New York, London and Paris boys. One of their large staff of watchful detectives. I was sent here to keep an eye on Mrs Gedge's jewels.'

'What!'

'That's my story, and I'm going to stick to it.'

'You can't get away with that.'

'Why not?'

'Why. . . . Well, darn it, I don't see why you mightn't,' said

Mr Gedge, awed. 'No, sir, I don't see why you mightn't, at that. Yessir, you might get away with it. How come you thought up that one so quick?'

'I've had detectives on my mind a little of late. They have figured rather prominently in conversations with my friends. And it sort of came to me.'

'Well, it's a chance.'

'I can't see a flaw in it. It's just the sort of kind-hearted thing an insurance company would do, to send a man to look after someone's jewels on the spot. Where do I find Mrs Gedge?'

'She's in the library.'

'I'll go to her at once. If you hear a dull thud coming from the library shortly, you will know that my story hasn't gone as well as we hope. But, personally, I am all optimism. I seem to hear the blue birds twittering and Old Man Trouble gnashing his teeth in baffled fury. Not,' said Packy thoughtfully, 'that I don't wish I could absorb just one quick drink – or perhaps two – before having this little chat. Because I do.'

2

The library of the Château Blissac was on the ground floor, looking out on the drive. Awnings hung over its windows, shutting out the sun and rendering the interior dim. But it did not render it so dim that Packy, entering, was unable to see Mrs Gedge and see her clearly. And at the spectacle his fortitude wavered a little. He had expected his hostess to be slightly on the formidable side, and this she unquestionably was. He did not like the expression in her eyes, nor the ominous tightness of her lips. For that matter, he did not like the way her hands were opening and shutting.

However, he advanced with what confidence he could muster and took a seat.

Sitting, he felt better. Not any too good, but better.

'How do you do, Mrs Gedge?' he said.

He received no first-hand information as to how Mrs Gedge did. The menacing woman did not even bow. She looked as if she had been hewn from the living rock.

'I have just been talking to Mr Gedge.'

Again no comment.

'He tells me you are aware that I am not the Vicomte de Blissac.'

This time there was a reaction. Quite unmistakably his hostess gave evidence of being flesh and blood. She had not expected this airy jauntiness, and she started perceptibly.

'He is a friend of mine, though. And when I explained to him how necessary it was that I should come to the Château, he agreed to let me take his place. I am . . .'

'Yes,' said Mrs Gedge, finding speech at last. 'I should like to hear your name. Or at least one of your *aliases*.'

Packy laughed. He hoped it was a merry laugh, but was not quite sure. It had sounded a little hacking to him.

'My dear Mrs Gedge! Are you under the impression that I am a criminal?'

'Yes.'

Packy smiled this time. Smiling was easier.

'Let me explain.'

'You can explain to the police.'

'They wouldn't understand me. I can't talk French. Mrs Gedge, you insure your jewellery with the London, Paris and New York.'

'You seem well informed.'

'Yes. You see, I am in their employment. And they sent me here.'

'What!'

'I am one of their large staff of detectives.'

Once more, astonishment gave Mrs Gedge that faint suggestion of being human after all.

'You expect me to believe that?'

'I hope you will believe it.'

'Well, go on.'

Her manner was not what in the strictest sense could be called encouraging, but Packy proceeded.

'They sent me here to keep an eye on your valuables. St Rocque, though you may not know it, is a great place for crooks in the season. They collect here in droves. The place is stiff with them. I'll bet you couldn't throw a brick in St Rocque at this time of year without hitting one.'

Mrs Gedge closed her eyes. She seemed to be trying to indicate by the action that she never threw bricks.

'My company had reason to believe that an attempt was to be made on your jewels. . . .'

'What reason?'

Packy wished this woman would not ask him questions. He found the going so much easier when he was allowed to deliver a monologue. This particular question seemed to call for a little quick thinking, and he did some.

'There is a criminal actually in the house,' he said impressively.

Again Mrs Gedge's eyes closed. This appeared to be her substitute for speech, and not a bad one, either. At any rate, she conveyed her meaning quite clearly to Packy. There was, indeed, her eyelids seemed to say, a criminal in the house.

He hastened to support his statement with corroborative detail. And it is one more proof of how irony is never far distant in this life of ours that not for an instant did he dream of casting aspersions on the Duc de Pont-Andemer. Mr Carlisle was an artist, and Packy had accepted him at face value without question.

'Senator Opal is a guest of yours.'

'Are you trying to suggest that Senator Opal is a criminal?'

'No. But he has one in his employment.'

It cost Packy something of a pang thus to throw Blair Eggleston to the wolves, but he consoled himself with the thought that any little added inconvenience which might ensue could scarcely affect a man who for nearly a week had been in the Senator's employment as a valet.

'When you have been here longer and have had leisure to take a look at the domestic staff, you will notice a small, furtive man, the Senator's personal attendant. Eggleston he calls himself. We know him as English Ed.'

Watching his hostess closely, he was gratified to observe another ripple pass over her surface. He took it to indicate the dawn of a feeling that there might possibly be something in this. He went on, encouraged.

'But I was explaining how I came to be here in the name of the Vicomte de Blissac. As I told you, he is a friend of mine, and happening to run into him and learning that he was about to be your guest, I saw a solution to the problem which had been bothering me. It was essential, you see, that I should find some way of establishing myself in the Château in such a manner that this English Ed would not become suspicious of me, and here it was. I put the whole thing to the Vicomte, and he readily agreed to allow me to come here in his place. And so far, I am glad to say, the man Ed has suspected nothing.'

'You are really a friend of the Vicomte de Blissac?'

'Known him for years.'

Mrs Gedge leaned forward keenly.

'What is his first name?'

'Maurice,' said Packy promptly.

Mrs Gedge leaned back again. The result of her test had left her uncertain. Still half sceptical, she was beginning to believe.

'Well, it all seems very extraordinary to me.'

'I suppose so.'

'Why did not the London, Paris and New York people tell me they were sending you here?'

There was faint reproof in Packy's voice as he answered the question.

'It is foreign to the policy of the London, Paris and New York management to alarm their clients unnecessarily. They do good by stealth.'

Mrs Gedge brooded.

'Are you sure about this man Eggleston?'

'Quite.'

'And what do you propose to do?'

'I shall keep him under close observation.'

'And in the meantime, no doubt,' said Mrs Gedge tartly, 'he will be murdering me in my bed.'

Something of the sensations which he had once had when in the Yale Bowl waiting for the whistle to unleash eleven corn-fed assassins from Harvard or Notre Dame upon him came to Packy. This was the moment when he must put his fortune to the test, to win or lose it all. Now or never must the balloon go up.

He clutched the sides of his chair.

'Why should he go near your bedroom? You don't keep your jewels there.'

'Yes, I do.'

Packy gasped.

'You do? You mean to tell me that you . . . My dear Mrs Gedge,' said Packy earnestly, 'you cannot realize the risks you are taking! It isn't safe for you, sleeping in that room with all that ice . . . I mean, it is most dangerous . . . Why, use your imagination. First thing you know, some heist-guy . . . some burglar will break in. You wake up and get set to scream, and what happens then? Either he does a dive . . . he is faced with the alternative of making his escape by the window, or else he is compelled to choke you. And from what I know of English Ed the latter is the course he would choose. On no account must you continue sleeping in that room.'

'But I can't leave it empty.'

'My advice would be that you changed rooms with Mr Gedge. After all, guarding jewels is man's work.'

Mrs Gedge brightened visibly at the suggestion. Packy, watching her tensely, felt how unerring had been Mr Slattery's knowledge of feminine psychology when he had said that he guessed that if there was going to be a murder in the home she would rather it was the old man than her.

'Yes,' she said meditatively.

'Yes,' said Packy, helping the thing along.

'Yes,' said Mrs Gedge.

'Yes,' said Packy.

'Yes,' said Mrs Gedge.

It might have been a Hollywood story-conference.

'I will tell Mr Gedge when I see him,' said the now quite

cordial woman. 'I can give him my revolver,' she added, with a pleasant touch of wifely consideration.

'Exactly,' said Packy. 'Well, I am very glad to have had this little talk,' he said, rising. 'I hope you will feel that if anything happens I am always here for you to call upon.'

'Thank you.'

'Not at all,' said Packy. 'It is nothing but my duty.'

He smiled a courteous, reassuring smile and walked out. He had scarcely gone when there was a slight fluttering noise from behind a large Spanish leather screen in the corner of the room, and there came into view the fragile form of Miss Putnam.

'Well, of all the hooey!' said Miss Putnam.

3

To most of those who knew her, Mrs Gedge's social secretary had always been a sort of agreeable wraith. Your senses told you that she was there, but the fact made no real impression on you. You caught the gleam of flashing spectacles, saw a mild, deferential smile floating in mid-air, and said to yourself: 'Ah, Miss Putnam.' Then you went about your business without giving her a second thought.

The woman who now took the chair opposite Mrs Gedge was quite a different Miss Putnam. Her eye was keen, her manner masterful. But the greatest change was in her behaviour. It was un-Putnamic to a degree. The normal Miss Putnam would never have sat down without being invited. She would never have laughed sardonically in her employer's presence. Above all, she would never have done anything to give the impression that she was testing her employer's reflexes. And that was what she was doing now. For, having seated herself, she leaned forward and tapped Mrs Gedge sharply on the knee.

'You didn't swallow all that apple-sauce, I hope, Mrs G.?' she asked solicitously.

The other's silent and wholly unexpected entry had caused Mrs Gedge to jump. She spoke with a sense of grievance.

'I didn't know you were there.'

'I was,' said Miss Putnam briskly. 'I wanted to hear what sort of a story that bird would spill. I've been on to him all the time. Believe it or not,' said Miss Putnam, 'when you engaged me to keep an eye on your jewels, you handed me one swell job. The way it looks to me, I'm going to be as busy as a cross-eyed man with the jim-jams trying to turn in a fire-alarm on the dial phone.' She shook her head reproachfully. 'When it comes to house-guests, Mrs G., you certainly are a great picker. First this bird, and then that Duke of yours!'

Mrs Gedge started.

'The Duc de Pont-Andemer? You don't mean . . . ?'

'Only Oily Carlisle, one of the best bunco-artists in the business, that's all. I recognized him the moment I saw him. How did you come to get mixed up with him?'

'I met him on the boat.'

Miss Putnam clicked her tongue. She did not seem angry, only pained.

'Didn't your mother ever teach you the facts of Life, Mrs G.? Because one of them is never to be too friendly to people you meet on boats. As for this fellow that says he's a Vicomte and then says he's a detective . . .'

'But are you sure he's not?'

'Then you did swallow his story?' said Miss Putnam with quiet censure. 'I thought you'd have had more sense.'

'But how do you know he is not?'

'Because I'm a dick myself, and I can recognize one a mile off.'

'But he is a friend of the Vicomte de Blissac.'

'He says he is.'

'He knew the Vicomte's first name.'

'And how long do you think it would take him to find out that? He could buy an *Almanac de Gotha* in any bookstore, couldn't he? And being a tough, strong young fellow he'd be quite physically able to open it and read up what it said about the Vicomte.'

'Why, of course. I never thought of that.'

'And remember how he couldn't keep up the smooth talk and had to start pulling that stuff about ice and heist-guys? I tell you he's a crook, all right. I know 'em. And he's getting set for quick action, too. All that about wanting you to change rooms with Mr Gedge. There isn't a real safe-blower I ever heard of that likes to work in a room where there's a woman. Women scream, and they can't get rough with them like they can a man.'

Mrs Gedge looked thoughtful.

'It seemed to me a good suggestion,' she said. 'I think I will change my room.'

'Sure, change your room. I'd have suggested it myself. What we want is to give these birds a chance to think they're sitting pretty, so's they can go ahead and we can get them in the act.'

'Do you think they are working together?'

Miss Putnam shook her head.

'No. And I'll tell you why. They don't act like it. What I mean, you don't see them going off for country rambles arm in arm. They behave sort of distant. No, how I figure it out is like this. The one that was in here just now is playing a lone hand...'

Mrs Gedge uttered an exclamation.

'The Senator!'

'No, he's all right,' said Miss Putnam. She seemed to speak with a certain regret, as if she would have liked him to be a criminal, too, so as to make the thing symmetrical. 'I've seen Senator Opal in Washington. This is him right enough. And I don't take any stock in what that fellow said about the Senator's valet being a crook. That was just eyewash.'

'What I meant,' said Mrs Gedge, 'was that I have a letter which Senator Opal would give anything to get back. Do you think this man can be somebody he has employed to steal it?'

'It straightens out the whole thing,' said Miss Putnam with gratification. 'You've hit it. That accounts for everybody nicely. This fellow is working in with the Senator, and Oily is after the ice. But Oily is a bunco-steerer. He doesn't blow safes. That means there's somebody on the outside he's teamed up with, and I think I know who it is. Did you ever hear of a fellow named Slattery? Soup Slattery?'

There was a pause. Mrs Gedge seemed to be searching in her memory.

'No,' she said at length. 'No,' she said slowly. 'Soup Slattery? What a very odd name. Why Soup?'

'Soup's what they blow safes with. Dynamite.'

'Oh, really?'

'And when I was down to the town the other day I could have sworn I saw this Slattery. His isn't a face you can forget. He was going into the Casino, or somebody that was his double. And now this has happened, Oily getting in here and all, I'm dead sure it was him. Oily's got himself into the house, and he's planning to let Soup in when he's good and ready. That's the way it's always done.'

'Is it?'

'It's what's known as the inside stand.'

'The inside stand?' murmured Mrs Gedge. 'Really?'

She spoke quietly, but Miss Putnam could see that she was much shaken. She was not surprised. A broadminded woman, she realized that the presence of criminals in the home, which gave her merely a sporting thrill, might affect otherwise the chatelaine of that home. The lay mind, she was aware, reacts differently from that of the professional. And women are a nervous sex.

She had been tapping Mrs Gedge's knee. She now patted it.

'There's no occasion to worry, Mrs G. I'm here. When you hire an employee of the James B. Flaherty Agency, you're getting something.'

'But what can you do?'

'Listen,' said Miss Putnam. 'You light a cigarette and smoke it and go on smoking it till there's hardly nothing left, only half an inch of stub, and I'll guarantee to shoot it out of your mouth at twenty paces. That's what I can do.'

Mrs Gedge seemed to recover herself.

'I am sure I can rely on you completely.'

'The slogan of the James B. Flaherty office is "Service",' said Miss Putnam devoutly.

Mrs Gedge rose.

'Then I will leave everything to you.'

'You couldn't do better.'

'I must go and find Wellington and tell him about the change of rooms. I think,' said Mrs Gedge, 'I will go to bed at once. I am a little tired after my journey.'

'You aren't worrying, are you?'

'Oh, no,' said Mrs Gedge.

Her strained eyes belied the words. Miss Putnam, watching her till the door closed, shook her head regretfully. She had had experience of nervous employers before. She wished now that she had kept her information to herself.

Then she brightened. Her spectacled face lifted itself, not unlike that of a war-horse sniffing the approaching battle. It looked to Miss Putnam as if stirring happenings were on the horizon. And stirring happenings, as she had often observed to intimates at the James B. Flaherty office on Forty-Fourth Street and Seventh Avenue, were her dish.

CHAPTER 14

I

DURING the momentous interview between Packy and Mrs Gedge, Mr Gedge had been hovering within easy distance of the library door; and the self-enrolled employee of the London, Paris and New York Insurance Company had no sooner emerged than he pounced upon him, fluttering with agitated curiosity.

Packy's report had brought new life to him. According to Packy, everything had gone like a breeze. Mrs Gedge, he stated with confidence, had swallowed his story, hook, line, and sinker. It made Mr Gedge feel as if he had been reprieved on the steps of the scaffold.

The information, conveyed to him some few minutes later by Mrs Gedge, that she proposed to occupy his bedroom and that he was to shift his belongings to the Venetian Suite, did nothing to diminish his elation. He could not understand why she wished to make this odd exchange, but then she did so many things of which he was unable to divine the motive. He put it down to a woman's idle whim, and went out into the grounds almost trippingly. He still had his worries, of course, but for the time being the greatest of them had been solved. As he rounded the corner of the house he was actually singing.

He would probably in any case not have sung long, for a man with so much to exercise his mind would have been sure quite soon to discover material for silent meditation; but he sang even more cursorily than might have been expected. For, as he sauntered along and drew near to the back premises of the Château, his eyes, roving idly to and fro, suddenly fell upon a sight which brought him back on his heels as if a fist had smitten him.

It was a sight which would have unmanned anyone in his unfortunate position. The fact, therefore, that he uttered a strangled squeak and tottered back against a tree, giving his head a rather painful bump, should not be taken as evidence of any lack of virile fortitude in his character.

For what Mr Gedge had seen was a gendarme. A gendarme who had just slipped back into the bushes outside the kitchen door with the sinister furtiveness of a hunting leopard.

2

Now, we, having had the advantage of that bird's-eye view to which allusion was made earlier, know all about this gendarme. We are aware that he was not a remorseless bloodhound on the trail, but merely a likeable young man of the name of Octave who was waiting for pie. We, therefore, are able to behold him calmly. Our eyes, like stars, do not start from their spheres, nor do our knotty and combined locks part and each particular hair stand on end like quills upon the fretful porpentine.

Mr Gedge's did. He was a mere jelly of palpitating ganglions. With the force of a sledge-hammer the frightful realization had come upon him that, despite all his pains and all his caution, the police had tracked him down.

To pass those bushes with their hideous contents was a task beyond his power. He wheeled and retraced his steps. And it was as he once more rounded the corner of the house that he encountered Packy, the one man with whom he was in a position to discuss this awful affair.

'Say!' he gasped.

Packy, like most people who saw the little man approaching, had been intending to throw him a word and hurry on; but the sight of the other's face arrested him. Mr Gedge's goggle-eyed horror perplexed him. It was only a few minutes since he had left him in what was virtually a state of mental peace, and he could not imagine what had caused so notable a relapse.

'Listen!' said Mr Gedge tensely. 'The cops are watching the house!'

Packy's bewilderment increased. All he could think of as a reply was, 'Surely not?'

'What do you mean, surely not?' said Mr Gedge warmly. There are moments when one is forced to speak with asperity even to one's accomplices. 'I saw him. With my own eyes.'

'You did?'

'Yessir.'

'Where?'

'He was hiding in the bushes outside the kitchen door.'

'Just one cop?'

'One's plenty.'

Packy could make nothing of this.

'Very odd,' he said.

Mr Gedge was not in a frame of mind to be finicky about the *mot juste*, but this adjective seemed to him so extraordinarily inadequate that he snorted wrathfully.

'Odd!'

'Wait here,' said Packy. 'I'll go and have a look at this fellow.'

'Don't let him see you.'

'All right.'

Packy made his way to a point of vantage from which he was able to observe the kitchen door. He had not been watching long when a pleasantly touching scene of love among the lower orders rewarded his vigilance. The cook came out of the house, carrying a smoking pie. As if drawn by the scent, a gendarme emerged from the bushes. The pie changed hands. The gendarme kissed the cook. The cook kissed the gendarme. The gendarme then moved off, heading south. He carried the pie, and he was crooning in an undertone what sounded like a sentimental ballad.

Packy understood all, and it was with a certain purposefulness in his manner that he returned to Mr Gedge. He had had another of those bright ideas which were becoming so frequent with him nowadays that he had almost ceased to be surprised at them.

'Well?' said Mr Gedge.

'He's there, all right,' said Packy. 'I see what this means. The fellow has been sent up here to make enquiries. Amazing how quick these French police work.'

Mr Gedge could not share this apparent enthusiasm for the smooth working of the French police machine. He danced a few silent steps.

Packy, who was evidently still trying to get to the bottom of this affair, now put a question.

'On the night of the crime . . .'

'I wish you wouldn't call it the night of the crime.'

'On the night of the unfortunate affair,' amended Packy, 'did you tell anyone you were going to the Festival?'

'No. But the butler let me in and put me to bed when I got back.'

'And he would have noticed that you were wearing an Oriental costume, complete with turban?'

'I don't see how he could have missed it.'

'Then that's how they have got on the trail. The butler must have laid information.'

'The hound!' said Mr Gedge emotionally. 'And he promised not to say a word about it.'

'You should have tipped him.'

'How could I tip him? Who do you think I am – John D. Rockefeller?'

'Well, it's too late to worry about that now. If the police are on your trail, there is obviously only one thing to do. You must make your getaway. You must edge off and lie low somewhere. And I'll tell you where you can do it. On my boat.'

'Your what?'

'I came to St Rocque on a yawl. It's lying in the harbour now. You would be quite safe there, and it's comfortable. Lots of canned food aboard. You could hide for weeks without being found. And when it was all right for you to come back, you could tell Mrs Gedge some tale about loss of memory or something. Aphasia, I believe they call it. Prominent business men disappear from their homes in New York and are found months later in Dubuque, Iowa, wandering round with a glassy look in their eyes, saying, "Where am I?" You could be thinking all that up on the boat. You'll have plenty of time to do a little thinking.'

Of all the suggestions that could possibly have been made to him, none could have exercised a more immediate appeal to Mr Gedge. The thought of being well away from the Château enchanted him. If Packy had been a financier offering to give him unlimited credit, he could not have eyed him with a more whole-hearted affection.

'Let's go!' he said, with simple enthusiasm.

'Wait a minute,' said Packy. 'How are we going to get you there?'

'Can you run a motor-boat?'

'Yes.'

'Well, there's one down at the boathouse on the lake.'

'Very possibly. But where's the sense of going joy-riding about the lake?'

'There's a channel leads to the harbour.'

'Oh, is there? That's great. Then you had better go and pack a few toothbrushes and pyjamas and any other little necessaries you may fancy, and we'll be starting.'

It was with quiet contentment that Packy watched Mr Gedge disappear into the house. At last, it seemed to him, he had got this rather complex little affair straightened out. All that remained to be done, after placing his host aboard the *Flying Cloud*, was to pay a call at the Hotel des Etrangers, find Mr Slattery, and inform him that he need have no further qualms. When he busted the Venetian Suite that night, he would be busting a room not only completely free from beazels but lacking even a masculine occupant.

He felt that he had done Mr Slattery proud. And turning his back to the breeze to light what in his opinion was a well-earned cigarette he perceived Blair Eggleston approaching.

3

It was quite obvious, as he came up, that the powerful young novelist was not in sunny mood. But this did not deter Packy from engaging him in conversation. He had sunniness enough for two.

'Hullo, Egg,' he said. 'How are you making out?'

The sombreness of the other's frown deepened.

'I wish you would not call me "Egg".'

'I'm sorry. But how *are* you making out?'

His companion did not reply for a moment. He winced a little, and his eye grew darker.

The fact was, Blair Eggleston had been deriving from the task which had been thrust upon him even less enjoyment than he had expected to derive. And that this should have been so affords one more proof of the truism that authors seldom resemble the books they write.

On paper, Blair Eggleston was bold, cold, and ruthless. Like so many of our younger novelists, his whole tone was that of a disillusioned, sardonic philanderer who had drunk the wine-cup of illicit love to its dregs but was always ready to fill up again and have another. There were passages in some of his books, notably *Worm i' the Root* and *Offal*, which simply made you shiver, so stark was their cynicism, so brutal the force with which they tore away the veils and revealed Woman as she is.

Deprived of his fountain-pen, however, Blair was rather timid with women. He had never actually found himself alone in an incense-scented studio with a scantily-clad princess reclining on a tiger-skin, but in such a situation he would most certainly have taken a chair as near to the door as possible and talked about the weather. And in his recent *tête-à-tête* with Medway by the lake it was only the knowledge that Senator Opal was listening-in that had lent any real warmth to his remarks.

So now, in response to Packy's question, he winced reminiscently.

'I can't think what to say to the damned girl,' he said with a burst of candour forced from him by the recollection of his sufferings.

Packy was surprised.

'But I thought you modern novelists were such devils with the beazels.'

Another point struck him.

'What are you doing here, anyway? Your place is by her side.'

'She sent me to get some cigarettes and a bottle of wine. She says she's thirsty.'

'Is there wine in this house?' asked Packy, interested. 'I haven't seen any.'

'It's locked up. But the butler can get at it.'

'My gosh, how I am going to cultivate that butler! This is worth knowing.'

He returned to the point at issue.

'Cigarettes? Wine? Why, this looks great. It's the old Omar Khayyam stuff. You must have been going better than you thought. You're probably one of those fellows who don't say much but do it all with the eyes. I shouldn't worry about not being able to think of things to say. Just continue swinging that alluring eye-ball of yours, and you can't lose.'

A sort of febrile spasm of fury stirred Blair Eggleston from his limp despondency.

'I've a dashed good mind to chuck the whole thing.'

'No, no. This is not your true self speaking. Think how we are all relying on you.'

'I have. A dashed good mind! I consider I have been very badly treated. I have been placed in a most unpleasant and undignified position, and I'm sick and tired of it. I feel . . .'

Blair Eggleston was a man of whom Packy could never have

brought himself to be really fond. At their first meeting he had sized him up as a pretty noxious sort of pustule, and as a pretty noxious sort of pustule he still had him listed. And a hundred times he had marvelled what a girl like Jane Opal could possibly see in him. Nevertheless, he had no wish to let him suffer unnecessarily. The inspiration which had carried him so triumphantly through his recent interview with Mrs Gedge had put him in a position to show Blair Eggleston the way out.

'Well, if you don't like making love to her,' he said, 'I can offer an alternative suggestion. Tell her you're a detective yourself.'

'What!'

'I have tested this ruse personally, and it works like magic. It carries the full Franklyn guarantee. Simply tell her that you are a detective in the employment of the London, Paris and New York Insurance Company, who have sent you here to keep an eye on Mrs Gedge's jewellery, and the results should be immediate. If she's in the same line of business, she will instantly give you the grip and say so. If she isn't, she will probably be so overawed that you won't be able to come within a mile of her again. Either way, you win out.'

If Packy had distributed in the last few days a certain amount of trouble and anxiety among these new acquaintances of his, he was certainly doing much this afternoon to restore the balance. He had just brightened Mr Gedge's whole outlook on life. He was about to bring tidings of great joy to Mr Slattery. After that, his revelations would have a tonic effect on Senator Opal and Jane. And now he had evidently taken an immense load off the mind of Blair Eggleston. After the first struggle to adjust his faculties to the suggestion, Blair Eggleston was plainly finding in it the source of infinite comfort and relief. His eyes lit up, and he seemed to be on the point of putting his approval into words, when there was a sound of panting and Mr Gedge came trotting up with a small suit-case in his hand.

'So you will do that, Eggleston?' said Packy.

'Very good, sir,' said Blair Eggleston.

He proceeded on his way to the house.

'Do what?' asked Mr Gedge.

'I was just giving him a word of advice on how to act so as to please Senator Opal.'

'I wouldn't be old Opal's valet,' said Mr Gedge, 'not if you gave me a million dollars. No, sir! Come on, let's go.'

CHAPTER 15

SOME few minutes before the meeting of Packy and Blair Eggleston, there had appeared, limping across the lawn of the Château Blissac, a dusty and travel-stained figure. It was Gordon Carlisle returning from his country walk. We have already stated that Mr Carlisle was not fond of country walks, and his latest experience of this form of exercise had done nothing to change his views. He had a blister on his heel and he was feeling red-hot.

He made wearily for the house. It was his purpose to collect the bathing-suit which he had bought on the previous day and to go down to the lake and enjoy a swim in its healing waters.

He went indoors, gathered up suit and towel, and presently emerged and started down the rustic path which led to his destination. Half-way there, he observed someone coming up it and saw that it was Senator Opal.

The Senator greeted him cheerily. What he had observed from his hiding-place had left him well content. The fellow Eggleston had seemed to be making excellent progress with the girl Medway, and he felt that his watching eye was needed no longer.

'Hello, there, Duke,' said Senator Opal. 'I'm just going to stroll down to the town. You off swimming?'

'Yais.'

'Well, take care where you undress. That maid of Mrs Gedge's is down by the lake.'

Mr Carlisle's eyes gleamed.

'Yais?'

'Yes. Flirting with that man of mine, Eggleston.'

'What!'

'Saw 'em at it just now,' chuckled the Senator, and passed on.

Mr Carlisle stood for a moment, rigid. Then he drew a deep breath and resumed his journey.

It was a red-eyed and tight-lipped Gordon Carlisle who some few minutes later burst through the bushes at the end of the rustic path and charged like an avenging fury into the clearing by the side of the lake. The blood of the Carlisles was up. A brief inspection of Blair Eggleston on the previous evening had satisfied him that the latter was just about the size he liked people to be on whom he planned committing assault and battery, and he was full of fight.

Having expected to interrupt a sentimental scene and having in the course of his brief walk keyed himself up to immediate action, he was not a little disconcerted to find only Medway standing there. She was throwing bits of stick into the water in the apparent hope of beaning a small water-fowl, an innocent occupation at which the most jealous of lovers could scarcely have cavilled. Wondering if by any chance he could have been misinformed, Mr Carlisle halted. Then he remembered those parting words of hers on the drive, those cruel, taunting words each syllable of which was graven on his heart, and he was firm again.

Medway had turned. He glowered at her sternly.

'Well,' he said with menace, 'where is he?'

Medway's eye was cold.

'What are you doing here, may I enquire, Mr Carlisle?'

'Where is he?'

'Where is who?'

'That guy Eggleston. They told me he was down here with you.'

'They did, did they?'

'Yes, and they told me something else. You've been flirting with him.'

Medway yawned.

'What of it?'

There was pain mingled with the sternness of Mr Carlisle's gaze.

'Necking with the help! I wouldn't have thought it of you, Gertie.'

'Mr Eggleston,' replied the girl with hauteur, 'is a gentleman in every sense of the word. I can't help it if he likes me, can I?'

A slight grating noise intruded itself on the quiet of the afternoon. Gordon Carlisle grinding his teeth.

'He seems to have taken quite a fancy to me,' proceeded Medway with a light, careless laugh. 'Most attentive he is being. He has nice eyes, and, funnily enough, he seems to think I have, too.'

The grating noise increased in volume.

'He was telling me about them when I sent him up to the house. He ought to be back any moment. Then he'll tell me some more, maybe.'

'He'd better let me hear him!'

'You'd do a lot, wouldn't you?'

'I'd break his neck.'

'Yeah? You and who else?'

The truculence of Mr Carlisle's manner gave way to a pleading softness.

'Don't do it, baby! Don't be this way.'

'I'll be any way I please. And perhaps you'll kindly lay off that "baby" stuff.'

'Is there any harm in saying "baby"?' protested Mr Carlisle, pained.

'Yes, there is. If you want to know how you stand with me, we're *pf' f' ft*, and don't you forget it. After you craw-fishing the way you did night before last. Not having the nerve to beat that guy up.'

'I explained that.'

'And after what happened a year ago.'

'I explained that too.'

'Yes, you did! Ankling into the hospital and eating my grapes with that woman's kisses hot upon your lips!'

'They were not hot upon my lips. I never kissed her in my life. It was nothing but a simple, straight forward business association. She happened to know a young canned-sardine millionaire, and I was trying to get her to quote her lowest terms for steering him into a card-game with me. Don't you believe me?'

'I wouldn't believe you even if I knew you were telling the truth. A nice sort of banana-split you turned out to be! If I'd had any sense, I'd of had you pegged for a wrong number the first day I met you.'

A sigh escaped Mr Carlisle.

'You'll be sorry for this, Gertie. One of these days you'll realize how you've misjudged me.'

'Well, when I do, I'll drop you a line. I can easily find out which prison you're at.'

Mr Carlisle stiffened. He loved this girl, but she had gone too far. She had insulted him in his capacity of Artist. The thing on which he had always prided himself was that great skill of his which kept him from making those blunders which brought inferior operators behind prison bars; and she had sneered at this skill. The slur was one he could not overlook. He raised his hat coldly.

'After that crack,' he said with quiet dignity, 'I will leave you.'

'Do,' said Medway. 'And if you never come back that'll be too soon.'

'Good-bye,' said Mr Carlisle.

Gentlemanly to the last, he raised his hat again and stepped haughtily into the bushes.

He had intended to retrace his steps up the rustic path, but just as he was about to do so he heard someone coming down it and paused. The next moment, Blair Eggleston came in view.

Mr Carlisle drew back into the shrubbery. He had changed his mind about leaving. Wounded pride had given place once more to the old jealous fury. His Gertie had given him the bird – what his friend Soup Slattery had so feelingly described on a previous occasion as the Bronx Cheer – and he no longer hoped for a reconciliation. But there still remained vengeance.

He stood there seething, and Blair Eggleston passed him and came out into the clearing. Mr Carlisle shifted his position to obtain a better view, and watched him with burning eyes.

It was unfortunate for Blair Eggleston that Packy's well-meant advice had had the effect of putting him in excellent spirits. His smiling face, taken in conjunction with the bottle of wine which he carried, conveyed to Gordon Carlisle the definite picture of a libertine operating on all six cylinders. It seemed to Mr Carlisle that he was about to be the spectator of an orgy.

The orgy, if such it was, began at quite a moderate tempo. Blair Eggleston uncorked the bottle, filled the lady's glass, filled his own, gave her a cigarette, took a cigarette himself, and sat down on the turf. His manner so far had been unexceptionable. And then, his words coming to Mr Carlisle only as a faint murmur, he began to talk.

For some moments, whatever he was saying appeared to be innocuous. Medway smoked her cigarette without exhibiting any of the emotion which a girl listening to the conversation of a libertine might be expected to display. And then suddenly the scene changed. To Mr Carlisle's ears there came the sharp sound of a woman's gasp. The cigarette fell from Medway's fingers. She stared at her companion as if what he had just said had shocked her maidenly modesty to the core. Distant though he was, Mr Carlisle could discern quite clearly the horrified expression in her eyes, and he waited no longer.

Gertie, he knew, was no prude. If this man had said something to make her look like that, it must have been something raw beyond the ordinary and it was high time for him to interfere. Glowing with the fervour which comes to men about to chastise libertines smaller than themselves, he burst from the bushes.

To Blair Eggleston, who had seen Mr Carlisle pottering about the Château and knew him to be the Duc de Pont-Andemer, a guest of Mrs Gedge, the spectacle of him advancing now did not immediately suggest danger. He was surprised to see him, because he had not known he was there, but he felt no apprehension. His first intimation that the new-comer's intentions were hostile was the latter's sudden spring. Something solid hit him in the eye, and for the next few moments the world became for Blair Eggleston a sort of nightmare knockabout sketch.

Your literary man is generally supposed to be a dreamy, absent-minded person, unequal to keeping his head in circumstances which call for practical common sense. Blair Eggleston was not this type of writer. He was capable of swift thought, and he thought swiftly now. And what he thought was that the soundest policy for a man of his physique, suddenly assaulted by an apparently insane Duc, was to remove himself as quickly as possible.

To attempt escape in an inshore direction was not feasible. Mr Carlisle, like Apollyon, was straddling right across the way. Making a sudden dash, accordingly, and choosing a moment when his assailant seemed to have paused for breath, Blair Eggleston galloped to the waterside and, hurling himself in, swam clumsily but vigorously to a small island which lay some fifty yards from the shore. Scrambling on to this, he stood panting. He was ankle deep in mud, for this sanctuary of his was covered twice a day by the tide, but at least he was alone.

Meanwhile, on the mainland, a tender scene was in progress. In Blair Eggleston, watching it, this scene increased the already definite conviction that everybody had gone suddenly mad, but to Gordon Carlisle's bruised heart it brought nothing but balm. Medway, who during the recent exchanges had been hovering on the fringe of the battle like some maiden of the Middle Ages for whose favours two knights are jousting, now flung her arms impulsively about Mr Carlisle's neck and with words appropriate to the gesture gave him to understand that the past was dead.

'Oily,' she said, 'you're a wow! I didn't know you had it in you. I take it all back.'

The cave-woman in her had been deeply stirred. She had always been aware that when it was a question of conjuring cash out of the pockets of his fellow-men her mate had no superior, but her doubts of his physical courage had done much to neutralize the admiration excited by his professional skill. These doubts he had now set at rest, and also her doubts as to the sincerity of his love.

She kissed Mr Carlisle. Mr Carlisle kissed her. The little episode did not impress itself on Blair Eggleston as idyllic, but idyllic it undoubtedly was.

'Oily!' breathed Medway.

'Gertie!' murmured Mr Carlisle.

And then, for in these practical modern days the business note is never far away even from lovers' reconciliations, Gordon Carlisle began to talk what he would have called turkey.

'Listen, baby,' said Mr Carlisle. 'We've got to get busy. There's no sense in wasting time hanging around. I'm going to open that safe to-night. Around one in the morning would be the best time. Do you think you can get one of the cars out of the garage?'

'Sure.'

'Then we'll have it waiting in the drive with the engine running. I'll drop down off the balcony with the stuff, and we'll be off to Paris.'

'You won't hurt yourself, sweetie?'

'Sure not. It ain't only a drop of a few feet. And let me tell you something. That letter I was telling you about that you wouldn't listen when I was telling you.'

In a few brief words he related the burden of what Mr Slattery had told him. Medway's eyes sparkled enthusiastically. She, too, had the business sense, and she could understand how admirable an asset to a young couple just starting housekeeping a compromising letter of Senator Opal's authorship would be.

Then a graver look came into her face. There was something which in the emotion of the recent reconciliation she had forgotten.

'Oily,' she said, 'there's something we'll have to watch out for. That bird over there is a dick!'

'A dick!'

'That's what he just told me. Employed by the London, Paris and New York Insurance Company to watch over Mrs Gedge's ice.'

Blair Eggleston, dripping on his island, was concerned to observe his late assailant turn and direct at him a stare which, despite the distance which separated them, was so unpleasant that he wished they could have been even further apart.

'He is, is he!' said Mr Carlisle tautly.

'What'll we do?'

'There's only one thing to do. Tie him up and park him somewheres till we've made our getaway.'

'But how will we get at him?'

Mr Carlisle surveyed the waste of waters with a thoughtful eye.

'Isn't there a boat anywheres around this pond?'

'There's a boathouse along there past those trees.'

Mr Carlisle became brisk.

'Baby,' he said, as Napoleon might have said to one of his Marshals when instructing him in his latest plan of campaign, 'I'll wait here and watch him so he don't get away, and you trot along to that boathouse and get you a boat and come back here and pick me up. Then we row along to that island and prod him with the boat-hook. He jumps into the wet and we haul him

aboard. Then we tie him up and leave him in the boathouse and
send the folks a wire from Paris to-morrow where to find him.
Get me?'

'I got you.'

'All straight?'

'All straight.'

'Then shoot,' said Mr Carlisle.

CHAPTER 16

I

IT was the fact that the Château Blissac was being run on lines of the strictest teetotalism that had taken Senator Opal to the town this lovely afternoon. Accustomed as he was in private life to deviate somewhat from those principles which he upheld so eloquently in public, the Château's aridity had occasioned him a good deal of inconvenience, necessitating as it did a tiresome series of daily visits to the cocktail bar of the Hotel des Etrangers, where more liberal views prevailed. It had become a practice of his to drop in there of an evening for the modest refresher which his system demanded, and it was thither that he had repaired after leaving Mr Carlisle.

As a rule, it was his habit to pass through the lobby to his destination at the speed and with something of the look of a steer approaching a water-hole in the Painted Desert; but this afternoon his progress was arrested by the sudden appearance of Packy. The latter, having stowed Mr Gedge away on the *Flying Cloud* and moored the motor-boat to the jetty, had proceeded to the Hotel to communicate the latest developments to Soup Slattery. His arrival in the lobby coincided with that of the Senator.

The Senator, who preferred to be alone on these occasions, was not too pleased at the encounter.

'Ah, Franklyn,' he said with a touch of reserve.

'Hullo, Senator,' said Packy. 'What brings you here?'

'I have just remembered an important cable which must be dispatched to New York without delay. I came down here to send it.'

'I've come to see Soup.'

'Soup?'

'My colleague. Mr Slattery. The man who's going to bust the safe for us.'

Senator Opal brightened.

'Capital! Have you – ah – made any plans?'

'Oh, yes. Everything's fine. Nobody will be sleeping in Mrs Gedge's room. The coast will be quite clear. You'll have that letter to-morrow.'

It was not only indignation that had the power to turn Senator Opal's face purple. Sudden joy could do it. As he extended his right hand to clasp Packy's and laid the other affectionately on his shoulder, rather in the manner of the president of the firm in a magazine advertisement congratulating a promising junior on having had the resourcefulness to take a Correspondence Course of Business Training, he was mauve to the roots of his hair.

'My dear boy!'

'I thought you'd be pleased.'

'Is this man in the hotel?'

'Yes. I'd better go and ask for him at the desk. I'll tell you all about everything later.'

'Quite right. Do not waste a moment.'

With feelings too deep for words, he watched Packy

approach the clerk. A fear that he had had that on a fine afternoon like this the expert of whom he was in search might not be at home, vanished as he saw the young man cross the lobby towards the elevator. Feeling that if ever an occasion justified an extra cocktail this was it, Senator Opal was turning to resume his journey when a voice spoke behind him.

'I beg your pardon.'

The Senator wheeled round, and for a space stood breathless. The voice had been a musical one, but it had not prepared him for its owner's overwhelming beauty. This was the loveliest girl Senator Opal had ever seen, and in an instant he was all courtliness and gallantry. Thirty years had passed since he had been really at the top of his form with beautiful girls, but in the flourish with which he removed his hat and the polished reverence of his bow there was a good deal of the old pep.

'I saw you talking to Mr Franklyn. Can you tell me where he is staying? They say at the desk that he is not at the hotel.'

If anybody had told Senator Opal a moment before that he would shortly be regretting having met this outstandingly handsome girl, he would have ridiculed the idea. Yet, as he heard these words, there did come to him a definite feeling that he was sorry their paths had crossed. The last thing he desired at this very critical point in his affairs was the arrival of persons aware of Packy's identity.

He choked a little. Then, recovering, he prepared to lie stoutly.

'Mr Franklyn?'

'You were talking to him just now.'

'Not to any Mr Franklyn, my dear young lady. To the best of my recollection, I do not know anyone of the name of Franklyn. My recent companion was the Vicomte de Blissac.'

'What!'

'The Vicomte de Blissac,' said the Senator firmly. 'A very old French family.'

The girl was staring at him, and he was sorry to observe that her stare was the stare of incredulity. However, he stuck to it bravely.

'These close resemblances are, I believe, not uncommon. Everyone has had experience of them from time to time. I myself... I remember once in Washington...'

The duty of a chronicler to his readers is to sift and select. Whatever of his material is not, in his opinion, of potential interest he must exclude. Out, therefore, *in toto* goes the story of what Senator Opal remembered in Washington. It would not grip. It was very long and inexpressibly tedious. Its only merit was that it served to give his narrator the breathing-space he so sorely needed. By the time it had wound to its conclusion, the mere sound of his own voice had made him his calm, comfortably pompous self once more.

'And that sort of thing,' he concluded, 'is happening all the time. I have no doubt that there must exist a very striking resemblance between the Vicomte and your friend, Mr Franklyn, but I can assure you that the young man you have just seen is the Vicomte and no other. I am in a position, I may add, to speak authoritatively on the point, for he is engaged to be married to my daughter.'

'Engaged to your daughter!'

'Precisely.'

'Are you sure?'

Of all the remarks which she could have made, this struck Senator Opal as perhaps the silliest. He chuckled fatly.

'You would not ask that if you had seen them together. It is beautiful in these cynical modern days to witness affection like theirs. They are completely wrapped up in one another. Never seem to be happy unless they are kissing one another all the time. And I like to see it,' said Senator Opal warmly. 'If two young people are in love, let them conduct themselves accordingly. That's what I say. I'm sick to death of this idiotic fashion that seems to be the thing nowadays of engaged couples behaving as if they were bored to extinction with one another. There's nothing of that about my daughter and the Vicomte.'

'It must be charming.'

'It is charming.'

'Well, I seem to have made a mistake. I must apologize.'

'My dear young lady!'

'I wonder if you could tell me where the writing-room is? I suppose there would be no objection to my writing a letter there?'

'None whatever. It is through those curtains.'

'Thank you.'

She bowed slightly and left him. Senator Opal, with a faint yearning pang for the years that were no more – years when he would certainly not have permitted a girl like that to pass out of his life without a struggle, proceeded on his way to seek that source of consolation which the philanthropic Monsieur Gustave affords to men who, even if they have passed the age when Love is king, can still swallow.

2

Soup Slattery was sitting up in bed, reading *Alice in Wonderland*. As Packy entered, he sneezed and turned to refresh himself from a glass of hot whisky.

'Hello,' he said. He held the book up. 'Ever read this?'

'Often. Where did you get it?'

'Found it downstairs in the lobby. Must belong to someone, I guess. Say, perhaps you can tell me. This White Rabbit. I don't get him. What's his racket?'

'Wasn't he going to tea with the Queen, or something?'

'But he's wearing a business suit and carrying a clock.'

'Yes.'

'Well,' said Mr Slattery, shaking his head, 'it don't seem possible to me.'

He sneezed again, and Packy looked at him with some concern.

'You've caught cold.'

'I certainly have.'

'I'm sorry,' said Packy. 'This complicates matters. I came to tell you that I wanted you to bust that safe for me to-night.'

Mr Slattery was of Spartan mould.

'Cheese!' he said lightly. 'You don't think a little thing like a cold is going to stop me? Sure, I'll bust it for you. Then you got the Gedge dame out of that room?'

'Not only that, but Gedge won't be there, either.'

'Good enough. How did you work it?'

'Oh, it's a long story,' said Packy deprecatingly. 'I showed extraordinary sagacity and resource. If you care to call it genius, it will be all right with me. Mrs Gedge will be in Mr Gedge's room, and Mr Gedge is in dead storage elsewhere. I'll leave the drawing-room window open for you, and all you'll have to do is walk in and collect. A soft job.'

'Well,' confessed Mr Slattery, 'they can't come too soft for me nowadays. Used to be the tougher an evening's work was the better I'd like it. Julia would razz me about it sometimes. All for a quiet life now. Getting old, I guess. If I could grab me a little bit of capital, enough to buy a farm, I'd retire. There's something about a farm. All those cows and chickens.'

He mused wistfully. Then some unpleasant thought seemed to intrude itself on his dreams, for his eye kindled.

'Say, I've been meaning to ask you. About that Chatty-o.'

'What about it?'

'Who would a guy up there be with white hair and black eyebrows? Sort of thick-set bird.'

'Oh, have you met him? That's Senator Opal.'

Packy paused, surprised. A whistling breath had escaped his companion. It might be pneumonia, but it had sounded much more like a strong man's wrath.

'What's the matter?'

Mr Slattery was still breathing in that odd, laboured way.

'Senator Opal? The fellow you want to get this copperizing letter for?'

'That's the man.'

'Brother,' said Mr Slattery, 'the whole thing's off. I won't do it.'

'What!'

'No, sir, not even to oblige you. Me get that white-haired bird out of a jam? Say, the worse jam he's in, the better it suits me. If he was drowning, the only thing I'd throw him would be a flat-iron.'

Packy was bewildered. He could make nothing of this startlingly unexpected display of feeling.

'But . . .'

'No, sir,' repeated Mr Slattery firmly. 'If that guy's in a spot, I'm glad of it. After what he done to me . . .'

And in crisp, telling sentences, to which an occasional sneeze merely lent additional impressiveness, he proceeded to relate the story of his night in the open. He told it well. You could see the window-sill, hear the cold breeze whistling about his dangling ankles. Packy, listening, found hopelessness creeping over him. After what had occurred, it was plainly not going to be easy to mollify this injured man.

'Tough,' he agreed.

'Tough,' said Mr Slattery, sneezing moodily, 'is right.'

'But surely you aren't going to get sore at a little thing like that?'

'Did you,' asked Mr Slattery, 'say "little thing"?'

'It was just his fun.'

'I don't like that sort of fun.'

Packy felt that he had tried the wrong line of reasoning. He struck a more personal note.

'But think of me. You wouldn't let me down, would you?'

Mr Slattery seemed to be puzzled.

'Say, just where do you come in on this? It's had me guessing right along. Why are you so steamed up about it? If this palooka has been writing letters he shouldn't have written, it's his funeral, not yours. I can't see what you're doing in the act.'

'Senator Opal has a daughter. She is naturally very much upset about this thing. I want to help her.'

'Are you stuck on her?'

'Certainly not,' said Packy.

It annoyed him that the purely Platonic friendliness which he felt towards Jane Opal should be so consistently misinterpreted. He himself knew, of course, that there was nothing between them except, on his side, a chivalrous desire to be of assistance to a distressed acquaintance and, on hers, a natural gratitude for such assistance. True, once or twice he had had occasion to pat her hand and, indeed, to hold it for a brief moment or two; but that had been the merest civility, such as he would have shown towards an aunt, had he had an aunt in trouble.

He endeavoured to impress this upon Mr Slattery now.

'Nothing of the kind. I'm just sorry for her.'

'Well, you'd best be sorry for old Opal.'

'Then you won't help us out?'

'No, sir.'

Packy regarded him reproachfully.

'I can't believe it is really Soup Slattery – good, trusty old Soup Slattery – who is talking like this.'

'It is,' Mr Slattery assured him.

'You really refuse?'

'Yes, sir.'

Packy turned to the door. He knew when he was beaten.

'Well,' he said with infinite sadness, 'this has broken me all up. I don't suppose I shall ever have another shock like this in my life.'

He was wrong. He had one almost immediately. It occurred when he stepped out of the elevator into the lobby and recognized in the lovely girl who advanced towards him his *fiancée*, Lady Beatrice Bracken.

3

The emotions of a young man who, separated from the beautiful girl to whom his troth is plighted, suddenly finds himself quite unexpectedly reunited to her ought to be unmixedly ecstatic. Packy's could scarcely have been so described. In a situation which has furnished a congenial theme for more than one poet, he merely felt as if some muscular acquaintance had just punched him solidly on the nose.

Beatrice was the first to speak.

'Well,' she said. 'You don't seem very pleased to see me.'

The words had the effect of causing Packy's stunned faculties in a certain measure to function again. He was still feeling far from tranquil, but Reason, limping back to her throne, told him that he ought to be exhibiting at least a modicum of hearty rapture. He endeavoured to do so. His brain was still numbed by this unbelievable disaster, but he contrived to smile tenderly.

'I'm tickled to death,' he said. 'It's simply wonderful, seeing you. But I didn't expect...I mean, I hadn't a notion...'

'No. I suppose you hadn't.'

'When did you arrive?'

'This afternoon.'

Packy began to regain his proper form. The one thing he must avoid, he recognized, was the display of anything that might suggest a guilty conscience. After all, things were not so bad as they might have been. Fortunately, he had his boat as an alibi. There was no reason why she should ever know that he had not been living on the *Flying Cloud* ever since his arrival.

His manner, though still not assured, became easier.

'How fine that you were able to come over. I hoped you would when I wrote and told you I was coming here. But I was afraid you might be tied up at your father's for weeks. How was the house-party, by the way?'

'Quite nice.'

'Lots of interesting people there?'

'Quite a number.'

'And how is everybody at home?'

'Quite well.'

'How's your father?'

'Quite well.'

'How's your mother?'

'Quite well.'

'How's your aunt Gwendolyn?'

This detailed solicitude, instead of touching Lady Beatrice Bracken, seemed to make her rather restless.

'Wouldn't it save time,' she said, 'if you simply accepted my assurance that *everybody* at Worbles is quite well?'

Packy recognized the reasonableness of the suggestion.

'Well, it's wonderful your having been able to get over here,' he said, abandoning the theme. 'I suppose you had some difficulty finding me, as I wasn't at any of the hotels. You see, I came over on a boat. You remember my saying I might charter...or did I tell you in my letter?'

'No. In your letter you simply mentioned that you were leaving for St Rocque.'

'Well, I chartered a yawl. She's lying in the harbour now.'

'Are you living on board?'

'That's right. Yes. Living on board.'

'Oh?' said Beatrice. 'I understood you were at this Château, passing yourself off as the Vicomte de Blissac.'

Once again, Packy experienced the sensation of having been punched on the nose. It seemed to him, moreover, that his unseen assailant, not satisfied with this buffet, had also brought his right up with a swing and got home on the point of the jaw. Through an enveloping mist he heard Beatrice continue.

'I happen to know that the Vicomte de Blissac is staying at his mother's Château with some Americans named Gedge. And I met an old man just now who told me that you were the Vicomte de Blissac and that you were engaged to his daughter. Don't you think, perhaps, that you had better explain?'

One of the drawbacks to Life is that it contains moments when one is compelled to tell the truth. Such a moment, Packy realized, had arrived now. There were few things he would not have preferred to telling the truth, but it seemed unavoidable.

'I'll tell you all about that.'

'I am longing to hear.'

'That old man was Senator Opal.'

'So you are engaged to Miss Opal?'

'No, no, no! He only thinks I am.'

'From what he told me, you seem to have given him very good reason to think so.'

'Senator Opal wrote a letter.'

'A curious coincidence. I have just written a letter.'

'It was a compromising letter, and Mrs Gedge got hold of it and talks of giving it to the papers, so he wants to get it back. I happened to meet his daughter...'

'How was that?'

'Well, it's a long story. I was cutting the old man's hair...'

'Doing what?'

'I can't go into that now. But while I was cutting his hair I met his daughter and she told me about this letter, so naturally I offered to get it back for her. And this, of course, gave old Opal the idea that I was Blair Eggleston.'

'What!'

Packy paused to marshal his thoughts. He felt he was not making this as clear as he should.

'When I say he thought I was Blair Eggleston, I mean that Jane...'

'Jane!'

'Her name is Jane. He thought I was the man to whom Miss Opal was engaged. She's really engaged to Blair Eggleston.'

'She certainly isn't. Mr Eggleston didn't say a word to me about it when I met him in London.'

'Naturally not. You see, it's a dead secret.'

'Well, go on.'

'Well, that's why he thinks we're engaged.'

Beatrice tapped her foot on the carpet, always a bad sign.

'Up to the present, all I have understood is that this Senator Opal wrote a letter and that Miss Opal wishes you to get it back.'

'Well, that's all there is to it.'

'Not quite. Isn't it rather a risky business, stealing this letter from Mrs Gedge?'

'You bet it's risky!'

'It might lead to your getting into serious trouble.'

'It certainly might,' said Packy, charmed by her solicitude.

Beatrice's lips tightened.

'And yet,' she said, in that soft, silky voice which women so often employ and which has never yet done any man any good, 'you were apparently quite prepared to take the risk for Miss Opal's sake. A girl who means nothing to you.'

Too late, Packy saw the quagmire into which she had led him. He felt some of the helpless desperation which comes to nervous witnesses when trapped by cross-examining counsel.

'Yes, but don't you see . . .'

'I think I see perfectly. To me, the inference is obvious. You are evidently infatuated with this girl. I think you had better take this letter and read it. It will save a lot of unnecessary talk.'

'But you don't understand.'

'Don't I?'

'I went into this business simply for the fun of it.'

'What *is* the fun of it?'

'Well, I mean . . . the spirit of adventure . . .'

'The spirit of absolute idiocy. It seems to me that you have not only been making love to this Miss Opal behind my back but are also a perfect half-wit. And it is quite plain to me that you are not the man I want to spend the rest of my life with. I thought I could make something of you, but evidently it's hopeless, and we might as well recognize it at once. Just glance at that letter, will you, when you have a spare moment. It says everything. Good-bye.'

'But listen . . .'

The objection to holding these intimate heart-to-heart talks in a public spot is that your movements are hampered by the necessity of observing the conventions. Even in France you cannot chivvy girls across the lobby of a hotel. Beatrice had begun to make for the door at a pace so brisk that Packy's only alternative to letting her go was to pursue her at a gallop. He let her go.

The envelope crackled in his hand. He opened it dully. He did not anticipate that it would add much to his existing information. After those last words of hers, so character-istically lucid, he presumed it to be the bird or raspberry in written form.

He had guessed correctly. The letter ran to three pages and a little over, but its gist could have been condensed into that poignant phrase so familiar to lovers of melodrama – *Those wedding-bells shall not ring out.*

The marriage which had been arranged between Lady Beatrice Bracken (who is, of course, the daughter of the Earl of Stableford) and Patrick B. Franklyn (who is, of course, the well-known young American millionaire and sportsman) would not take place.

Statisticians, who have gone carefully into the figures – the name of Schwertfeger of Berlin is one that springs to the mind – inform us that of young men who have just received a negative answer to a proposal of marriage (and with these must, of course, be grouped those whose engagements have been broken off) 6.08 per cent clench their hands and stare silently before them, 12.02 take the next train to the Rocky Mountains and shoot grizzlies, while 11.07 sit down at their desks and become modern novelists.

The first impulse of the remainder – and these, it will be seen, constitute a large majority – is to nip off round the corner and get a good, stiff drink. Into this class Packy fell. The imperious urge to put something cold and stimulating inside him swept over him within ten seconds of his perusal of the opening sentences of Beatrice's letter. Two minutes later he was in the cocktail bar entreating the kindly Gustave to come to the aid of the party. And it was while the latter was reaching for bottles and doing musical things with ice that he observed Senator Opal bearing down on him.

He was not surprised to see Senator Opal. To the other's thin story about having come to the Hotel des Etrangers to dispatch a cable he had attached little credence. He was perfectly aware that if he entered the cocktail bar one of the first sights which met his eye would be the great Dry legislator with his foot on the rail and his head back, restoring his tissues. All he felt on perceiving him now was merely that well-marked sensation of nausea which comes to broken-hearted young men who see would-be conversationalists making in their direction. He had no wish to chat with the Senator, and only the intense desire to get outside a Gustave Special immediately held him where he stood.

Before proceeding to the more vital agenda, Senator Opal had a word of warning to impart.

'There was a girl out there just now, asking about you,' he said. 'I stalled her all right, but better keep out of the way.'

Packy's Gustave Special had arrived. He drained it without replying and asked for another. The kindly Gustave, who could read faces, had foreseen the repeat order. He filled it instantaneously, and Packy snatched at the glass like a frightened child reaching for its mother's hand.

'I don't know who she was. She knew you all right. But I told her you were the Vicomte de Blissac, and she went off quite satisfied. You go out by this door here, and she'll never see you.'

Having disposed of this minor matter, Senator Opal came straight to that other which was nearest his heart.

'Well, have you fixed everything up?'

Packy, now dealing with his third Gustave Special, stared with no human sparkle in his eye. The Senator's choler, always near the surface, began to rise.

'What the devil,' he demanded, 'are you goggling like a fish for?' A faint mauve, the first beginning of that royal purple which was wont to suffuse it in his Berserk moments, came into his face. 'Are you doped?' he asked sharply. 'Can't you talk? You went up half an hour ago to arrange things with that man of yours. What happened?'

With an effort, Packy contrived to bring his mind to bear on the question. The strain of this made him feel as if the top of his head had worked loose. But something told him that only when he had supplied the desired information would he be permitted to return to his sorrow unmolested.

'Oh, that's all off,' he said.

The Senator was now completely purple.

'All off?'

'Yes. He says he won't do it.'

'Why not? He's a burglar, isn't he?'

'Yes. But apparently when he was doing some burgling the other night you planted him out on a window-sill and he didn't like it.'

'Goosh!' The Senator paused for a moment, aghast. 'You don't mean that was the fellow?'

'Yes.'

'And he's sore?'

'Very sore. He says if you're drowning he'll throw you a flat-iron, but outside of that he doesn't want anything to do with you.'

Senator Opal fermented silently. How true it is, he was feeling, that we never know how devastating the results of our most trivial actions may be. Just because he had done an ordinary everyday thing like putting a burglar on a window-sill, the sort of thing one does and forgets about next minute, ruin stared him in the face. He mourned, as many a stout fellow had mourned before him, over the irrevocability of the past.

Packy welcomed his silence. It enabled him to turn his mind to his own troubles. He was brooding on these, when an insistent noise at his side brought him to earth and with considerable annoyance he saw that the Senator was still there. And not only that, but he had begun to ask questions again.

'But what'll we do?'

'I don't know,' said Packy. He was relieved to find the conundrum so simple and easy to answer.

The Senator appeared dissatisfied. Observing that his young

friend had fallen in some sort of a trance or day-dream, he secured his attention by the simple expedient of kicking him sharply on the right ankle.

'Ouch!' said Packy, and ceased to dream.

'We must do something,' said the Senator fretfully. 'We've got to have that letter.'

'Oh, the letter?' Packy could put this straight, and he did so. 'I got that.'

'You *got* it?'

'Yes.'

'When?'

'Just now.'

'My letter?'

'No, not your letter. Beatrice's letter.'

The Senator moaned a little.

'Are you mad?'

'I'm not any too well pleased,' admitted Packy. 'You see, it's the bird.'

'What's a bird?'

'The letter.'

It was possibly his presence of mind in clutching his temples at this point that prevented Senator Opal's head coming apart. He snatched at the vanishing skirts of sanity.

'Somebody's got to open that safe,' he said, returning to the one aspect of the matter about which there could be no argument or misunderstanding. 'Can't you open a safe?'

'No.'

'Why not?' said the Senator querulously, as if it were one of the things which every young man ought to know.

'It's a very complicated business, opening safes,' said Packy. 'Keesters and pressure-bolts and all that sort of thing enter into it. You have to have dynamite and gauze and thick things and thin things . . . all very complicated.'

'Goosh!'

'Unless it's the other kind of safe.'

'What other kind of safe?'

'The kind Mrs Gedge has. Then it's easy.'

'Easy?'

'Oh, very easy. Perfect pie. All you have to do is find out the combination.'

'And do you know how to do that?'

'Me?' Packy looked at him in mild surprise. 'Oh, no. I haven't the remotest idea.'

The Senator's hopefulness faded. Packy's attention wandered again.

'Then do you mean to say there's nothing to be done?'

'Eh?'

'Is there nothing to be done?'

'Absolutely nothing. She says she thought at one time that she might make something out of me, but she sees now it's hopeless.'

Senator Opal's goggling stare was almost Gedge-like.

'What the devil are you talking about?'

Packy's mind cleared. He saw that he had been on the verge of imparting to this white-haired old Nosey Parker the inner history of a tragedy too sacred and intimate for human ear. With a little difficulty, for Gustave of the Hotel des Etrangers mixes a pretty potent Special, he detached himself from the bar.

'Good-bye,' he said.

'Here, wait!'

But Packy had gone. He had passed to where beyond these

voices there was peace – or if not peace, at any rate uninterrupted leisure for musing in solitude on his fractured heart. As he made his way back to the jetty where he had moored the motor-boat, he wondered a little why Senator Opal should have been so interested in Beatrice's letter. Putting it down to mere idle curiosity, he dismissed the matter from his mind.

He started the motor-boat and, laying a somewhat zigzag course, drove it to the Château Blissac's boathouse. He was now completely distrait and unable to contemplate any mundane phenomena.

This was the reason why the faint gurgle which Blair Eggleston, lying tied hand and foot in a dark corner of the boathouse, contrived to cause to filter through the gag in his mouth, made no impression on his consciousness. If he heard it, he gave it no attention. He moored the motor-boat and walked up to the house, brooding.

5

Several hours later, when darkness had settled upon St Rocque, a lissom form might have been observed emerging stealthily from the Hotel des Etrangers and making its way with equal furtiveness towards the harbour.

Enforced detention in his room had long since started to prey upon the nervous system of Maurice, Vicomte de Blissac. He was a young man who all his life had liked mirth and gaiety, and there are few things less mirthful and gay than a protracted sojourn in a French hotel bedroom.

To-night, he had suddenly cracked under the strain. Days of contemplation of the ceiling, the wash-hand stand, the arm-chair, the other chair, the flowered wall-paper and the steel engraving of the Huguenot's Farewell had reduced him to a state of desperation when he was prepared to take any risk, no matter how fearful. Like the heroine of a modern play, he wanted to get away from it all.

And it was as he wrestled with this mood of recklessness that there came to him what he recognized as quite the brightest idea he had ever had in his life.

Why should he not steal off under cover of darkness to Packy's boat and in the name of their ancient friendship implore Packy to up anchor and take him over to England out of the jurisdiction of the *gendarmerie* of St Rocque?

The more he contemplated the idea, the better it looked. He wondered why he had not thought of it before. There would, of course, be a certain amount of danger in the passage of the streets that led to the jetty, but he scoffed at danger. All he wanted was to be away from that ceiling, that wash-hand stand, that arm-chair, that other chair, that flowered wall-paper and that steel engraving of the Huguenot's Farewell.

So here he was now, sidling with infinite caution through the crooked little streets that wound down to the harbour.

Luck was with him. No stern official voice bade him halt, no hard official hand descended on his shoulder. He reached the jetty, found a boat, climbed in, loosened the rope and rowed off. It was a task of some little difficulty to discover the *Flying Cloud* among all the craft that rocked at anchor on the incoming tide, but he managed it at last.

He called Packy's name cautiously, but there was no answer. Packy, it seemed, was on shore. He decided to go aboard and wait for him.

Arriving on deck, he recollected something very vital which he had learned on his previous visit to the yawl – the location of the cupboard where Packy kept his whisky. He made for it at his best speed. His whole soul was crying out for a restorative.

It was some moments later that he discovered that he was not the only person on board who had been thinking along these lines. The first thing he saw as he charged into the main cabin was a little man of tubby build whose fingers clutched a brimming beaker of the right stuff. His back was to the Vicomte, but at the sound of the latter's footsteps he sprang up in a flurry of arms and legs, spilling the contents of his glass over the tinned tongue which had constituted his modest dinner.

The Vicomte found himself looking into the protruding eyes of J. Wellington Gedge, the man whom, he had been informed by a usually reliable source, he had murdered three nights ago at the Festival of the Saint.

6

It was some four hours later, when the hands of a watch which he had stolen in Cincinnatti were pointing to twenty-five minutes after midnight, that Soup Slattery's better self, which had been stirring uneasily within him ever since Packy's departure, suddenly sprang to life and took charge.

He saw now that he had been within an ace of committing the sin which had the distinction of being almost the only one which his elastic code recognized as such – the unforgivable sin of refusing help to a buddy in trouble. A pal had given him the distress sign and he had ignored it.

There were many things about Soup Slattery at which a moralist would have pursed his lips and raised his eyebrows.

His views on the sanctity of personal property were fundamentally unsound, and he was far too prone to substitute a left hook to the jaw for that soft answer which the righteous recommend. But there was one thing, he had always flattered himself, which nobody could say of him, and that was that he had ever let a friend down in his hour of need.

He burned with shame and remorse. In spite of Packy's statement that only the purest altruism animated him in his desire to assist Jane Opal, he had read between the lines and come to the conclusion that love was the motivating force. Packy, he was convinced, was that way about this squab, and he, Soup Slattery, just because he was at outs with the squab's old man, had been planning to throw sand in the gear-box. As he put on his trousers and reached for his little kit of tools, Soup Slattery was groaning in spirit.

It was with the inward glow of a penitent, the quiet elation of one who at the eleventh hour has seen the light, that he left the hotel some ten minutes later and started to walk up the hill to the Château Blissac.

This time, he knew, there would be no open window waiting for him, but he anticipated no difficulty in climbing on to that balcony which had so immediately won his approval on the occasion of his first visit. Nor did he find any. The thing might have been placed there purely for the convenience of the visiting heist-guy. He negotiated it noiselessly in a matter of seconds. And it was as he stood there, breathing a little heavily, for he was past his first youth, that he noticed that the window of the room was open.

This puzzled him. Packy had assured him that the Venetian Suite would be unoccupied that night. He crept closer and was further mystified to see that there was a light behind the curtains. Odd, felt Mr Slattery, and parted the heavy folds sufficiently to enable him to inspect the interior.

There was an electric torch lying on a table, so placed that its rays fell on the safe. And over the safe, fiddling with the handle, was bending a dim figure.

CHAPTER 17

I

Packy Franklyn had retired to his room early that night. But he had not gone to bed. To one in his state of mental upheaval sleep was out of the question. At the advanced hour when Mr Slattery was setting out with his little bag of tools, he was still in a chair at his open window, fully clothed, gazing over the moonlit grounds with a pipe between his teeth and in his eye that strange, goofy gleam which had been its predominant expression ever since Beatrice had terminated the engagement.

In that world-famous brochure of his, to which we have already referred, Schwertfeger of Berlin writes as follows:

'Having round the corner nipped and the good, stiff drink taken,' says Schwertfeger – he is still on the theme of the young man disappointed in love – 'the subject will now all food-nourishment refuse and in 87.06 per cent of cases will for a long and muscle-exercising walk along the high road or across country at a considerable rate of speed and in much soul-agitation go.'

How true this is. It was what we saw happen in the case of Gordon Carlisle, and it had happened with Packy. Immediately on his return to the Château, he had started out on a walk which, lasting as it did for several hours, had caused him to absent himself from the dinner table. The dinner hour had come and gone without his noticing it. If he gave it a thought, it was merely to let his mind rest for an instant on the idea of food and then wince disgustedly away again.

And now, in the small hours, sitting smoking at his window, he was surprised and a little revolted to find that the agony had abated to so noticeable an extent that it was only by prodding his wounded soul that he could still succeed in feeling adequately miserable.

This change of mood puzzled him. It would not have puzzled Schwertfeger.

'The long and muscle-exercising walk concluded,' writes Schwertfeger, 'and the subject having to his room in much physical exhaustion returned, it now frequently happens that he will in a chair with his feet up sit and a pipe light, and in 65.09 per cent of cases examined it has been established that at this point he will with clarity and a sudden falling of scales from the eyes the position of affairs re-examine and to the conclusion will come that he is *auge davonkommen*' – or, as we should say in English, hazarding a translation of an untranslatable phrase, 'jolly well out of it.'

And it was this stage that Packy had now reached.

For several hours after his parting with Beatrice gloom had enveloped Packy Franklyn like a fog. Now, abruptly, he had begun to feel absolutely fine.

He marshalled the facts. Beatrice had broken off their engagement. There was no getting round that. But – and this was the point, he saw, that hitherto he had overlooked – what of it? The more he examined the thing from this angle, the more clearly did he perceive that, so far from being a tragedy, what had occurred was nothing more nor less than the good, old-fashioned happy ending. For the second time in his career as a wooer, it was plain, Fate had granted him a most fortunate escape. To have become the husband of the present Mrs Scott – or Pott – or even Bott – would have been bad. Would it have been any better to have become the husband of Lady Beatrice Bracken, of Worbles, Dorsetshire?

All that business of enlarging his soul. . . . All those concerts and picture galleries. . . . That marked tendency of hers to thrust him into the society of the side-whiskered and intellectual. . . . Would not these be things which, after the first fire of passion had died down, might make a man consider that in replying in the affirmative to the clergyman's 'Wilt thou?' he had given the wrong and injudicious answer?

Undoubtedly.

And her family – what of them? Was not a man to be congratulated rather than pitied who had escaped a lifetime of the huntin', shootin', and fishin' anecdotes of the Earl of Stableford, the parish gossip of Lady Stableford, the searching eye and nasty cracks of that pre-eminent blister, the Lady Gwendolyn Blinkhorn?

A thousand times yes, felt Packy, and a sudden great peace seemed to descend upon him. It was as if he had taken off a pair of tight shoes.

The fragments of his broken heart came together with a click, as good as new. And at the same moment he became aware of a soft, insistent knocking. The door opened, and Jane Opal came in.

'Sh!' she said.

She closed the door.

'Sh!' she said again.

The admonition was unnecessary. Packy could not have spoken. Like Soup Slattery, now softly making his way to the balcony of the Venetian Room, he was in an agony of remorse, and it completely deprived him of speech.

For hours and hours, he realized, he had not given this girl so much as a thought. Concentrated on his own selfish sorrow, he had neglected altogether the consideration of her distress, of the blow she must have received when her father informed her that Soup Slattery had torn up his contract and that there was now no hope of recovering the letter, on the recovery of which her happiness depended. It was a reflection that did not make him think well of himself.

He eyed her mournfully. She was wearing a blue negligee, and in a blue negligee, as the records have already shown, she looked charming. So charming, indeed, that something suddenly seemed to explode inside Packy like a bomb, and remorse was swept away on the tide of another emotion.

Let us turn to Schwertfeger for the last time.

'This stage reached,' writes Schwertfeger, concluding his remarks, 'and the subject being now in this state of earnest, eyes-raised-thankfully-to-heaven gratitude for his fortunate escape, it is extremely probable that he will immediately in love with somebody else fall.'

But Packy would have denied that he had fallen in love. It was his view that he had loved this girl all the time without happening to notice it. He saw now that the Vicomte de Blissac had been right, that Mr Slattery had been right, that Beatrice had been right. Even the Senator had been right, though working on false premises. They had all assumed that he was in love with Jane Opal, and how unerring their instinct had been. Nobody could have been more surprised than himself, but it was a fact – and he recognized it – that Jane, if not the only girl he had ever loved, was most certainly the girl he loved now.

He gazed at her emotionally. He saw wherein her attraction lay. In the past, now this and now that attribute had lured him in the girls he had met. Jane had everything. The vivacity which had been the charm of Mrs Scott (or Pott or Bott) . . . she had that. The thoroughbred quality of Lady Beatrice Bracken . . . she had that, too. And in addition there were all the bewitchments that were hers alone. She was a sort of *macédoine* of everything feminine that he most admired. She was one hundred per cent, the right girl, the only possible girl, the girl he had been looking for all his life. She was absolutely It.

Against all which, however, must be set the fact that she was in love with Blair Eggleston.

It was a jarring thought to intrude on the moment of a man's realization that he has found his soul-mate, but it did intrude, and it sent Packy back into his chair as if he had been hamstrung.

'What's the matter?' asked Jane anxiously.

'Nothing,' said Packy.

Jane had gone to the door and was listening. Satisfied by the quiet without, she came back, her face determined.

'I was talking to Father to-night,' she said.

Packy nodded sadly.

'He told me your friend Mr Slattery had refused to get that letter. And he told me you had told him that Mrs Gedge's room would be empty to-night.'

Packy nodded again.

'That,' he said, 'is the bitter thought. I worked like a dog to that end, and now it's all no use.'

'You have been wonderful,' said Jane. 'You've been wonderful all along. I don't think I've ever admired anybody so much.'

Her eyes were shining, and Packy averted his gaze. In the circumstances, he felt, the less he saw of shining eyes, the better. The Honour of the Franklyns was just equal to the task of keeping him from picking this girl up in his arms and kissing her, if he looked the other way. It was best not to put too great a strain upon it. That blue negligee alone had been sufficient to make it wobble.

'And it isn't all no use,' continued Jane, 'because everything's fine.'

This remarkable statement succeeded in overcoming Packy's resolve not to look at her. He looked, and his tortured spirit moaned within him. She was standing with her chin up and her eyes sparkling, and the blue negligee was bluer than ever. He looked away again.

'Because, I mean, when Father told me that, I had an idea. I thought, "Well, darn it, there was a burglary in the house only a couple of nights ago, so she can't think it funny if I'm nervous." So I went to Miss Putnam and told her I wanted to put my brooch and things in Mrs Gedge's safe because I was frightened of having them lying around loose. And she said certainly, of course, and she took me to Mrs Gedge's room and opened the safe and put the things in. And I watched her all the time, and what she did was she sort of twiddled a bit and there was a sound like something dropping, and then she twiddled some more and the door came open. I'm sure I can remember how it was done. So what I mean is, why shouldn't we go there now and have a try?'

Packy could not speak. The thought that a girl capable of thinking up a fast one like that should be madly throwing herself away on Blair Eggleston, a man who wore side whiskers and, if the truth were known, was probably a secret beret-wearer as well, was infinitely saddening.

And to secure the Senator's letter would be to remove all obstacles to their union.

He bit the bullet. The Queen could do no wrong. If she wished thus to throw herself away, so be it. And if Fate in its irony insisted that he must be the one to help her do so, the thing had to be faced.

He saw now the part he must play. He must stand by her to the end, and then join her hands to Blair Eggleston's and give them his blessing and wander out into the sunset with a stifled gulp of renunciation. And many years later a white-haired wanderer would peer through the hedge of an old-world garden and see children playing on the lawn with their mother – grey now, but still beautiful – and would wipe away a tear and pluck a rosebud from a bush and place it next his heart and go off and do a lot of good somewhere.

But he wished it had been someone except Blair Eggleston.

Jane misinterpreted his silence.

'Don't you think it's worth trying?'

Packy came to himself with a start.

'Of course, it's worth trying.'

'Then what are we waiting for?'

'We aren't waiting,' said Packy. 'Come on.'

3

Soup Slattery stood gazing at the dim figure, and it is interesting to record that his first emotion on beholding it was one of almost maudlin pity. Unable to distinguish anything for the moment beyond a shapeless outline, he had leaped to the conclusion that Packy, deprived of his professional aid, was trying as a forlorn hope to accomplish something in his blundering amateur way for himself. And the pathos of the thing touched his kindly heart. He felt like a father brooding benevolently over his infant son.

Then the figure turned for an instant; the light of the torch disclosed the features of Gordon Carlisle: and Mr Slattery ceased to feel paternal.

Mention has already been made of the dislike Soup Slattery had for trade rivals. For partners and business associates who suddenly displayed themselves in that capacity his antipathy can scarcely be expressed in words. The discovery that Gordon Carlisle, whom he had trusted freely, was attempting to double-cross him was so unnerving that he had to sit down on the balcony wall to assimilate it.

For that this was Mr Carlisle's purpose Soup Slattery had no sort of doubt. Not once had the other given him so much as a hint that he, too, possessed the ability to open safes. Right from the start, therefore, he must have been planning this vile betrayal: and there and then Soup Slattery added another maxim to that little store of wisdom which he had been accumulating in the course of an active life. Never again, he told himself, would he trust Confidence Trick men. They weren't honest.

But this was not the time for moralizing. Action was demanded. He rose and approached the curtains once more, and without a sound drew them apart and stepped into the room. Only when he had tip-toed to within a few feet of Mr Carlisle's bent back did he speak.

His actual observation it is not necessary to record. It was Biblical in its general nature and delivered through clenched teeth. It is sufficient to say that it caused Gordon Carlisle to jump like a Mexican bean.

From the very beginning of this undertaking, Gordon Carlisle had been extremely nervous. This sort of thing was out of his line, and he did not like it. Only the thought of what his Gertie would say if he backed out had been able to steel him to the task. As he twisted the handle of the safe and listened for the falling of the tumblers, not even the knowledge that Gertie was outside in the passage, keeping watch, had been able to soothe his agitation. Subconsciously, he was expecting anything to happen at any moment.

But he had never expected anything like this. In all his mental list of the unpleasant things which might occur he had not included the possible appearance of Soup Slattery. It seemed to him, as he heard the other's voice, that it was only the fact of his teeth having snapped together with his tongue in between them that had prevented his heart leaping out of his mouth.

It was Mr Slattery who for the next few minutes monopolized the conversation. In a stream of well-selected words his opinion of his friend's duplicity rumbled hollowly through the room. The occasion was one when the orator would have preferred to express himself at the full capacity of his lungs, but the circumstances of the encounter precluded that.

Even when whispered, however, Mr Slattery's remarks were effective. After all, when you are calling a man a low-down, horn-swoggling, double-crossing skunk, it is the actual words that count, not the volume of sound.

Gordon Carlisle edged back against the wall. He was not a sensitive man, and mere verbal criticism had never hurt him yet. But what was weighing on his mind was the growing suspicion that all this was mere preamble. All too soon, he feared, the speaker would realize the futility of talk and proceed to action. And he was aware what the word 'action' signified in the simple lexicon of Soup Slattery.

And then suddenly hope dawned. Behind Mr Slattery's menacing form he perceived that his Gertie had stolen silently into the room, and – what was so particularly reassuring – she was carrying in her hand a good, stout vase.

From hard-won experience, Gordon Carlisle knew what his loved one could do with a vase. And this was a particularly large, hard, thick, solid vase, in every way superior to the one which a year ago she had bounced on his head. It was one of those vases which a Zulu chieftain would have been perfectly satisfied to make shift with while his knobkerrie was being cleaned at the club-maker's. The impact of it on a skull even so tough as that of Mr Slattery could scarcely fail to produce results, especially when wielded by one who believed in taking the full Vardon swing and getting plenty of follow-through.

All that was needed was for him to keep the prospective victim's attention engaged for just those few seconds which would enable this Angel of Mercy to gauge the distance and take her stance. And so stimulated was Mr Carlisle by the sight of rescue so close at hand that inspiration descended on him.

'No, no!' he said protestingly. 'You got me wrong, Soup, you got me wrong.'

He saw that the girl behind the vase had stepped on to the tee and had begun her preliminary waggle, and the sight lent him eloquence.

'Surely you don't think I'd double-cross you, Soupie? It was like this. After you told me what had happened that other night – you out on the window-sill and all – I said to myself: "The way it looks to me, poor old Soup may feel he don't want to come visiting here again. . . ."'

Mr Slattery's was a single-track mind.

'Why didn't you wise me up that you could open petes?'

'I can't open petes.' Mr Carlisle's voice was all musical reassurance. 'But some guy once told me that if you listened for the tumblers you could get the combination, and I thought it was worth trying. You see, after what happened that night, it struck me that you might want to wish yourself out of the thing and . . .'

He had no need to say more. And if he had said more he would have been addressing an inattentive audience. There was a sound like the collision of two heavy pieces of wood, and Soup Slattery slid to the floor. Mr Carlisle expelled a long, whistling breath and passed the sleeve of his coat across his forehead.

''At-a-girl!' he said reverently.

His bride-to-be had no leisure to listen to verbal tributes. She was as brisk as Lady Macbeth giving instructions on what to do with the guest in the spare bedroom.

'Push him under the bed and get a move on,' she said crisply. 'I'll look after the broken china. You've got to work quick, Oily. Somebody may have heard that smash. How long'll it take you getting that thing open?'

'Coupla minutes.'

'Then snap into it. I'll be going down to the car. We may have to run for it any minute now.'

She hurried through the curtains, and Mr Carlisle, having disposed of his unfortunate friend as directed, returned to the safe.

His boast that only a period of two minutes would be required for its opening was completely justified. Ninety seconds had not gone by when the steel door swung free, revealing the interior.

And it was at this moment that there came to his straining ears the sound of soft footsteps in the passage outside.

Gordon Carlisle was primarily a man of intellect, but he could act. He switched off the torch and joined Mr Slattery under the bed.

He was not in darkness long. A half-minute later, light flooded the room. Somebody had pressed the electric button by the door.

4

It was Packy who had pressed the electric button. Arrived at his destination with the door shut behind him, he saw no reason why the proceedings should not take place with the fullest illumination possible. The house was asleep, and nobody could see through those curtains that the room was lighted.

All seemed quiet on the Venetian front. Despite her haste, the efficient Gertie had gathered up every vestige of the broken vase, and the hangings of the bed, reaching to within an inch of the floor, effectually concealed the Messrs. Slattery and Carlisle. Nevertheless, there came to Packy that same feeling of unreasoning nervousness which had gripped him on his first visit to this room. Now that he had actually met Mrs Gedge, the intimidating atmosphere of this boudoir of hers seemed intensified.

Jane, whose reaction to the vibrations of a woman's room was less pronounced, had hurried to the safe. And now, observing its condition, she uttered a squeak of astonishment.

'Why, it's open!'

Packy, too, had made a discovery.

'So,' he pointed out, 'is the window.'

Jane's eyes met his. He was touched to note that, brave girl though she was, she moved a little closer to him.

'Somebody,' she said with a slight quiver in her voice, 'has been here.'

'Must have heard us coming and dashed out of the window,' agreed Packy.

'Perhaps they're on the balcony!'

'I'll look.'

'Oh, do take care!'

'No,' said Packy, returning, 'there's no one there. They must have got away. It's an easy drop.'

The pallor of her face attracted his notice. If ever there was a girl who needed a strong man to clasp her little waist and draw her to him and stroke her hair and breathe comforting words to her, it was the hitherto intrepid Jane Opal: and it was gall to Packy to think that, simply because she had got herself tangled up with the unspeakable Blair Eggleston, the honour of the Franklyns must cause him to censor the first three items on the list.

However, he could breathe comforting words, and he did so.

'Don't be scared,' he said. 'There's nothing to be frightened about. They have gone. I never saw anything like this house for burglars. They absolutely congest the place. The Château Blissac seems to have burglars the way other houses have mice. However, it's all for the best. They have very conveniently opened the safe for us, so I don't see what we've got to grumble at.'

Jane's composure had returned.

'Quick! Look inside and see if it's still there. The letter, I mean.'

Packy did so.

'Yes, this must be it. Yes, this is it, all right.'

'Are you sure?'

'Quite.'

'Then,' said Gordon Carlisle, emerging from beneath the bed, 'just hand it over.'

He pulled himself to his feet. There was an automatic pistol in his hand. He directed it at Packy.

'And make it snappy,' he said.

To a young couple engaged in burgling their hostess's bedroom the sudden appearance of an armed desperado is always disconcerting. Neither Packy nor Jane bore the experience with perfect composure. Jane made an odd little noise like a startled kitten and backed slowly towards the window. Packy stood where he was, regarding Mr Carlisle, astounded.

'Stand still,' said that nervous but determined man.

Jane ceased to retreat. She cast a questioning look at Packy. He had proved himself in these last few days so noteworthy a man of resource that she was not without some faint hope that he might be able to do something about this.

But Packy had no immediate plans. He was still staring at the Duc de Pont-Andemer with bulging eyes. This sudden transformation of one on whom he had looked till now as a respectable member of the French aristocracy had paralysed him.

His sojourn under the bed had not toned up Mr Carlisle's nervous system. Such close proximity to even an insensible Soup

Slattery had affected him unpleasantly. More than ever, he wanted to get this business finished and return to his own less exacting walk in life. Growing panic lent a sharpness to his voice.

'Hand over that letter!'

'I won't,' said Packy, finding speech.

He wished that Mr Carlisle could have been just a few feet closer. He was just too far away for tackling purposes.

'I'll count ten.'

'Count all you want.'

'One ... two ...'

Packy attempted to appeal to his reason.

'You don't really want it. It's just a letter.'

'Three ... four ...'

'If you're collecting autographs ...'

'Five ... six ... seven ...'

Packy began to feel irritated.

'Do stop imitating a cuckoo-clock, and let's sit down quietly and talk it over. You can't possibly want a letter that's of no value whatever except to the owner.'

'Eight ... nine ...'

'Ten,' said Miss Putnam in the doorway. 'You're out!'

She walked composedly into the room, followed by Mrs Gedge.

5

On occasions when any little group of men and women are gathered together, nothing spoils the evening more than the absence of introductions. The perfect hostess will always attend to this branch of her duties first of all. Miss Putnam lost no time in making her identity clear.

'Presenting Kate Amelia Putnam, of the James B. Flaherty Detective Agency of New York,' she said amiably, holding the pistol in her hand on a steady line with Mr Carlisle's pelvis. 'Drop that gun. And you,' she added to Packy, 'keep your hands up.'

Mr Carlisle's automatic dropped to the floor. Miss Putnam seemed well content.

'Now we're all set,' she said. 'Mrs G., might I trouble you to step across and pick up that cannon. And while you're there...you see that little ninctobinkus on the writing-table...'

She indicated a small woollen rabbit of rather weak-minded aspect which had apparently been designed as a penwiper.

'Put it on top of his head. We may as well have a little demonstration in case any of them are tempted to try any funny business.'

Mrs Gedge laid the object on Mr Carlisle's hair and backed away.

'Now, then,' said Miss Putnam. 'William Tell stuff.'

There was a sharp report. The rabbit seemed to explode.

'That'll show you,' said Miss Putnam, simpering slightly.

There is always a somewhat breath-taking quality about a pistol shot. Miss Putnam's entire audience were visibly affected. The first to recover was Mr Carlisle. He turned to Mrs Gedge, spluttering.

'This is an outrage!' he said, speaking in the justly incensed tone which French Ducs always employ when they have had woollen rabbits shot off their heads. 'Figure to yourself, Madame, I hear a noise and I come at great risk and I find this man burgling your safe and I defend your property, and now this woman comes and shoots at me.'

Miss Putnam could not let this pass.

'I didn't shoot at you. If I had of, I'd of hit you.'

'By what right,' demanded Mr Carlisle, 'am I treated as if I were a...'

'All this,' said Miss Putnam, 'would go a lot stronger with me if I wasn't hep that you were Oily Carlisle. Take off those whiskers, Oily, we know you.'

'Oh, you do, do you?' said Mr Carlisle, starting with some violence and ceasing abruptly to portray a French aristocrat in a state of righteous indignation. He was aware that the retort was a weak one, but he was not feeling in good debating form.

Packy now spoke. He had had time to collect himself, and he saw his line of action clearly.

'Smart work!' he said in a crisp, approving sort of voice. 'Capital, capital! I dare say Mrs Gedge has told you that I, too, am in your line of business. I am one of the staff of detectives employed by the London, Paris and New York Insurance Company, and they sent me here to look after Mrs Gedge's jewels. Miss Opal came to me just now and told me she had heard noises in here, so I came down to investigate, and this fellow covered me with his gun. Most fortunately, you arrived, so all is well. You have done splendidly, Miss Putnam,' said Packy, hoping that he was not being too patronizing. 'I shall advise my employers to write a special letter to your firm commending you highly for your work to-night. Very smart work, indeed.'

'I could listen for ever,' said Miss Putnam, 'but I know all about you, too, buddy. I got the London and Paris on the wire this evening, and they've never heard of you in their lives. So don't bother about that letter.'

Packy subsided. He was blaming himself. The fact that Miss Putnam had not been drowned at birth was the fault, of course, of her parents. But to his personal negligence was due the fact that she had not been drowned in the Château Blissac's leaky cistern.

'Well,' said Mrs Gedge, 'you were right.'

'I always am,' said Miss Putnam.

'You said they would try to burgle the safe tonight.'

'I knew they would, as soon as I heard Mr Gedge hadn't been at dinner. One of them got him out of the way somehow. I don't know which of them it was, but it doesn't matter.'

'Where is Mr Gedge?' demanded the bereaved wife.

'Search me,' said Mr Carlisle sullenly.

'He's on my boat,' said Packy, feeling that nothing was to be gained by concealing this minor point.

Miss Putnam eyed him keenly.

'If you beaned him and tied him up, boy, that'll make things a lot worse for you.'

'No. He went quite willingly.'

'Well, we'll go into that when we get him back.'

She appeared to be about to speak further, but at this moment a voice spoke in the doorway.

'Goosh!'

Senator Opal was standing there in a mauve dressing-gown that matched his face. He stared in horror at the scene before him. An intelligent man, he had no need to ask what had occurred. He came totteringly into the room, and Miss Putnam uttered a piercing cry.

'Get out of the way, you mutt!'

It was too late. He had wandered across her line of fire, and Mr Carlisle was a swift thinker.

Of what occurred in the next few second it is reluctantly that the historian brings himself to write. He has been at pains all through this chronicle to lay stress on the intense gentlemanliness of Gordon Carlisle, and Mr Carlisle's behaviour now fell far below its customary standard. For, seeing a heaven-sent Senator in between him and his formidable foe, Gordon Carlisle definitely lapsed.

Darting forward, he seized Jane. Employing her as a shield, he dashed to the window. Then, reaching the window, he hurled her at the on-coming Miss Putnam with such force and shrewdness of aim that the efficient woman went down as if she had been pole-axed. And long before she had succeeded in regaining her feet the window had slammed and there came faintly from beyond it the sound of a heavy body dropping to earth.

Miss Putnam did what she could. In the execution of their duties the employees of the James B. Flaherty Agency do not spare themselves. The window opened and slammed again, and this time from out of the night there sounded a fusillade of shots, mingled with the roar of an accelerated motor engine.

She came back into the room, drooping a little.

'They got away,' she said.

Her attention was attracted to the fact that in the interval of her absence a brawl appeared to have broken out in the Venetian Room. Packy was still where she had left him, but he had now been joined by Mrs Gedge, who was pulling at his arm. The liveliness of the scene was increased by the fact that Senator Opal was pulling at Mrs Gedge.

'Stop him!' cried Mrs Gedge, seeing her ally. 'He's eating it!'

'Eating what?' said Miss Putnam, mystified.

'Don't worry,' said the Senator buoyantly. 'He's through.'

He gripped Packy's hand and shook it warmly.

'All finished?'

'That was the last mouthful,' said Packy, swallowing. 'As palatable a letter as I ever tasted.'

'Nice work, my boy!'

'Packy,' said Jane, 'you're wonderful!'

'I wonder,' said Packy, addressing Mrs Gedge, 'if I might have a glass of water?'

Mrs Gedge had regained command of herself. She stood there, a statue of Doom.

'You'll be sorry,' she said.

'Here, what is all this?' asked Miss Putnam.

'He has eaten Senator Opal's letter.'

'He has? Buddy,' said Miss Putnam, eyeing Packy with severity, 'you must like trouble, the way you keep right on asking for it.'

She suspended her remarks once more. She had spied strangers. The doorway had come a staring mass of them. The butler was there. The cook was there. So were what seemed a regiment of the lesser servitors. You cannot fire pistols in a country house during the small hours without exciting interest among the domestic staff.

'Get out of here,' said Miss Putnam, annoyed. She was always opposed to the presence of the general public on these occasions. 'What do you think this is – a circus?'

She removed herself temporarily from the centre of operations. She could be heard out in the passage and on the stairs driving a reluctant mob before her.

Mrs Gedge's eyes were hard. Her lips quivered.

'Yes, you'll certainly be sorry,' she said.

'I'm glad,' said Senator Opal, correcting this view. 'You won't be long. I'll give you your choice. You make my husband Ambassador to France, or this man and your daughter go to prison. Think quick.'

'Miss Opal had nothing to do with it,' said Packy. 'She just came down because she heard a noise.'

'I didn't,' said Jane. 'I came with you.'

'Fathead!' said Packy. 'What did you want to say that for?'

'Do you think I'm going to run out on you?'

'Yes, but . . .'

'Well?' said Mrs Gedge.

Something stirred beneath the bed. A battered head appeared, followed by a massive body. Soup Slattery was back in the world of men.

'Cheese!' he observed, rising slowly to his feet and passing a meditative hand over his skull.

Then it seemed to come to him that he was not alone. He looked about him dazedly. His eye fell on Mrs Gedge, and he backed against the safe, his eyes widening.

In Mrs Gedge's demeanour, also, a close observer might have noted an equal consternation. Her rigidity now was not that of righteous wrath. She seemed paralysed, as if by the sight of a ghost.

Twice Mr Slattery's mouth opened, and twice no words came. The third time, he was luckier.

'Julia!' he gasped.

Miss Putnam came back into the room, swinging her revolver like a clouded cane. She halted, and a pleased smile played across her face.

'In person!' said Miss Putnam. 'I thought so. We were expecting you, Mr Slattery.'

6

It was an observation which seemed to call for a reply, but Soup Slattery did not give one. He was still staring with that expression of profound amazement.

'Julia!' he said. 'Julia! What are *you* doing here, Julia?'

To Miss Putnam this seemed mere trifling.

'My name is not Julia,' she said curtly.

Packy saw all.

'No, but hers is,' he said, pointing at Mrs Gedge. 'And our Mr Slattery told me all about her. Ladies and gentlemen, permit me to introduce Long-Lost Julia, the best inside-worker a safe-blower ever had.'

'What,' enquired Miss Putnam, 'are you gibbering about?'

'I am not gibbering. If this is really Mr Slattery's Julia – and it is?'

'Sure,' said Mr Slattery. 'What are you doing here, Julia?'

'. . . she was for years Mr Slattery's partner in his enterprises. She used to get herself invited to all these swell homes, having class. And if the pete was in a dame's room she would slip in first and put a sponge of chloroform under her nose, so that by the time Mr Slattery arrived everything was hotsy-totsy. But in the end she walked out on him, and this is where she walked to. Ladies and gentlemen, featuring Mrs Gedge, the many-sided. Am I right, Mr Slattery?'

'Sure.'

The safe-blower was still dazed, but this did not prevent him from displaying a nice gallantry.

'You look just the same as ever, Julia. Not a day older.'

It was a handsome tribute, and well deserved, for Mrs Gedge, though not looking her best at the actual moment, was an exceedingly attractive woman. It was plain, however, that she did not appreciate the compliment. Her face twisted, her eyes shone with a baleful light, and those shapely hands of hers tightened into two fists.

'You poor goop,' she said, in a hard, strained voice, 'I'd like to paste you one.'

To Miss Putnam, watching her thoughtfully, the remark brought conviction. It was as if the veneer which for want of a better word Mr Slattery had described as 'class', had fallen from Mrs Gedge like a garment. Doubtful before, Miss Putnam now accepted the truth of Packy's words.

Mr Slattery was concerned.

'I'm sorry if I've caused trouble, Julia.'

Packy reassured him.

'You've caused anything but trouble. You've saved the situation. You've brought the good news from Aix to Ghent. I hardly think our hostess will carry out that scheme of hers for having us all arrested for burglary now.'

Miss Putnam nodded.

'Better give up the idea, Mrs G. They've got the goods on you. I see now why you took it so big when I mentioned that Soup Slattery was in the neighbourhood.'

Senator Opal had stepped forward like one about to bestow the Freedom of the City.

'I would like to shake hands with you, Mr Slattery.'

'Yeah?' said Soup, giving him a hard stare.

He put his hands behind him. The Slatterys did not lightly forget.

'Well,' said Miss Putnam, speaking with regret, for it was not thus that she had hoped the night would end, 'seeing everybody's old friends here and there's nothing doing in my line, I'll be off to bed and catch up with my beauty-sleep.'

She walked pensively to the door. Reaching it, she turned to deliver a parting homily.

'This is what comes of having a past, Mrs G. No good to anyone, a past. Never know when it'll crop up. And me explaining to you what an inside stand was! Well, good night, all,' said Miss Putnam, and passed from the scene, a disappointed woman.

In the room she had left there was silence for some moments.

'Well...' said Mr Slattery.

He left the sentence uncompleted. But that it had been intended for a speech of farewell was shown by the fact that he now moved towards the window.

'Yes, get out of here,' said Mrs Gedge.

Mr Slattery paused with his hand on the curtains.

'So you quit me to marry some rich guy, did you, Julia? Well, I'm not saying you wasn't right. It's a mug's game, this pete-blowing business, what I mean. Me, I'm retiring myself. Going to buy a farm. Good-bye.'

The curtains fell behind him.

'And now you get out, all of you,' said Mrs Gedge.

'Madam,' said Senator Opal, 'rest assured...that...'

He broke off and stood staring. There had come from the passage outside the sound of uncertain feet. A hand clutched the door-frame, appearing from nowhere like a hand in a mystery play. There came the sound of an amused laugh, and across the threshold walked J. Wellington Gedge.

He navigated towards the bed and propped himself up against it. To the discerning eye, it was all too clear that Mr Gedge was many fathoms beneath the surface.

The mutual recognition of J. Wellington Gedge and the Vicomte de Blissac on Packy's boat some hours earlier had had the natural effect of relieving both their minds to a very marked extent. After the first moment of panic, when each had thought the other a visitant from another world, the thing had become a joy-feast. For perhaps half an hour they had sat side by side, telling each other their frank opinion of Packy and sketching out roughly what they would do when they returned to the Château together and confronted him; and at the end of that period the Vicomte had suggested that they could not possibly confront Packy as he should be confronted without first fortifying themselves with food and drink.

Mr Gedge had received the suggestion well, and a pleasant dinner for two had begun at the Hotel des Etrangers at about nine-thirty. It was still in progress at midnight. At one a.m. the Vicomte had slipped silently to the floor with a peaceful expression on his face, and it was so evidently his intention to remain there that Mr Gedge felt that the time had arrived for home and bed. And here he was, about to turn in.

The sight of his room full of people seemed to puzzle him for a moment. He stared from one to the other with a questioning look. Then, seeming to say to himself that optical illusions like this were only to be expected at such a time, he removed his collar by the simple process of seizing both wings and pulling. Then he climbed into the bed and fell into a peaceful sleep.

Packy was the first to advance a comment.

'And that,' he said, 'is the man you want to make Ambassador to France! You seriously propose to let him loose on Paris! If this is how he goes on in St Rocque, think what he could accomplish with all the vast resources of Paris at his disposal. I advise you to take him back to California and keep him there. In fact,' said Packy, 'I'm afraid I must insist. The poor devil is pining for the old home town, and it's cruelty to keep him away from it. I should like your assurance, Mrs Gedge, that you will return with him to Glendale at the earliest opportunity.'

His eye met Mrs Gedge's. She saw the menace in it. She was a clear-thinking woman, and she realized how subversive to domestic discipline would be the confiding of her secret to Mr Gedge. Her teeth clicked together, but when they parted again it was to enable her to give the assurance required.

'And now,' said the Senator, with something of the manner of a pleased guest reluctantly tearing himself away from a party, 'we will be going. I have no doubt that we can find beds at the hotel.'

'I have a better idea,' said Packy. 'Come back to my boat for the night. Room for all, and very snug.'

'Capital!'

'If Mrs Gedge will allow us to borrow her motor-boat...? Then we will meet when you are ready at the boathouse.'

'And meanwhile,' said Senator Opal, 'I will be doing my own packing personally. There are several little valuables which I should be sorry to lose.'

He gave Mrs Gedge a meaning look. But Mrs Gedge made no answer. Without a word, she turned and strode from the room. A snore from the bed seemed to speed her on her way like a benediction.

7

Through the scented night Packy walked down the hill to the boathouse. The stars were shining peacefully, and there was peace in his heart. True, he had now lost Jane Opal for ever, but what did his personal misfortunes matter when weighed against the Niagara of sweetness and light which had suddenly flooded his little world? As far as the eye could reach, that little world's inhabitants, with the solitary exception of himself, were sitting pretty. The cloud had passed from the sky of Senator

Opal. Mr Gedge, when he woke, if he ever did, would find happiness to console him for the rather severe headache from which he would be suffering. The Veek was himself again. And Jane and Blair would live happy ever after.

A pretty good bag, felt Packy. A very fine bag, indeed.

He reached the boathouse and opened the door. And as he did so his attention was attracted by an odd, strangled noise which seemed to proceed from a dark corner.

Advancing cautiously, he was able to discern what appeared to be a large-sized cocoon. And closer inspection revealed this as none other than Blair Eggleston. He was securely tied with stout cords, and there was a gag of some description in his mouth.

Packy cut the cords. He removed the gag.

'Egg!' he exclaimed solicitously.

Blair Eggleston did not reply. He was going through an intricate system of physical jerks and massage. His mood was plainly not radiant.

It was Jane who eventually broke an embarrassing silence. She had just reached the boathouse door.

'Blair!' she cried.

Packy had delicacy. He could recognize a sacred moment when he saw one. He withdrew silently, and, moving some little distance along the lake front, sat down and lit his pipe.

It was some ten minutes later that he heard a voice calling his name.

CHAPTER 18

JANE OPAL came out of the shadows.

'What was it all about?' asked Packy.

Jane seemed troubled.

'I couldn't make out half he said. He was so angry, I mean. He just bubbled most of the time.'

'And if ever a man had an excuse for bubbling...'

'Oh, I'm not blaming him. Do you know he had been there like that for hours?'

'But who did it?'

'He says it was Medway...'

'Medway!'

'... and the man who called himself the Duc de Pont-Andemer. They just jumped on him and left him like that.'

'Poor devil!'

'He's very cross,' said Jane meditatively.

'I'm not surprised.'

'He says it's all our fault.'

This was a new aspect of the matter to Packy.

'Ours?'

'Yours and mine and Father's, because we got him mixed up with Medway. Apparently, Medway and this man Oily something are going to be married.'

'Tell Eggleston to take a strong line and not send them a wedding present.'

'I don't suppose I shall see Blair to tell him anything,' said Jane, gazing out over the dark water. 'He's going back to Bloomsbury.'

Packy's heart leaped.

'You mean he's broken off your engagement?'

'Yes.'

For an instant, all Packy could feel was an exquisite elation. Then he told himself sternly that this was unworthy of a modern Sidney Carton. Not for Sid to rejoice at such a breach, but rather to do all in his power to heal it.

'I shouldn't worry,' he said soothingly. 'He spoke without thinking. You can't expect a man who has been tied hand and foot in a smelly boathouse for goodness knows how many hours to be a little sunbeam right away. Leave him lay for a day or two, and you'll be surprised. You know how it is about the milk of human kindness. Something starts a leak and out it goes with a hoosh. But give it time and little by little it will flow back till the reservoir is full again. You take my word for it, in a day or two he will be twanging a guitar beneath your window.'

Jane was silent.

'He will come to you and say, "Forget those cruel words!"'

Jane kicked at a twig.

'But I'm not sure that I want to forget them.'

'What!'

'I rather think this may be the best thing that could have happened.'

Packy swallowed a jagged something that was interfering with his vocal cords.

'You don't mean—?'

'Yes, I do.'

'Don't you love Egg any more?'

'I'm not so sure that I ever did love him. You know how it is. You meet somebody and they seem to you all chock-a-block with wonderful ideals and you get sort of infatuated.'

Packy was stunned by this added proof that this girl and he were twin souls.

'You don't have to explain that to me. Boy, as good old Slattery would say, could I write a book! It was just that way with me and Beatrice.'

'But you haven't stopped loving Beatrice.'

'Yes, I have. With a sort of jerk at around twelve p.m. last night.'

'What!'

'And it's just as well,' said Packy, 'because my engagement has conked, too.'

'You don't mean that?'

'Yes, I do. Beatrice gave me the bird face to face at, I should say, about six-fifteen yesterday evening.'

'But she isn't here?'

'She was then.'

'But why did she break the engagement?'

Packy hesitated.

'Well, there were several reasons. Somehow or other she got the impression that I was a half-wit. And then ...'

'Then?'

'Well, you see, she happened to run into your father, and he told her one or two things about ...'

'About what?'

'Well, about you and me. She accused me of making love to you behind her back.'

'But you haven't made love to me.'

'I know. Silly idea. But you know what women...'

Jane looked pensively out at the lake.

'I wish you would,' she said.

A curious sensation came upon Packy. It was out of the question, of course, that some invisible man should suddenly have beaned him with a blunt instrument, but he had all the emotions of one who has undergone such a beaning. Somebody had also removed all the muscle from his legs.

He forced himself to be calm.

'Did you say,' he asked carefully, 'that you wished I would?'

'Not,' said Jane, 'if you don't want to.'

The muscle returned to Packy's legs. His head cleared. He felt like a giant.

'But I do,' he cried. 'Gosh ding it, you don't mean to tell me that you – er – that you – ah – that you, as it were... how shall I put it?'

'I believe I've been in love with you ever since I was a kid and used to go and watch you play football.'

'It's exactly the same with me. I mean, I didn't watch you play football, but... well, you know what I mean.'

'And when you came here and were so marvellous, I suddenly realized it.'

'Isn't it a scream, the way these things sort of dawn on you!' said Packy enthusiastically. 'I can see now that I really loved you from the moment you walked into your father's suite that day and sat down on the table. Something told me that we were soul-mates. Jane!' said Packy.

It was some moments after he had clasped her to him that Packy felt that there was something that remained to be said.

'You realize the sort of chump I am, don't you?' he asked anxiously. 'You aren't going into this with your eyes shut?'

'I think you're a precious angel pet.'

'I am a precious angel pet,' admitted Packy, 'but that doesn't alter the fact that I've been engaged twice before this. Once to Beatrice and once to the current Mrs Scott or Pott or Bott. In fact, getting engaged had become with me something of a habit, and many people would say I was a flippertygibbet.'

'What's a flippertygibbet?'

'It's something I used to be before I met you. But what I'm driving at is that all that sort of thing is over now. This is the finish.'

'The third time,' said Jane wisely, 'is always lucky.'

'Why,' asked Packy, 'does your nose turn up at the tip like that?'

'I don't know. It always has. Don't you like it?'

'I love it. I love every bit of you.' A fresh spasm of ecstasy seized Packy. 'Oh, gosh, what fun we're going to have! *You* won't make me go to concerts and lectures, will you? Of course you won't. We'll just roam about the world together for the rest of our lives, raising Cain hand in hand. Did I say that we were soul-mates?'

'I believe you did.'

'Well, we are. Young Jane,' said Packy, holding her at arm's length and gazing searchingly into her eyes, 'are you sure you love me?'

'Of course I am.'

Packy expelled a deep breath.

'This,' he said, 'is like being in heaven without going to all the bother and expense of dying.'

Something vast and shadowy loomed up beside them in the darkness.

''Scuse me!'

The shadowy something revealed itself as Mr Soup Slattery.

'I knew you were kidding me when you said you weren't that way with this beazel,' observed Mr Slattery with satisfaction.

Packy turned on him with a touch of not unjustifiable annoyance. It is not pleasant for an ardent young man to have safe-blowers popping up out of traps in his moments of deep emotion.

'What do you think you're doing here?'

'Just thought I'd say Hello and Good-bye.'

Packy's annoyance vanished.

'I'm glad you did,' he said. 'I haven't thanked you for coming and trying to help us. It was sporting of you.'

'Aw, hell!' said Mr Slattery modestly. 'I thought it over and I seen where I was doing you dirt, so I come along.'

'I'm afraid you had a wasted evening, Mr Slattery,' said Jane sympathetically.

'Her gentle woman's heart,' explained Packy, 'is touched at the thought that you hadn't time to snitch anything out of that safe.'

Mr Slattery seemed piqued. He bridled a little.

'Hadn't time? Hadn't *time*? Say, how much time do you think I need to dig into a pete? I just let me fingers flicker and there I am. I got away with a necklace, two rings, a pendant and a sunboist. You won't see me around these parts no more. Me, back to the old country. Going to get me a farm, that's what I'm going to do. It's the only life – the farmer's. Eggs, milk, chickens ... and brew your own applejack. Swell! Well, pleased to have seen you, boy. Wish you luck, miss. I'll be going.'

The night swallowed him up, and Packy gazed reverently after him.

'What a man!' he murmured.

A hideous noise woke the birds in the tree-tops. Senator Opal was coming down the path with a song on his lips.

P. G. Wodehouse

IN ARROW BOOKS

If you have enjoyed *Hot Water*, you'll love
Money for Nothing

FROM

Money for Nothing

I

The picturesque village of Rudge-in-the-Vale dozed in the summer sunshine. Along its narrow High Street the only signs of life visible were a cat stropping its backbone against the Jubilee Watering Trough, some flies doing deep-breathing exercises on the hot window-sills, and a little group of serious thinkers who, propped up against the wall of the Carmody Arms, were waiting for that establishment to open. At no time is there ever much doing in Rudge's main thoroughfare, but the hour at which a stranger, entering it, is least likely to suffer the illusion that he has strayed into Broadway, Piccadilly, or the Rue de Rivoli is at two o'clock on a warm afternoon in July.

You will find Rudge-in-the-Vale, if you search carefully, in that pleasant section of rural England where the grey stone of Gloucestershire gives place to Worcestershire's old red brick. Quiet – in fact, almost unconscious – it nestles beside the tiny river Skirme and lets the world go by, somnolently content with its Norman church, its eleven public-houses, its pop. – to quote the Automobile Guide – of 3,541, and its only effort in the direction of modern progress, the emporium of Chas Bywater, Chemist.

Chas Bywater is a live wire. He takes no afternoon siesta, but works while others sleep. Rudge as a whole is inclined after luncheon to go into the back room, put a handkerchief over its face and take things easy for a bit. But not Chas Bywater. At the moment at which this story begins he was all bustle and activity, and had just finished selling to Colonel Meredith Wyvern a bottle of Brophy's Paramount Elixir (said to be good for gnat-bites).

Having concluded his purchase, Colonel Wyvern would have preferred to leave, but Mr Bywater was a man who liked to sweeten trade with pleasant conversation. Moreover, this was the first time the Colonel had been inside his shop since that sensational affair up at the Hall two weeks ago, and Chas Bywater, who held the unofficial position of chief gossip-monger to the village, was aching to get to the bottom of that.

With the bare outline of the story he was, of course, familiar. Rudge Hall, seat of the Carmody family for so many generations, contained in its fine old park a number of trees which had been planted somewhere about the reign of Queen Elizabeth. This meant that every now and then one of them would be found to have become a wobbly menace to the passer-by, so that experts had to be sent for to reduce it with a charge of dynamite to a harmless stump. Well, two weeks ago, it seems, they had blown up one of the Hall's Elizabethan oaks and as near as a toucher, Rudge learned, had blown up Colonel Wyvern and Mr Carmody with it. The two friends had come walking by just as the expert set fire to the train and had had a very narrow escape.

Thus far the story was common property in the village, and had been discussed nightly in the eleven tap-rooms of its eleven public-houses. But Chas Bywater, with his trained nose for news and that sixth sense which had so often enabled him to ferret out the story behind the story when things happen in the upper world of the nobility and gentry, could not help feeling that there was more in it than this. He decided to give his customer the opportunity of confiding in him.

'Warm day, Colonel,' he observed.

'Ur,' grunted Colonel Wyvern.

'Glass going up, I see.'

'Ur.'

'May be in for a spell of fine weather at last.'

'Ur.'

'Glad to see you looking so well, Colonel, after your little accident,' said Chas Bywater, coming out into the open.

It had been Colonel Wyvern's intention, for he was a man of testy habit, to inquire of Mr Bywater why the devil he couldn't wrap a bottle of Brophy's Elixir in brown paper and put a bit of string round it without taking the whole afternoon over the task: but at these words he abandoned this project. Turning a bright mauve and allowing his luxuriant eyebrows to meet across the top of his nose, he subjected the other to a fearful glare.

'Little accident?' he said. 'Little accident?'

'I was alluding—'

'Little accident!'

'I merely—'

'If by little accident,' said Colonel Wyvern in a thick, throaty voice, 'you mean my miraculous escape from death when that fat thug up at the Hall did his very best to murder me, I should be obliged if you would choose your expressions more carefully. Little accident! Good God!'

Few things in this world are more painful than the realization that an estrangement has occurred between two old friends who for years have jogged amiably along together through life, sharing each other's joys and sorrows and holding the same views on religion, politics, cigars, wine, and the Decadence of the Younger Generation: and Mr Bywater's reaction, on hearing Colonel Wyvern describe Mr Lester Carmody, of Rudge Hall, until two short weeks ago his closest crony, as a fat thug, should have been one of sober sadness. Such, however, was not the case. Rather was he filled with an unholy exultation. All along he had maintained that there was more in that Hall business than had become officially known, and he stood there with his ears flapping, waiting for details.

These followed immediately and in great profusion: and Mr Bywater, as he drank them in, began to realize that his companion had certain solid grounds for feeling a little annoyed. For when, as Colonel Wyvern very sensibly argued, you have been a man's friend for twenty years and are walking with him in his park and hear warning shouts and look up and realize that a charge of dynamite is shortly about to go off in your immediate neighbourhood, you expect a man who is a man to be a man. You do not expect him to grab you round the waist and thrust you swiftly in between himself and the point of danger, so that, when the explosion takes place, you get the full force of it and he escapes without so much as a singed eyebrow.

'Quite,' said Mr Bywater, hitching up his ears another inch.

Colonel Wyvern continued. Whether, if in a condition to give the matter careful thought, he would have selected Chas Bywater as a confidant, one cannot say. But he was not in such a condition. The stoppered bottle does not care whose is the hand that removes its cork – all it wants is the chance to fizz: and Colonel Wyvern resembled such a bottle. Owing to the absence from home of his daughter, Patricia, he had had no one handy to act as audience for his grievances, and for two weeks he had been suffering torments. He told Chas Bywater all.

It was a very vivid picture that he conjured up. Mr Bywater could see the whole thing as clearly as if he had been present in person – from the blasting gang's first horrified realization that human beings had wandered into the danger zone to the almost tenser moment when, running up to sort out the tangled heap on the ground, they had observed Colonel Wyvern rise from his seat on Mr Carmody's face and had heard him start to tell that gentleman precisely what he thought of him. Privately, Mr Bywater considered that Mr Carmody had acted with extra-ordinary presence of mind and had given the lie to the theory, held by certain critics, that the landed gentry of England are deficient in intelligence. But his sympathies were, of course, with the injured man. He felt that Colonel Wyvern had been hardly treated and was quite right to be indignant about it. As to whether the other was justified in alluding to his former friend as a jelly-bellied hell-hound, that was a matter for his own conscience to decide.

'I'm suing him,' concluded Colonel Wyvern, regarding an advertisement of Pringle's Pink Pills with a smouldering eye.

'Quite.'

'The only thing in the world that super-fatted old Black-hander cares for is money, and I'll have his last penny out of him, if I have to take the case to the House of Lords.'

'Quite,' said Mr Bywater.

'I might have been killed. It was a miracle I wasn't. Five thousand pounds is the lowest figure any conscientious jury could put the damages at. And, if there were any justice in England, they'd ship the scoundrel off to pick oakum in a prison cell.'

Mr Bywater made non-committal noises. Both parties to this unfortunate affair were steady customers of his, and he did not wish to alienate either by taking sides. He hoped the Colonel was not going to ask him for his opinion of the rights of the case.

Colonel Wyvern did not. Having relieved himself with some six minutes of continuous speech, he seemed to have become aware that he had bestowed his confidences a little injudiciously. He coughed and changed the subject.

'Where's that Stuff?' he said. 'Good God! Isn't it ready yet? Why does it take you fellows three hours to tie a knot in a piece of string?'

'Quite ready, Colonel,' said Chas Bywater hastily. 'Here it is. I have put a little loop for the finger, to facilitate carrying.'

'Is this Stuff really any good?'

'Said to be excellent, Colonel. Thank you, Colonel. Much obliged, Colonel. Good day, Colonel.'

Still fermenting at the recollection of his wrongs, Colonel Wyvern strode to the door: and, pushing it open with extreme violence, left the shop.

The next moment the peace of the drowsy summer afternoon was shattered by a hideous uproar. Much of this consisted of a high, passionate barking, the remainder being contributed by the voice of a retired military man, raised in anger. Chas Bywater blenched, and, reaching out a hand towards an upper shelf, brought down, in the order named, a bundle of lint, a bottle of arnica, and one of the half-crown (or large) size pots of Sooth-o, the recognized specific for cuts, burns, scratches, nettle-stings and dog-bites. He believed in Preparedness.

The P G Wodehouse Society (UK)

The P G Wodehouse Society (UK) was formed in 1997 to promote the enjoyment of the writings of the twentieth century's greatest humorist. The Society publishes a quarterly magazine, *Wooster Sauce*, which includes articles, features, reviews, and current Society news. Occasional special papers are also published. Society events include regular meetings in central London, cricket matches and a formal biennial dinner, along with other activities. The Society actively supports the preservation of the Berkshire pig, a rare breed, in honour of the incomparable Empress of Blandings.

MEMBERSHIP ENQUIRIES

Membership of the Society is open to applicants from all parts of the world. The cost of a year's membership in 2008 is £15. Enquiries and requests for membership forms should be made to the Membership Secretary, The P G Wodehouse Society (UK), 26 Radcliffe Rd, Croydon, Surrey, CRO 5QE, or alternatively from info@pgwodehousesociety.org.uk

The Society's website can be viewed at www.pgwodehousesociety.org.uk

Visit our special P.G. Wodehouse website
www.wodehouse.co.uk

Find out about P.G. Wodehouse's books now
reissued with appealing new covers

Read extracts from all your favourite titles

Read the exclusive extra content and immerse
yourself in Wodehouse's world

Sign up for news of future publications
and upcoming events

arrow books